ANGEL AMONG US

ANGEL AMONG US

Katy Munger

This first world edition published 2012
in Great Britain and in the USA by
SEVERN HOUSE PUBLISHERS LTD of
9–15 High Street, Sutton, Surrey, England, SM1 1DF.

British Library Cataloguing in Publication Data

Munger, Katy.
  Angel among us. – (The dead detective mysteries)
  1. Fahey, Kevin (Fictitious character)–Fiction.
  2. Delaware–Fiction. 3. Detective and mystery stories.
  I. Title II. Series
  813.6-dc23

ISBN-13: 978-0-7278-8201-1 (cased)

All Severn House titles are printed on acid-free paper.

Severn House Publishers support The Forest Stewardship Council [FSC], the
leading international forest certification organisation. All our titles that are printed
on Greenpeace-approved FSC-certified paper carry the FSC logo.

Typeset by Palimpsest Book Production Ltd.,
Falkirk, Stirlingshire, Scotland.
Printed and bound in Great Britain by
MPG Books Ltd., Bodmin, Cornwall.

For Zuzu, my angel on earth – may your life always be filled with love and joy.

PROLOGUE

She had known unimaginable pain before and survived it. She had known day after day of deprivation and survived that, too. She had known fear so deep that it infiltrated her dreams at night like a vulture seeking flesh. She had endured all of it and come out of those terrible months with an unshakeable confidence in her own strength. She had survived.

This time was different. All she endured in the past – the beatings, rape, torture, the threats to her family – had all been directed at her. She had proved she could take anything and live. But things were different now. A life so precious it made her own seem irrelevant hung in the balance, depending on her for its survival.

She must not panic. The walls around her were damp and caked with clay. The floor was tamped down to rock. The air was thick with her own exhalation and so devoid of life that she felt as if she were spiraling down, down, down into a deep black hole. She splayed a palm wide against the dirt walls of her prison. It comforted her to feel the coolness of the earth and to know that, however far she was beneath its surface, she was still alive. She still breathed and the child inside her remained oblivious to their captivity.

The child. She forced herself to shut out everything but the life that stirred within her. The baby had been restless for the past two days, as if it, too, wanted to escape confinement. It would not be long now, she thought. And with that realization, fear overtook her. That was what he was waiting for. He had not yet said so, but she knew it to be true. As soon as the baby was born, he would take it from her and she would be left, forgotten beneath the earth. No one would ever know she was there.

Panic welled in her. The room was no bigger than half a boxcar and she was chained to one wall of it. She shifted the hand bound by metal and flexed her fingers, seeking relief from the pain. Her fingers brushed against something sharp in the dirt and she froze. She could use anything for a weapon. Anything at all. She began to brush the dirt away from the protrusion with her fingertips, moving carefully to avoid cutting herself on the object's sharp edges. She worked mechanically and did not know for how long, but at last she had smoothed away the earth enough to slide her fingers along a slender object buried just below the floor's surface. She willed herself to memorize its contours and tell her what it was. It took less than a minute to understand and, when she did, her panic was absolute.

It was a finger bone and it led to a hand. Just beneath the surface of the dirt floor, she had discovered a human hand now reduced to nothing more than bone, bone that was part of a skeleton. She knew it. She could feel it.

Others had died in this dark hole before her.

She wrapped her free arm around her belly and began to pray.

ONE

As time ticks onward, taking me further and further away from my death, I have started to lose even the memory of what it was like to have a body. Flesh. Bone. Blood. Pain and arousal. They are nothing but words to me now. Like a man examining a car he is thinking of buying, I have taken to studying the bodies of the living with no motivation other than nostalgia. There is no more excitement in watching a young girl as there is in watching an old man in the park feeding the pigeons. Yes, I see beauty in the human form – but it is an unpredictable call as to what I find beautiful these days. Appreciation comes upon me unexpectedly, in places I never expected to find it.

For example, babies (once sticky, squalling messes best left to others) seem like miracles to me now, with their faces open to all the world and their spirits radiating joy at being alive. Young people are beautiful to me, too, even as they struggle to understand who they are inside the bodies they wear. There are times when I stop by the high school to watch the young men training on the baseball field, marveling at how effortlessly strong their bodies are as they dart across the field. They accept their physical perfection with the careless grace of those who do not yet understand that youth does not last forever.

Perhaps because of my own, all too tortured life, I often find myself turning away from the perfection of youth. I am drawn to those who have suffered the slings and arrows of misfortune long enough for it to show in their splotchy faces and sagging skin. They have lived life to the fullest, however unwillingly, and it shows.

There are two old men I sometimes watch as they soak in the baths of a downtown Russian men's club. They carry the scars of a long-ago war on fireplug bodies covered with skin so tough they look upholstered in hide. They do not seem to notice the gouges of shiny flesh from old bullet wounds that mar their torsos like miniature mouths. Their spirits fill their war-torn bodies with a resigned acceptance, as if they have signed a treaty with their limbs not to complain so long as they draw breath.

But now that I am dead and I know what awaits them, it can be painful for me to view those whose blood and bones and tissue have betrayed them. Their strength sometimes seems to ebb before my very eyes. I can spot the sickly cast to their skin from across a room and feel how their blood falters in their veins. There is a weariness emanating from them that is unmistakable, for it is tinged with the fear of what lies ahead. I find I cannot stay long in the company of the ill, not just because, if they are too close to my world, there is a chance that they will see me, but also because I sometimes think that I feed on the life force of others in some way and I do not think that they have any to spare.

In truth, though, my very favorite place to watch the glory that is the human body is the playground of an elementary school on the outskirts of town. It is located in a neighborhood where the Irish and Italian meet, and where, in recent years, housefuls of Mexican immigrants have taken up residence, each home seemingly holding a dozen or more of them. The neighborhood school reflects their hopes for the future, regardless of where their pasts have taken them. Sturdy children shriek and chase one another across the playground, hugging just to feel the newness of their bodies together. They hold hands and form friendships blind to both color and physical beauty. If you catch them soon enough, that is. By second grade, I can see that their capacity for unbridled affection is gone, replaced by a sometimes cruel judgment of others. But if they are younger, they do not care whether the object of their affection is fat or poor or ugly. They bestow their love abundantly and it is a joy to watch.

I was doing just that one morning when I first caught a glimpse of a beautiful Mexican woman with skin the color of honey, whose flawless face was made even more exquisite by a hint of sadness that showed in her eyes. I could feel a deep love for the children on the playground emanating from her like the rays of a sun, yet I could feel her sorrow, too, as if something treasured had been taken from her and she knew that she would never get it back. The children called her 'Seely' and clustered around her, clutching her legs, stroking her hair, kissing her cheeks when she lingered long enough. They adored her as she herded them to and fro, soothing their scrapes and intervening with gentle admonishments during the rare fights. She was possessed of such patience it astonished me. No matter how chaotic the playground became, she sailed through it, calm and reassuring to all.

For a while, I watched her with the children morning after morning until, at last, I felt all there was to feel from their unfettered exuberance. I left to learn more elsewhere. But I took the memory of Seely's face with me when I left. It was, I thought, the face of an angel.

I did not see her again for half a year, not until the day I felt compelled to follow a visibly sick woman home from the market to make sure that she would be OK. Watching her struggle up the steps that led to her front door had wearied me. I left her and sought out the bustle of her neighborhood's main street, needing to feel the energy of the thriving around me. I found myself near the elementary school where I had stood for over a month watching the children play. School had let out for the day. The streets around me were filled with people from a dozen different countries. My little town was changing. Everyone seemed in a generous mood, as if they were glad to be sharing the streets with others.

It was June and the sun bounced off the store windows in bursts of glory. A pregnant woman caught my eye. She was standing in front of a Korean greengrocer whose business thrived thanks to an endless selection of vegetables and fruits wildly unfamiliar to me. Each night he took his displays down as carefully as if they were jewels, and then put them back up again early the next day, never seeming to weary of building his colorful pyramids. I envied him his contentment at this daily task.

I drifted closer to the pregnant woman, drawn by a feeling that I knew her. She was well along, although I am no expert in such things, having left every aspect of childbearing to my wife. I did not recognize her at first and so I saw her through the eyes of a stranger. Her cheekbones were high and angular, sloping down to a chin exquisitely carved below a wide mouth the color of strawberries. Her hair gleamed like chocolate in the sun and swayed as she picked her way through a crate of oblong fruit with an orange tint and intoxicating smell. She examined each fruit carefully, holding it to her nose and inhaling its fragrance before putting it back down again in search of something better. She was slender and her belly protruded out in front of her as if it, too, was a fruit ripening in the sun. She wore a yellow sundress that contrasted with the creamy tan of her skin and made me think of lemons.

As I stood, drinking in her beauty beneath the June day, I realized that I did know her – it was the preschool teacher from the nearby elementary school, the woman the children had called Seely.

Pregnancy had filled out her frame and crowded out her nascent sorrow.

She still had, I thought, the face of an angel. Wide sleepy eyes and a drowsy smile that lingered at the corners of her mouth. There was still sadness there, after all, I decided, though further underneath than before, perhaps hidden by daydreams of her life to come.

When she finally selected her fruit and made her way down the block, I followed – when you are dead, there is not much else to do. She loaded her purchases into the back seat of a battered green Volvo and I decided to hitch a ride. I sat next to her, unseen, as she drove out of my town and into the gently rolling hills of Delaware growing thick with corn, soybeans and wheat. She did not use air-conditioning but rolled all four windows down. I enjoyed the wild rush of air as much as she did and perhaps even more, for I could watch the silken strands of her hair whipping wildly in the wind as she drove.

Ten minutes outside of town, she turned and we bumped merrily down a rutted road gouged by tractor tires that wound through fields of new growth. She pulled up in front of a white farmhouse and unloaded her groceries from the car with the same placid calm she had shown in choosing them. She had not bothered to lock her back door and pushed her way inside with a bump of her hips. Clearly, this house was home.

Leaving her bags on the counter, she wandered languidly down the hall. I could feel the sleep starting to overcome her. As she entered a cheery yellow bedroom decorated with bright quilts and flowers, she pulled her sundress over her head and fell on to bed. She was asleep almost instantly, her body as still as the cool afternoon air that held the room in abeyance. That was when I saw them – dozens of scars criss-crossed against the creamy brown skin of her back that wound their way over her swollen abdomen and breasts, some long and an angry pink, others dark welts or mounds of puckered tissue from old burn marks.

I was paralyzed by what I saw. Above, she had the face of an angel. Below, a devil had surely been at work.

TWO

Her name was Arcelia. I learned that when – just as the sun had lost its bite and the afternoon had turned into an early summer evening – a tall man with brown hair in need of a haircut entered the farmhouse covered in dust from the fields. The door banged shut behind him and I came back out into the kitchen to see who had arrived. He was standing in the center of the room, clearly at home, looking around for his wife. When he found her in the bedroom, fast asleep with her hands cradling her belly, he left without a sound. He returned to the kitchen and began preparing the evening meal. He ate no meat. He pulled vegetables from drawers and washed them reverently. He sautéed them in restaurant-quality pans, adding seasonings and sauces with such ease I knew he had once worked as a chef.

Wonderful smells filled the kitchen and I could feel the hard labor of the day falling from him as he paid homage to the bounty of the earth. I wondered if he had grown the vegetables he was eating. He didn't look like any of the farmers I had ever known. He was in his mid-thirties, with clear blue eyes, an angular nose and a close-cropped beard that he seemed, somehow, to hide behind.

When the dinner was done, he prepared a plate and carried it in to his still sleeping wife. He sat on the edge of her bed and gently touched her shoulder. 'Arcelia,' he whispered.

Her eyes flew open – she was instantly awake. For a moment, I saw the fear in her eyes and knew she was close to panic. Then she saw her husband's face and relaxed again. 'I fell asleep,' she mumbled.

'Good,' the man said. He smiled lovingly at her. 'I made dinner.'

She struggled to sit upright, her belly making it difficult to maneuver. 'I'm as big as a house,' she admitted as she reached for the plate and ate hungrily. Her husband smiled, amused at her appetite. 'I'm not sure how much longer I can take it,' she said, but was instantly distracted. 'Are these the purple potatoes you told me about?'

The man nodded. 'What do you think? I've got three restaurants in Wilmington that say they'll take all I can grow. It was a little early to pull them, but I wanted you to try them.'

'They're amazing.' She looked down at her dinner plate ruefully. 'And they're all gone.'

The man laughed and reached for her plate. 'I'll bring you more.'

'And more butter?' She said this hopefully, widening her eyes a little, knowing it would melt him into submission.

He laughed again as he left the room. Her eyes followed him with a love I envied. If anyone had ever felt that way about me, I could no longer remember it.

This time, the man returned with two plates and they sat side by side on their bed together, watching the shadows grow on the lawn outside their windows. They ate in silence, content in each other's company. The room felt filled with safety and love.

I understood then how it was that she could continue, that she could bring a child into this world, when she still bore the scars of what a terrible place it could be.

I fell in love with her a little that evening as I watched how she surrendered to her love for her husband. He returned that love and I was reminded, for the millionth time since my death, of how poorly I had measured up in that department when I was alive, of what a wretched father and husband I had once been.

Being reminded of my failures is sometimes more than I can take. I left before dark, but in the end, I could not stay away.

I returned in the morning in time to see Arcelia stepping from the kitchen door, a piece of toast still in hand as she struggled with a pocketbook, a tote bag of fresh vegetables and a comically large ring of keys. When she drove away in her old Volvo, I rode shotgun and enjoyed the cool morning breeze alongside of her. She headed back toward town to the elementary school where she worked, parked in the lot set aside for teachers and trundled slowly toward the entrance, her pregnancy slowing her down. The janitor hurried out the door and took her packages from her, ignoring her protests as he gallantly led her inside. Children and their parents began arriving soon after. As they were delivered to Arcelia, their cries of delight told me that the children still adored their Seely.

Arcelia ruled her classroom the way she did the playground: with gentle admonitions, warning glances and frequent smiles. The children gravitated toward her as if she were a beacon and absently wrapped their arms around her legs for comfort.

I had not been so clueless as a father that I did not remember school typically ended in mid-June. The school year was winding down. I knew there were only a few days left to watch her at work and so I decided to return the next day and spend another pleasant morning watching the children barrel about in their sturdy bodies, testing the boundaries of their world. But when the next morning dawned, I was distracted by a family of rabbits exploring the clover in a nearby park. After that, I followed a pack of feral dogs to see where they went during the day (deep into the park bushes to sleep). By the time I reached the elementary school that day, it was already mid morning. Arcelia had not yet arrived. Parents stood in annoyed clusters, looking at their watches, anxious about being late to work. The children were less concerned. Any extra time to swing or slide was fine with them. The principal was the only one who looked anxious. He was a tubby man with close-cropped gray hair and kept offering his opinion that Arcelia must have gone into labor early; there was no other explanation for her tardiness. She had never been so much as a minute late before.

A substitute teacher finally arrived and the remaining parents fled, leaving the principal to deal with where his teacher was and why. He handed over the care of the children to the substitute and returned to his office. I followed and watched as he searched through his emergency contact files until he found the one for Arcelia. Improbably, her last name was Gallagher and her husband's name was Daniel. He did not answer his phone. The principal's agitation was growing and I wondered at his anxiousness. She was only three hours late at that point, but I saw fear in the way he dialed number after number looking for her.

He spoke briefly to someone on the other end of his last phone call without success, then hung up and stared at the wall across the room. A woman poked her head in the doorway and asked, 'Any word?'

The principal shook his head. 'A neighbor said he would try to find her husband. He thinks he may be in the fields.'

'I called the hospital,' the woman said. 'She's not there.'

The principal and his secretary exchanged a glance I could not understand. A silence filled the room. 'Perhaps she had car trouble?' the man suggested.

His secretary nodded, acknowledging the possibility. She did not look convinced.

'If we don't hear from her soon, I'm calling the police,' the principal decided, sounding like he was trying to find the courage to do so. 'You never know.'

The woman's hand flew to her mouth, as if she were trying to suppress her opinion. She did not want to agree with whatever it was the principal was thinking, but they knew more than I did. That much was obvious. They were both deeply afraid.

THREE

The principal was a plump little man with soft round hands that looked like a woman's. He sat at his desk, unable to move, unable to act. Occasionally, his secretary would look in on him, then close the door, leaving him to his indecision. If he dithered this much about every matter, the school was in trouble. Once or twice, he started to reach for the phone but held back.

I could not understand what had him so worried. As lunchtime came and went, he still did not move. He went back to work on other papers of inconsequential nature. It was not until early after-noon that he phoned the police.

Two cops I did not know arrived quickly. The school was served by a new substation I had never visited. One cop was young, skinny and white. His partner was an older Hispanic man putting on weight in his middle age. Both seemed bored with their assign-ment, especially since the principal did not help his case. Whatever was bothering him, he was having trouble spitting it out to the cops.

His secretary, who had been listening in at the door, finally took matters into her own hands. She entered the room and interrupted her boss's utterly baffling attempts at explaining what he feared.

'Sir,' she said to the principal, 'I apologize for interrupting, but the other teachers and I have discussed the situation and I feel perhaps I could add some information here.'

The two cops looked as if she had about thirty seconds before they shut their notebooks and left. So far, they had learned nothing from the principal to make them the least bit concerned about the teacher who had failed to show that morning.

'We have long noticed that Arcelia was afraid of something,' the secretary explained. She patted her hair anxiously. 'There were times when it seemed as if she was in physical pain, as if it was difficult for her to move. We thought she was suffering from some illness, but then one of the teachers suggested that maybe she was being, well, abused.' She exchanged a glance with the principal, who had flushed red at the idea. 'She hasn't been married long. I think maybe two years or so. She's been working here for a year now and, to be fair, she's never said a word about her husband being abusive in any way. But once we started watching her more closely, it did become obvious. Arcelia was afraid of someone and she was often in physical pain.'

'Now, now, Mrs Trafton, everything you say is simply hearsay,' the principal said. 'There is no proof that her husband is doing anything to her.' He looked up anxiously at the police. 'I have been through this before,' he sputtered. 'I lost the best teacher I ever had due to unfounded accusations. It was awful. I simply cannot let that happen to another person.'

Mrs Trafton wasn't buying it. 'The police need to know,' she said firmly. She faced the two beat cops and took a deep breath. 'Arcelia is married to the mayor's son.'

The youngest cop dropped his notebook and his partner looked at him in disgust.

'Are you telling me that the missing teacher is married to Mayor Gallagher's son?' the older cop asked. He turned to the principal in exasperation. 'Couldn't you have told us that right away? Don't you think that was important?'

The principal looked stricken, but no one was paying attention to him any more. The news that the missing teacher was married to an important man's son took precedence.

That was my town for you. There were the men who were elected and served in obvious seats of power. And then there were the men who knew better than to run for office, who understood they could hold power longer if they simply controlled those who did. Mayor Gallagher was the latest in a long line of local leaders controlled by men in my town who, I suspected, live here so that they can launder money for even scarier men who lived a few states north. No one who wanted to keep their job ever voiced this theory out loud. But when I was alive, everyone on the force had understood that if certain cases involved certain men, you didn't look into them with the kind of obsessiveness that had gotten you your detective badge. Of course, doing a half-assed job had come naturally to me and my partner. We had been given more than our share of the hands-off cases simply because assigning them to us was extra insurance that they would never be solved.

How had a loud, aggressive man like Mayor Gallagher fathered the lanky, quiet farmer I had seen a few nights before tenderly serving his pregnant wife dinner in bed?

'This is above my pay grade,' the older cop decided. He shut his notebook and stored it in his breast pocket. 'You should have called this in sooner.'

The principal looked ashamed. Mrs Trafton looked grim. 'We didn't want to think the worst. There isn't a teacher more loved by her students,' she said. 'They are all so excited about the baby.'

The cops looked startled. 'She's pregnant?' the younger one stammered.

The principal and his secretary nodded in unison.

'Don't move,' the older one warned them. 'We're going to call this in and I can guarantee you they are going to send someone with a gold shield down to question you. And don't warn the husband.'

Neither the principal nor his secretary admitted that they had already tried to contact her husband – and that he could not be found.

There are at least eight senior detectives in my town, men who have served for decades and would understand the minefield this case represented. But I knew that our commander, a natural-born politician named Gonzales, would not send any of them. A missing pregnant schoolteacher married to the mayor's son? Gonzales would be intent on presenting a façade of professional independence while simultaneously doing god-knows-what maneuverings behind the scenes. There was only one person he would trust with a case this tricky – Maggie, my replacement on the force. Sure, she came with a partner Gonzales absolutely loathed, but Maggie Gunn had turned Adrian Calvano into a pretty decent detective. At least if she kept a close eye on him.

Sure enough, they arrived within the hour: Maggie, with her square muscled body and plain face made beautiful by her insanely good health, and Adrian Calvano, with his lanky frame, expensive suits and maddeningly thick black hair. He drove me nuts, but apparently Maggie saw something genuinely worthwhile in him and I trusted her judgment.

Maggie and Calvano questioned the principal and his secretary about the missing teacher's reliability, her past record of absences, any rumors they had heard about her marriage and what they knew about her husband. Eventually they came to the same conclusion I had come to – that Arcelia Gallagher was a very private woman, who had not disclosed a single personal detail about herself to any of her co-workers. All anyone really knew was that she was married to Danny Gallagher, the mayor's only son, and that she lived on a farm outside of town, where her husband worked long hours to grow organic produce that he sold to local restaurants. Arcelia had helped him in the fields after school until she had grown too pregnant to be much use. Other than that, no one knew where Arcelia had been born, how she had met and married her husband, if she had any other family, where she went on her vacations or, indeed, where she went during the summer when school was out for three months. All anyone really knew about her was that she was very sweet-natured and the children loved her.

Maggie and Calvano looked grim – they had learned little of use.

'She goes to St Raphael's,' the secretary offered meekly. 'I noticed her saying the rosary last Wednesday and I asked her if she was Catholic. She told me she was and that she went to St Raphael's.'

'No kidding?' Calvano said. 'I went there as a kid. I was an altar boy. I still go there now and then.'

No one in the room seemed impressed.

'Good,' Maggie told him. 'You can go talk to the priest there while I go talk to her husband.'

'No way,' Calvano protested. 'For all we know, he's the reason she never showed up for work. I'm not letting you go out there alone.'

Maggie looked insulted. The principal looked like he might have a stroke. The secretary looked relieved.

'Seriously?' Maggie asked her partner. 'Did you seriously just say that?'

'I mean it,' Calvano said. 'I know Danny Gallagher. He lived in my neighborhood when we were kids. He's bad news. He always had a temper and people don't change that much.'

I found that hard to believe about Danny Gallagher. I had watched him in the privacy of his own home, a place where people are always themselves. He had seemed to be a content and gentle man. Calvano was just being an ass. He did that quite well.

'If you know him, then you are not going out there to question him, either,' Maggie decided. 'The last thing we need is for someone to claim favoritism.'

'No one has to come out to question me,' a voice said quietly from the doorway.

I was as startled as everyone else to see Danny Gallagher standing at the edge of the room, staring down at his muddy work boots. 'What's this about? Where is my wife? She should have been home an hour ago. She's not answering her phone.'

When they told him his wife had not shown up for school that day, he collapsed. All six foot three of him froze in what I was pretty sure was pure terror, then he slid slowly to the floor and put his face in his hands. A shocked silence filled the room.

Maggie was the first to break it. 'What is it?' she asked him. 'What do you think has happened to your wife?'

'They've got her,' he whispered. 'She always said they'd come for her.'

Maggie and Calvano looked grim at this news. They knew that no one was that good an actor. Chances were good that Arcelia Gallagher was in real trouble.

As if he could read their minds, the husband let out a sound that stopped just short of a scream. I could feel him fading into the darkness. As the others watched in disbelief, he gave himself up to his fear and slipped to the floor unconscious.

Maggie and Calvano stared at him, unsure of what to think.

Once again, it was the school secretary who finally acted.

'For God sakes,' she commanded the principal. 'Call an ambulance.'

FOUR

I had been a professional disaster when I was alive and a detective on the force. I had bungled nearly every case, seldom finishing an assignment and pretty much living in the bottom of a bottle. Having a partner just like me had not helped. We had gone down in a blaze of infamous glory. But even on my worst days, those days when I was still drunk from the night before and smelled like the bottom of a bar's bathroom floor, I still had the wherewithal to be terrified of Commander Gonzales.

He was the perfect police commander. Tall, urbane, impeccably dressed and of Latino heritage – which was no small advantage when our little Delaware town was rapidly filling up with immigrants in search a better life for their families. Many of them had drifted down our way after trying New York and finding it too large for their tastes. Enough of them were voters that the traditional Irish and Italian power brokers in town had anointed Gonzales as their golden boy.

In truth, Gonzales had as little in common with the Mexican and Central American newcomers as I did. He shared their skin color, but that was it. Rumor had it that his grandfather had owned most of some Mexican state once upon a time. Certainly, he lived in the wealthiest neighborhood in town and knew how to move among the most powerful circles. He also knew when to deliver a favor.

He had scared the crap out of me. Anger fueled him and he needed someone to blame whenever things did not go as he planned. He liked to choose a whipping boy and go after him unmercifully until the poor bastard crumpled.

Right now, it was Adrian Calvano who was feeling his wrath. I hated feeling sorry for Calvano. He annoyed me to no end. But there you have it – I could not help but empathize with him. Gonzales was staring at him with utter contempt, his eyes flickering over every inch of Calvano's frame as if he were seeking a soft spot so he could go in for the kill. I had been shredded by Gonzales on many occasions and I knew how it felt. I did not wish that on anyone, not even Adrian Calvano.

'*Where* did you take him?' Gonzales was asking in disbelief.

'The hospital,' Calvano said defensively. 'What else were we supposed to do? The guy totally collapsed. He was in a catatonic state. The principal called the ambulance before we could stop him and then, well . . .'

'Things got out of control?' Gonzales suggested sarcastically.

Maggie took over. 'Sir,' she said. 'I don't know if the husband is faking it. But I do know that we were not going to get anything out of him at the scene.'

Gonzales stared at them both. I was impressed at how unflappable Maggie seemed. She was his favorite on the force, in no small part because Gonzales had known her since she was a little girl and her father had once been his mentor. As such, Maggie was not used to his disapproval. She was feeling it now, but she was taking it well.

'If the press gets wind of this situation,' Gonzales warned them, 'this town is going to turn into a circus. Again. I won't have it. The two of you are on this case until it is over and I don't want you to so much as eat lunch until you find out where Arcelia Gallagher is and if someone took her.'

'And if it turns out it's her husband?' Maggie asked. 'Which we all know is the most likely answer?'

Gonzales knew she was really asking what the hell they were supposed to do if it turned out that the son of the mayor, Gonzales's biggest political backer, had killed his wife.

'If you start uncovering evidence that leads to him,' Gonzales said, 'I want to know it by the end of the day and I will expect hourly updates after that. Is that clear?'

'Oh, he did it,' Calvano predicted. 'I knew Danny Gallagher when he was a kid and he was a bad one.'

Maggie flashed him a look that meant, 'Shut your mouth or I will strangle you.' It usually rolled off him like oil and this time was no different.

Gonzales looked mildly interested. 'How long did you know him?' he asked.

Calvano looked nervous. He was not used to Gonzales actually paying him attention. 'We grew up on the same block for the first nine years of our lives,' Calvano explained. 'But his parents got divorced and he moved away, I think to live at his grandfather's house.'

'When he was ten, he went to live with his mother and grand-father on the family farm,' Maggie explained calmly. 'It's the same farm he owns and works now. Apparently, he is a highly respected organic farmer who is some sort of leader in something called the farm-to-table movement. It's embraced by restaurants that believe in only using local produce.' Maggie was smart enough to have already done some background checking.

Gonzales looked mollified that Maggie was on the case. 'Where is the mother now?' he asked, knowing that the mayor's ex-wife was a clear candidate for the 'most likely to throw a wrench into our cog' award.

'She's dead,' Maggie said. 'She died about two years ago of cancer and left the farm to her son. He'd already been living there and, apparently, working it pretty hard for years until about two and a half years ago, when he disappeared for a month and came back with his wife. No one quite seems to know where he went to get her, or how he knew her, or what the situation was.'

'How do you know all this?' Calvano asked, sounding annoyed. As hard as he tried, he could never catch up with Maggie and there were days when it really bothered him.

'My father,' Maggie said, with a glance at Gonzales. They both knew that if Colin Gunn had provided the information, then it was true. Colin had been on the force for over forty years before he retired and he knew the importance of reliable information.

'How does Colin know the family?' Gonzales asked. He was always on the lookout for potential problems and a conflict of interest was a big one.

'He knew the mayor's first wife, Danny's mother, from growing up,' Maggie explained. She hesitated, not sure of how much to share. 'They were friends, and maybe even more than that when they were young. I think they kept in touch, especially after my mother died. But then she got sick and passed soon after. It was a lot for my father to take.'

Gonzales nodded thoughtfully. He had thought he knew all the players in what was sure to be a tricky situation, but now he was calculating even more possibilities, thinking up ways to head off potential trouble.

'I want you both to go talk to the husband,' he finally decided. 'Find out where he met his wife and see if you can uncover a reason why she was so afraid. So far, all I'm hearing are a bunch of rumors from the teacher's break room at an elementary school. That's not good enough for me. We have to be very, very careful here. I don't have to tell you what would happen if Terrence Gallagher lost the mayor's race to some immigrant rights candidate next year because we offended the Latino community.'

No, he didn't have to tell Maggie or Calvano what would happen. They all knew it would mean drastic budget cuts and a lot of new paperwork for justifying the frequent stop-and-searches they all knew the front line of the force was getting away with at the moment. And they wanted those traffic stops to stay. No one in our town wanted it to become part of the drug highway that led from New York City straight south down I-95 into Florida. It was not uncommon for any driver who looked like a stranger – never mind what their skin color was – to be stopped on some pretense if they lingered too long in town. And a stop was almost always followed by a search of their car. It bordered on the illegal, hell, it was illegal, but the policy had inspired the drug trade to give our town a wide berth and helped preserve its almost eerily wholesome nature, at least if you lived in the right neighborhoods.

'Sir,' Calvano said suddenly. His eyes were focused outside the window.

'What, son?' Gonzales demanded, making it obvious he didn't even remember Calvano's name. 'Spit it out.'

'You know how you said you were afraid our town would turn into a media circus?' Calvano asked. He swallowed. His mouth had gone dry.

Gonzales stared at him like he was a giant cockroach. 'Spit it out.'

'They're already here.' Calvano pointed out the window. Down the street that ran in front of the main station, a television news van from a national cable station specializing in crime was having a stand-off with a van from a major news network. Both wanted the parking spot that offered a full view of the front door of the station and neither was willing to give way.

'Shit,' Maggie said.

No one argued with her.

'How did they get here so quickly?' Calvano asked. He was not politically savvy enough to know the answer, but both Maggie and Gonzales had already figured it out.

'The mayor probably called them,' Gonzales said. 'He thinks it will put pressure on us to work faster.'

'This isn't going to help,' Maggie predicted. 'If they start getting to the witnesses before we do, we'll never get a straight story out of anyone.'

'I'll assign two more teams to help you question witnesses,' Gonzales promised. 'And I'm going to ask the FBI to look into the Mexican angle so you two are free to work the local angle. In the meantime, go out the back door. Go see the husband and stay there until you get him to talk. I want to know if you think he's involved.'

The Mexican angle? I didn't know what Gonzales meant by that remark, but I did know what it meant for this case: Gonzales hated that the victim was Latino and he was going to make it a problem for everyone involved.

FIVE

'I think Danny Gallagher did it,' Calvano predicted as we were heading toward the hospital where he had been taken. 'He just didn't figure on being caught.'

'How can you be so sure?' Maggie asked. 'If you get that in your head now, you're going to do a crappy investigation and you know it. You need to have an open mind.'

'Danny Gallagher was famous on our block,' Calvano said. 'He hit first and asked questions later. He stole my bike so often I ended up keeping it at his house. It was easier that way. He stayed on the streets until dark, just looking for someone to hassle. Once, he decided he liked my little sister Gina and followed her everywhere for weeks until my mother went over to his house to talk to his mother about it.'

He had left something out and Maggie sensed it. 'And what?' she asked curiously.

Calvano looked uncomfortable. 'When my mother got to his house, she said she heard Danny's parents fighting so loudly she was afraid to knock on the door. Things were being thrown and were crashing to the floor so she came right back home. About a month later, Danny's father left him and his mother. I heard my parents talking. Danny's father had moved in with some girl about twenty years younger than he was. Danny and his mother left town soon after. I wasn't sorry to see him go. No one was sorry to see him go. He was a bully and obsessed with finding the perfect girl. Leopards don't change their spots.'

Actually, Calvano had changed his spots. At least a little. Unfortunately, I was in no position to point that out.

'Did you ever think that maybe he was a bully because he was unhappy, and that he was unhappy because everything sucked at home?' Maggie asked. 'Did it ever cross your mind that maybe his father was taking it out on him and that Danny stayed out until dark because he couldn't bear to go home?'

'Hey, don't put that on me,' Calvano protested. 'I was a kid. It wasn't my problem. Don't make me feel sorry for the guy.'

'Yeah, well I remember when his father left his mother too. It was a big scandal. My parents talked about it all the time. Danny's father was on the city council then and the woman he ran off with was some college student who had interned for the summer. It was pretty public, if I recall. It must've been hard on Danny if he was just a kid.'

'Why do you care?' Calvano asked. 'It's not like you're the product of a broken home.' Everyone knew that Maggie's parents have been married for nearly fifty years before her mother died of cancer a few years before.

'I just think that people should be allowed to change,' Maggie said. Her hands were gripping the steering wheel tightly. 'Not everybody stays the same. Some people change.'

'Whatever you say,' Calvano decided. But then, in typical Calvano fashion, he added under his breath, 'He did it.'

Danny Gallagher didn't look like much of a killer. He was laid up in his hospital bed, pale and propped up against a mountain of pillows like he was too weak to sit up on his own. A Catholic priest was helping him sip water from a cup. I can't say I had much respect for the dude. His wife was missing and the best he could do was collapse like some weak old lady and be carted off to the hospital?

Danny's eyes took a moment to focus on Maggie and Calvano. Clearly, he had been given something to calm him down. 'I think the police are here,' he told the priest.

When the priest looked over his shoulder, I was startled by what I saw. It was as if someone from another century had stepped into the modern world. The priest had a long, thin face and jet black hair. His features were prominent and clearly Eastern European. But it was his eyes that captivated me completely as he focused them on Maggie. They were the bluest eyes I had ever seen, but neither the blue of the sky nor the teal of rock quarry waters. They were something in between, yet somehow also darker. His gaze was like the mouth of a deep well, as if you could fall into those eyes and tumble downward and downward into infinity. I wondered if he could see me, his gaze was that intense, but he made no sign of recognition.

Maggie seemed as startled as I was. She said nothing and Calvano came to the rescue. 'Father Sojak,' Calvano said in a respectful voice as he extended his hand. 'I'm Detective Calvano and this is my partner, Detective Gunn.'

The priest shook Calvano's hand and looked at him quizzically, wondering how he'd known his name.

'I see you at St Raphael's,' Calvano explained. 'I sometimes attend the eleven a.m. service.'

'Oh yes, of course,' the priest said, rising to his feet, though I did not think he recognized Calvano. 'Father Lansing still does the eleven a.m. I'm with the early risers.'

'That would not be me,' Calvano admitted. I was curious at the transformation in him. He deferred to Maggie in most situations. But he was clearly comfortable talking to the priest. He was far more Catholic than I had realized.

'We need to talk to Mr Gallagher about his wife,' Calvano explained. 'Would you like to stay while we question him?' I wasn't convinced Maggie was on board with his offer, but she said nothing to contradict him.

The priest exchanged a glance with Danny Gallagher and sat back down. Danny wanted him to stay.

'I know you,' Danny said to Calvano weakly. 'We grew up together. We lived on the same block.'

Calvano sat down in a chair next to his bed. 'That's right. I remember you well.'

'You must think I'm a terrible person,' Danny said. He glanced at the priest and I wondered what they had been talking about before we entered the room. 'That was a bad time in my life. A very bad time and I wasn't a very good person because of it.'

Maggie looked at Calvano with no small sense of satisfaction.

'But that stuff doesn't matter right now,' Danny continued. 'Whatever you need me to do, I'll do. I just want you to find my wife.'

Maggie interrupted. She was afraid he was going to say all the things that husbands say when their wives go missing, and she knew there was no time to go through the motions. 'You looked completely terrified when you found out your wife was missing,' Maggie said. 'Why? You have to tell us what it was you were afraid of. You have to tell us everything you know about your wife's life. It's the only thing that might bring her back.'

The priest and the husband exchanged another glance. They were hiding something, and they both understood that what they did next would likely determine whether the world thought Danny Gallagher innocent or guilty in his wife's disappearance.

A silence filled the room until Father Sojak nodded at Danny. 'Go on,' he said encouragingly. 'Tell them about your wife's history.'

Calvano took notes as Danny Gallagher told them the story: he had met his wife, Arcelia, four years ago while attending an agricultural college in Mexico. He was learning about new hybrid variations of vegetables hardy enough to be grown in the United States and sold to its growing Hispanic population. Arcelia had been working in the fields for one of the farmers Danny Gallagher had visited with his professor and class.

'It was just like in the movies,' Danny said, his voice breaking. 'I looked at her and it was as if the world changed from black-and-white to color. She looked back at me and I could see it in her eyes. She felt it, too. We had been meant to find one another.' His voice grew stronger as he talked. He did not seem embarrassed at how sentimental his story sounded. He did not seem the least in doubt that what he was saying was true.

'We didn't talk to each other that first day, but I came back the next week and she was sitting on a bench outside the gate of the farm, waiting for her ride home. I stopped my truck and sat next to her and we ended up talking for hours. She told me she was in school, studying to be a teacher, and was working at the farm to make money to pay for college. She told me about her family, they were poor with lots of kids, and I told her about mine. When

her ride came, she waved it on. It was dark by the time we ran
out of words. I don't even remember everything we talked about.
My Spanish was pretty bad back then and her English was no
better. But we understood each other perfectly. Somehow she
sensed what I was going to say before I even opened my mouth
and I could feel her thoughts in the same way.'

I watched the priest during this speech, curious to know how
he reacted to a world he would never experience himself. His eyes
never left Danny Gallagher's face. It was as if he was willing him
the strength to go on.

'So you got married?' Calvano interrupted. He was anxious to
get to the part that would help them.

'No,' Danny explained. 'Not at first. She couldn't leave her
family. Arcelia has twelve brothers and sisters and her father is
too old to work anything but part-time. She was needed at home
to support them and she had her school and I still had to finish
getting my graduate degree. So I went back to the States and we
made arrangements for her to visit at Christmas.'

'And you sent her money in between?' Maggie guessed, not
quite disguising her belief that there was a possibility he had been
scammed.

'Of course I did,' Danny said angrily. 'You have no idea what
it's like to live down there. There is no running water in her village
and no way to find work. She rode almost a hundred miles each
way on a bus just to go to our equivalent of community college
two days a week. The only money to be had where she comes
from is from drug gangs, and if you don't cooperate with them
your life is always in danger. I couldn't send her much money at
first, a couple hundred a month, but it made all the difference to
her family. It made it possible for them to survive.'

Calvano had perked up at the mention of drug gangs. 'I'm
gathering she didn't cooperate with the drug gangs?' he asked.

'She did not,' Danny Gallagher said. He closed his eyes and
laid his head back against the pillow. 'Her parents thought she
was, though. She didn't tell them about us because she knew they
would panic if they realized she was planning to leave. So they
just assumed that the money I sent her was from drug activity
somehow. They didn't like it but they took the money. I should
never have left her behind when I returned to the States. But she
told me a lot of Mexico was like that. That people were used to

it. That there was no way to get away from the drug gangs and
she wasn't afraid of them. She said they would leave her alone so
long as she steered clear of them.'

'That doesn't sound like the Mexican drug gangs I know,'
Calvano said drily.

For the first time, Danny Gallagher almost lost his temper. 'I
know what you're thinking, that she had a boyfriend in a gang or
something like that. But she just said she had a friend who would
make sure that she was safe and I believed her.'

Arcelia had clearly believed it, too, but the scars I had seen on
her body told me that either she had been mistaken to trust her
friend, or that friend had not remained one for long.

'Then what happened?' Maggie said. 'Did she get involved with
a gang?'

The priest intervened, an act of mercy I hoped was designed to
give Danny Gallagher some peace and not just an attempt to make
sure he didn't reveal more than the priest wanted him to reveal.

'A drug gang kidnapped Arcelia about three years ago,' the
priest explained. Danny Gallagher's eyes were closed. 'They held
her for a few months. We don't really know why, because she will
not speak of that time, but it could be as simple as someone saw
how beautiful she was and wanted to use her for a few months.'

I thought of the scars I had seen criss-crossing her body, of
how her tormentors had been careful to maim her only in places
where it would not show. Whoever had wanted to use her had
been sick. He had wanted to have her beauty, and yet destroy it
at the same time.

'When they grew tired of using her, they went to her family
and demanded five thousand dollars for her return,' the priest said.
'The family had no money, of course, certainly nothing approaching
that sum, and so they contacted Danny.'

'How did they find you?' Maggie asked Danny. 'You said that
they did not know of your existence.'

'I had been frantic,' he explained. 'I had not heard from Arcelia
in months. She did not reply to my letters and she had stopped
showing up for our weekly phone calls at her village's bodega I
went a little crazy when I didn't hear from her. It had been so real
and then, just as suddenly, I felt like a fool. I called the bodega
constantly for a few weeks, begging the owner to find her and get
her on the phone for me. He kept saying he had not seen her but

I did not believe him. I think he told her parents about me, so they knew she'd had a boyfriend from America. After a few months of trying to get her on the phone without luck, I just assumed she had met someone from down there and moved on. But when her parents were trying to find a way to raise the money for her ransom, they went through all of her things and they found the letters from me. Between the letters and what the bodega owner knew about me, they tracked me down here in Delaware.'

Danny's voice strengthened with anger as he told Maggie and Calvano the next part. 'My father refused to give me the money. Can you imagine? He said it was a scam. That Arcelia made her living setting up rich Americans by pretending to love them. He could not believe that what we'd had was real. He could not believe that such a thing actually existed.'

'So how did you get the money?' Calvano asked. He was staring at Danny Gallagher thoughtfully, fighting his own prejudices and trying to keep an open mind as Maggie had asked him to do. I was pretty sure Calvano was warming to Danny Gallagher, too. He loved women in all their many forms and, out of all the people in the room, I think Calvano was the one who believed Danny the most when he talked about the love he and his wife had shared. Calvano understood how great Danny's loss threatened to be if they could not find her.

'I went to my mother,' Danny explained. 'She didn't have that kind of money, but she sold a parcel of land on the edge of our farm to a developer who had been itching to get his hands on it. It was just a couple of acres and he paid cash. My mother never doubted me for an instant. She had the money within two days.' His voice cracked as if he were about to cry.

'Danny went down there personally with the money and brought Arcelia back,' the priest continued for him. He glanced at Danny. It was too much for him to remember. 'He was asked to leave the money at some tiny shop in a godforsaken village in the middle of nowhere and, in return, they were supposed to leave Arcelia at another village a few miles away. They kept their word. It's better for business that way, you see. If they kill everyone, then no one would ever give them money. Danny and Arcelia returned to the States and I married them the day after they arrived here. That was just over two years ago. Arcelia spent several weeks being treated for her wounds. She does not speak of that time. But she devotes almost every free moment she has to counseling Mexican immigrants who come here, helping them file reports for missing loved ones still in Mexico. She helps them provide identification and DNA and other information whenever the US authorities find the bodies of people along the border that might be missing relatives. She is a very strong woman. She has helped many people in our congregation. You must find her. She's gone through enough.'

'How did you get over the border?' Maggie asked.

It was clear that Danny had rehearsed his answer. Too quickly, he said, 'We got married in Mexico before we came back, so legally she was my wife. Between that and the papers I got from the consulate, she was able to come into the States with me. We got married again by Father Sojak, once we got here, just to be safe.'

I'm not sure anyone believed that answer. It usually took years to get travel documents from a consulate. But both Maggie and Calvano knew that they would never get the details out of Danny Gallagher if he and his wife had entered the United States illegally. Besides, there was no doubt that they were married and that Arcelia had the right to be here.

'Could she have run away?' Maggie asked him. 'Sometimes pregnant women start to have second thoughts. It's pretty common, in fact.'

'Never,' Danny said. 'I think maybe her worst fears came true – maybe the drug gang that took her somehow found out she was pregnant and living in the United States. Maybe they figure I'm rich and will give them even more money now.'

'You think a drug gang came up here and got her?' Calvano asked skeptically. 'Why bother? They'd be taking a huge risk for an uncertain payout. And if she had known something, or seen anything that might hurt them, they would have killed her long ago.'

'I don't know why they would come up here for her,' Danny Gallagher suddenly shouted. 'I just know she lived in fear, every day, fear that they might come for her and now the worst has happened.'

A nurse came running in at the sound of Danny Gallagher's cries and she looked at Maggie and Calvano with disgust. 'He needs his rest,' she told him sternly.

'I can arrange for him to talk to you again as soon as he is able,' the priest told them. 'I give you my word.'

A priest's word was good enough for Calvano. He stood, stowed the notebook back in his pocket and extended his hand to the priest once again. 'Thank you, Father Sojak.'

'Call me John,' the priest said quickly, shaking Calvano's hand. He held out his hand to Maggie, suddenly shy. I had seen it in priests before: the younger ones, fresh from the seminary, often had little experience with women. I wondered if that was what was making Father Sojak so nervous. He had a direct, forthright manner that I thought few people could resist, and yet, I could feel that he was hiding something from them. Was it Maggie or his omissions that made him so nervous?

'Father,' Maggie said respectfully as she left the room. She, too, had been raised a Catholic, though I knew she no longer attended church and preferred instead to spend her Sunday mornings running along the shores of our town's reservoir.

The doors had barely shut on the elevator before Calvano asked Maggie, 'Did you see the eyes on that priest? I bet the nuns go crazy over him.'

'Yeah, I saw his eyes,' Maggie admitted. 'And I could tell from them that he was hiding something. So was the husband.' She sounded grim. She was not looking forward to telling Gonzales how she felt.

'You think he did it,' Calvano said almost triumphantly.

Maggie gave him a look of half disgust and half affection. 'I didn't say that. I just said he was hiding something.' She stared at the floor numbers lighting up as they descended toward the ground floor. 'If I had to put my money on it, I'd say he was innocent. What about you?'

He shrugged. 'I don't think he did it, either. But I definitely don't think drug cartels would send someone to Delaware to snatch a kindergarten teacher.'

'I don't think so either,' Maggie said. 'But they might if she was more involved than she told her husband. For all we know, she's the kingpin.' She realized what she had said and started to laugh. 'A beloved preschool teacher would be a good cover, right? I really don't think that's the case, but I do have a friend at Quantico I can call. She'll run her name through the system and let us know if it's popped up in an investigation before. That will allow us to at least evaluate whether that angle is a real possibility.'

'Without actually having to work with the FBI, right?' Calvano

said. He, like Maggie, believed that the answer to virtually every
case that crossed their desk could be found locally, and that locals
were the best people to find out the truth.

'Right. What did you think about the priest?' Maggie asked.
'You two seemed to hit it off, you brown-noser, you.'

Calvano looked vaguely ashamed at what he was about to say.
'He's lying about something. But I think it's probably got to do
with how Danny brought her back over the border. I'm not buying
that story.'

'Me either,' Maggie said. 'And I think Father Sojak is a lot
more involved in this whole thing than he lets on.'

'You don't go to church any more, do you?' Calvano asked.

'What's that have to do with anything?' she said.

'I never met Father Sojak until today, but I've heard about him.
The nuns at St Michael's and St Raphael's all think he has the
touch.'

'What the hell is the touch?' Maggie asked.

'He can heal people just by laying on his hands. He can reach
people in comas. He can communicate with people close to death
and reassure them before they go. They say he's filled with the
light and has the gift.'

'That sounds a little New Age for any of the nuns I know,'
Maggie said drily. Her view of nuns tended toward the unfavorable.
I had eavesdropped many times on her conversations with her
father and her memories of Catholic school were mixed.

'It happens,' Calvano said, a little defensively. His faith was
pretty important to him. 'A lot of the saints were rumored to have
a gift like that when they were mortals.'

'You think Father Sojak is a saint?' Maggie asked skeptically.

'No. I just think it's possible he has powers we can't understand
and I definitely think it's possible he knows something he's not
telling us.'

'Which all leads us to one conclusion,' Maggie said. 'Arcelia
Gallagher was not taken at random or by a Mexican drug gang
going way off the reservation.'

'Definitely not,' Calvano agreed.

Maggie looked thoughtful. When the press found out that Arcelia
Gallagher's disappearance was not a random kidnapping, they
would go after her husband with a vengeance. A beloved preschool
teacher killed by a husband who had close family ties to the mayor

in town was a way better story than a drug king kidnapping or whatever the truth might be. Everyone in town would become part of the spectacle. The television cameras would be around for a long time to come, which meant that Gonzales would be looking over Maggie's shoulder for just as long.

SIX

I rode with Maggie and Calvano back to the station, listening to their easy banter and wishing that I'd had the chance to experience a partnership like theirs when I was alive. But it's tough being a good partner when you're drunk all the time and your partner is either joining you in alcohol-fueled lunches or looking at you with disgust because it's either judge you – or take a hard look in the mirror.

The closest I would ever get to having a real partner would be as an unseen observer in the back seat of their patrol car, feeding on their camaraderie as a bird might fall upon seed.

Maggie was telling Calvano about the emergency room doctor she had met during a case a year before. He had been the first person Maggie had felt like dating since her divorce four years previously but as she could not take the witness stand and say she was involved with another witness, they'd put the relationship off. Eventually the realness of what they had felt faded into the past and the potential of what they could be had withered under the long wait until trial. She sounded resigned about it – and that worried me. She had the tendency to make work her whole life. I had started to hope for more for her. In my opinion, when Adrian Calvano is your closest friend and your partner, you are in trouble. I knew Maggie didn't like people to get close to her, but she was too young to go through life alone and way too supportive of others to not know what it felt like to have others want to support her.

'You'll just have to date enough people for the two of us,' Maggie was telling Calvano. 'It's a sacrifice, I know. But you're up to it.'

'Are you being sarcastic?' Calvano asked. 'Because you're not

usually sarcastic and it indicates a level of bitterness about my
love life I did not realize you had.'

Maggie smiled. 'I was only being half sarcastic. Please, date
away. I wish you the best of luck.'

'Do you believe in all that stuff the husband was saying?'
Calvano asked. 'The part about true love and seeing someone and
knowing instantly that they were meant for you?'

'Maybe. But I don't hold out much hope that it's going to
happen to me.'

'Why do you say that?' Calvano asked. 'Any guy would be
lucky to have you.'

'You know, Adrian, that is so sweet. I will say this for you –
you're a gentlemen. But my choices in love so far in life have
proved to be disastrous and I hate making mistakes, so I prefer to
avoid it if at all possible.'

'That's terrible,' Calvano declared, shaking his head. 'How can
you work all the cases we work and see all the things we see, and
not believe in something good to counteract it?'

'I didn't say I didn't believe in love,' Maggie corrected him. 'I
just don't believe it for myself.' She looked at him thoughtfully.
'What about you, Adrian? You go out with an awful lot of women.
I'm guessing you haven't been hit by the thunderbolt yet?'

'I might have been hit by the thunderbolt. She just wasn't hit
by one in return.'

'Seriously? The way all those women throw themselves at you,
you're telling me you have never really been truly, madly, deeply
in love?'

Calvano was just about to answer when Maggie screamed, 'Son
of a bitch!' and slammed on the brakes.

Calvano lurched toward the dashboard and stopped himself just
in time. 'What the hell, Gunn?' he complained.

Maggie didn't hear him. She was staring at a well-muscled man
with feathered brown hair and that kind of square jaw I thought
only existed on cartoon superheroes. He was directing a camera
crew down the sidewalk toward the front doors of the station. The
guy was handsome in that weird way that makes him almost
uncomfortable to be around because you can't help but think he
is either shallow or, possibly, plastic.

Maggie was staring at the man with an expression I could not
decipher. Not admiration, that much I knew, because I could feel

the turmoil in her roiling at the sight of him. It was more like an explosion of emotions – anger, sadness, confusion and more. I had never seen her so rattled.

'What the hell is the matter with you?' Calvano asked. 'You almost made me chip a tooth.'

'I can't believe he's here,' Maggie muttered. She inched the car along, following the handsome man as he strode along the sidewalk, the hapless camera crew scurrying after him like ducks. He was wearing tailored pants and a really expensive sport shirt, the kind television reporters wear when they want to look like regular people. There was definitely something about the guy that I absolutely and completely loathed on the spot. I think it was the way he walked, as if he owned the world and everyone else was just there to serve him.

'Who is that guy?' Calvano asked. He craned his neck trying to get a better look, but Maggie was going so slow that they had yet to pass him. 'He looks like a giant freaking G.I. Joe doll. How many plastic surgeries do you think he's had?'

Maggie glanced over at Calvano. 'Zero. He was born that way.'

'You know him?' Calvano asked.

'Yeah, I know him,' Maggie said grimly. 'His name is Skip Bostwick.'

'Who the hell is called "Skip" at our age?' Calvano said. 'That name is as fake as he is.'

'Oh, it's real. He's been called that since he was a kid. His real name is Sydney.'

'How do you know so much about him?' Calvano asked curiously. 'Don't tell me he's one of the disastrous choices you were just talking about?'

'Oh, he is *the* disastrous choice.' Maggie was silent for a moment, trying to decide how much she should tell Calvano. 'He's my ex-husband, Adrian. He's why I moved back here. He's what I was trying to get away from when I left Wilmington.'

'No shit!' Calvano shouted, unable to help himself.

I felt exactly the same way. Maggie didn't have a personal life, at least not one I had been able to discover after many months of trying. I knew she had an ex-husband and that he had acted badly, I'd heard snippets of that disaster in conversations with her father. But I had never thought of the ex-husband as real. I'd thought of him more as a figure fading away in her rear-view mirror. To see him now, standing six feet tall and so inertly good-looking he may as well have been a wax figure in that London museum, well – I couldn't process it. Neither could Calvano. He just sat and stared at the guy.

Maggie didn't want to talk about it. 'It's true, and we are definitely going in the back door. I'd crawl through the air vent to avoid him if I had to.'

'We'll have to tell Gonzales,' Calvano said. 'If he finds out, he'll read you the riot act about not talking to the guy or giving him any information.'

'There is absolutely, positively no chance in hell that I will ever talk to him,' Maggie said. 'Trust me on this one, Adrian.'

But it was Calvano's turn to look surprised. Maggie had pulled even with the station house, giving them a clear view of the news crews that had set up camp on the sidewalk in front. 'Oh, Mother Mary. Gonzales is going to shit a brick. Look who's here.'

Maggie was trying to avoid a cluster of pedestrians who had started to gather to stare at the television cameras. 'Who?' she asked. 'Son of a bitch, get the hell out of my way.' She blasted her horn and a fat man taking his sweet time trundling across the street shot her the bird. Nice. Already, people were posturing for the cameras.

'It's Lindsey Stanford,' Calvano said, pointing at a stocky woman in a butt-ugly brown pants suit who was holding a microphone and practicing her intro while the sound man checked his levels. Middle age had hit her hard since I'd last seen her on TV. She had interesting features, if you were in a charitable mood, and a mean face if you were not. Snarling was her preferred expression. She also had one of those awful bowl haircuts that are round at the top like a Nazi war helmet. Her hair was dyed a frosted blond. But regardless of her looks, she was one of the most popular crime commentators in the country. She had her own show on a cable outlet and if Lindsey Stanford was here, it was Gonzales's worst nightmare come true. Every single element of the Arcelia Gallagher case would be subjected to Lindsey Stanford's ruthless speculation about who was to blame. If past history was any indication, she would zero in on someone and persecute them on air, contaminating the investigation and causing witnesses to invent details just for a little air time. It was not good news that she was in town.

'Why the hell is she here?' Maggie muttered.

'The mayor,' Calvano guessed. 'It's just like Gonzales said. He's called in the media to put pressure on us.'

Maggie pulled into a parking spot as far away from the cameras as she could get. 'You know what, Adrian?' she asked. 'I'd give my eye teeth to find out that, in the end, Mayor Gallagher was involved in his daughter-in-law's disappearance. Because he deserves payback for this, big time.'

'Look out,' Calvano said, pointing to a cluster of reporters who had rounded the corner and were heading for their car. Maggie's ex-husband led the pack. 'We've been spotted.'

'I'm not doing this,' Maggie decided. She put the key back in the ignition and revved the engine. 'Where are the other teams right now?'

'Tom and Terrence are at the elementary school, talking to the kids. Elton and Sandy are canvassing the neighbors.'

'Then we're going to the school,' Maggie decided. 'Better hold on.'

Calvano knew enough about Maggie's driving to take the warning seriously. He braced himself as she accelerated toward the main exit of the parking lot, then took an abrupt U-turn and screeched out the side entrance, leaving the news crews standing in a cloud of exhaust. They stared after her dumbfounded.

'Nice move, Gunn,' Calvano said. 'Way to make your ex eat your dust.'

'He's lucky that's the only thing I'm making him eat,' Maggie snapped back.

I was suddenly very glad that I had never been in a position to get on her bad side.

SEVEN

The school where Arcelia Gallagher taught was crowded with families waiting in the hallways to talk to the police. It seemed as if everyone wanted to find Seely. I was not the only one who had been captivated by her.

The children were still too young to understand what might have happened to their teacher. They raced up and down the hallways playing and their parents were too distracted to stop them. They had been forced to hurry past a gauntlet of television cameras as they entered the school with their children in tow and the experience had driven home the realization that Arcelia Gallagher's disappearance was real.

Two of the classrooms had been converted into staging areas where the detectives could question the children in the hope that at least one had seen something that might prove useful in the investigation.

The two men questioning the kids seemed an unlikely choice at first glance, but if you knew them, like I did, it made sense. One was tall and gaunt with a cadaverous face, but he was the father of four children, the last I'd heard, and comfortable with their fanciful flights of imagination – all of which had to be sorted out from the truth to reveal useful leads.

The other officer was a bear of a man whose father owned the Polish restaurant in town. Terrence Palicki must have eaten at it five times a day growing up because he was well over six feet tall and as wide as a grizzly. He was also a gentle giant. I remembered him as one of the few people who had been unfailingly kind to me back when I was alive and bumbling through my cases. He didn't have a mean bone in his body. At the moment, he was questioning a small boy with a remarkably round head and runny nose. Two of his classmates stood nearby, gazing at Terrence with awe.

'What did he look like?' Terrence was asking the little guy, who mostly seemed interested in the gold badge pinned to the detective's jacket pocket. Maggie and Calvano were waiting against one wall for Terrence to finish before they checked in. Both were the subjects of unabashed staring by a line of five-year-olds. Maggie barely seemed to notice their presence, but Calvano winked at a few and flashed his gun at a row of little boys. He had a lot of nieces and nephews and was comfortable with humans that barely reached his waist, even though he had none of his own.

The little boy with the round head picked up a crayon and bashed it into the top of the desk, enjoying the opportunity to smash something. 'I don't know,' he told Terrence, concerned solely with the destruction of his crayon. 'He looked like my dad.'

Now if it had been me, I would've torn my hair out long ago and left the task to someone else, but Terrence had unlimited

patience. 'What does your dad look like?' he asked the child.
'What color hair does he have? Is he taller than me?'

The little boy stared at Terrence. 'No one is taller than you.'

'What about his hair? What color was it?'

'Like mine. I look like my daddy so my daddy looks like me,'
the boy explained proudly.

Terrence sighed. He had limits after all. He shifted in the chair,
which was way too small for him, and the whole room seemed to
tremble. 'You have blond hair,' he pointed out. 'Did the man you
saw at the fence also have blond hair?'

The little boy nodded, but one of his classmates could no longer
stand by and listen to his nonsense. 'Liar!' an Hispanic boy with
a buzz cut interrupted. 'The man had brown skin like mine and
his hair looked like mine.'

The first boy looked at his classmate with scorn. 'I think I can
tell the difference between a Mexican and a 'Merican.'

Oh yes, it started young.

'So you saw the man at the fence talking to Seely, too?' Terrence
asked the second boy.

The boy nodded. His skin was the color of dried autumn leaves.
His eyes were huge and he stuck his thumb in his mouth for
comfort as he contemplated Terrence's size.

'Was this a few days ago?' Terrence said encouragingly, his
voice gentle as he tried to wheedle more information out of the
boy.

'No,' the little boy said stubbornly. 'It was the day we had the
birthday cake for Amy.'

Terrence sighed and wrote something down in his notebook,
but the first little boy felt his honor had been maligned and was
not going to let the matter stand.

'Edgar's lying,' he said, glaring at his classmate. 'I saw the man
and he had blond hair like me.'

'Did not!' Edgar shouted back.

Terrence was starting to sweat. Two little alpha boys were about
to go at it and he was trying to figure out what he could do about
it, given that the stun gun and pepper spray were out of the
question.

'Boys are so dumb,' a high-pitched voice interrupted. A little
girl with curly red hair stood a few feet away, arms crossed as she
shook her head at them like she was their mother.

The little girl looked from one boy to the other. Her voice dripped with scorn as she said to Terrence, 'Did you ever think that maybe there were two men at the fence. Huh? Did *any* of you think of that?' She was actually tapping her foot on the floor, a caricature of a movie mother. She was going to make someone miserable one day.

'Good point,' Terrence told the little girl. 'Why don't you come over here and talk to me some more?'

Like I said: infinite patience.

With Maggie and Calvano's help, they finished questioning the children within an hour while I amused myself by making faces at the little squirts – to no avail, as they could not see me – and then wandered outside to haunt the media crowd for a while. Maggie's ex-husband, Skip Bostwick, was there, being an even bigger jerk than he looked like. He was sucking up to the better-known newscasters with a zeal that only lifetime brown-nosers can achieve. I wandered back inside where the families were gradually trickling out, until just the detectives were left in the classroom discussing what they had learned. The only possible lead they had uncovered came back to the two little boys and their belief that the missing teacher had been talking to a man, or two men, depending on who you believed, through the back fence of the playground at various times the week before. One boy insisted the man had been blond and that Seely had been angry at him, shouting at him to go away and leave them all alone. The other little boy had stuck fast to his insistence that the man had been Mexican and that his teacher had seemed sad, not angry, after she had talked to the man. Neither boy, nor the red-haired girl, knew more and their classmates had not noticed anyone talking to their teacher at all.

'It's not a lot to go on,' Maggie said with resignation.

'Better than nothing,' Calvano said. 'And it might mean something.'

'Did any of the parents know anything?' Maggie asked.

Terrence shook his head. 'We didn't have time to talk with them one-on-one, but I asked anyone with information to come forward and I gave them plenty of opportunity to do so. I am sure they would have spoken up if they had anything. There is not a parent in the school who doesn't love that woman. I don't know what else she had going on in her life, but our missing girl must've been one hell of a teacher.'

Maggie's frustration was obvious. She glanced out the window where the camera crews were starting to pack up in the distance.

'What's that all about?' Terrence asked. 'The camera crews got here soon after we did.'

'Apparently, there is nothing else going on in America right now,' Maggie said bitterly. 'We're the main show until some moron who thinks he's smarter than everyone else kills his wife and hides her body.'

'You sure that's not what happened here?' Terrence asked.

'We're not sure of anything,' Maggie admitted, shaking her head in dismay.

EIGHT

D anny Gallagher was ready to go home, but home was out of the question. I had claimed the back seat of Father Sojak's car when he arrived at the hospital to pick up Danny later that night. I thought I might learn something useful if I tagged along with them. Unfortunately, Danny sat silent, still in shock, throughout the entire ride and Father Sojak turned out to be the kind of person who doesn't like to push someone into sharing. The silence had been heavy and depressing. Now, the three of us were staring at a gauntlet of media blocking the entrance to Danny's farm.

'Oh, God,' Danny muttered.

'I'll take you to the rectory,' Father Sojak decided. 'You can stay in one of our guest bedrooms.'

Danny did not answer. Someone in the crowd had recognized him and a camera crew started sprinting toward the car. Danny shielded his face while the priest turned the car around in a cloud of dust and sped back toward town, leaving the cameraman covered in dirt. I peered out the back window and stuck my tongue out at the media pack, enjoying one of the perks of not being seen. I was certain we would be followed, but none of the news vans took chase. It did not take long for me to realize that we had another tail, however. Maybe they didn't care whether or not they were spotted, or maybe they were just lousy at it, but it was pretty

obvious that Maggie and Calvano intended to follow Danny
Gallagher wherever he went. They picked us up on the highway
and followed us all the way through town. But when we reached
the parking lot of St Raphael's, Maggie pulled their car behind a
van where it would not be seen and stayed put. The priest was
leading a still-silent Danny Gallagher inside the church, so I took
the opportunity to see what Maggie and Calvano were up to.

They were arguing. I was astonished to find that Calvano wanted
to go inside alone to talk to the priest. He usually depended on
Maggie to take the lead in everything they did. But this time he
was adamant. 'Look, I don't want to offend you, but the dude is
clearly uncomfortable around women,' he said. 'You make him
nervous.'

'Gee,' Maggie said sarcastically. 'I wonder why that is?'

'Look, you have to respect his religion. Isn't it your religion,
too?'

Maggie gave Calvano a look of disgust. 'Fine. Go in and talk
to the guy alone if you think it will get us anywhere. But steer
away from Danny for now. I'll stay out here and wait to see if he
leaves, just in case.'

'Don't be mad at me. I just want to get another take on if he's
hiding something,' Calvano said.

'Oh, he's hiding something,' Maggie told him. She slumped
back against the seat, pulled out her cellphone and began reading
what I suspected was a string of e-mails from Gonzales. I had
seldom seen her in such a bad mood and I knew the appearance
of her ex-husband had everything to do with it. I was tempted to
keep her company – after all, that's what invisible friends are for
– but I was curious to watch Calvano in action.

I had never been a very good Catholic, not even when I was
young and the ultimate honor had been to be chosen by the priests
to serve as an altar boy at Christmas and Easter mass. I had always
argued with my parents, kicking and screaming, in fact, as I was
dragged from the car and forced to report for duty. Needless to
say, I had never been chosen for important masses. Then again, I
had never had to spend time alone with a priest, either, and maybe
that was good. Our town had become fiercely divided on the topic
of priests in recent years, with half of them – the Catholic half
– vigorously defending the local fathers from speculation even as
scandal gripped the church worldwide. The other half pretty much

just assumed they were all perverts and kept their children as far away from them as possible. It was a sad state of affairs.

Calvano clearly weighed in with the pro-Catholic half. It was as if he pulled himself together and solidified somehow before he entered the church, his steps slowing as he reached the front doors. I slipped in behind him, curious to know what it felt like to be in St Raphael's again after so many years. I had been there a few times as a child and it was, by far, the most beautiful Catholic church in the county. A high dome soared above floor-to-ceiling stained-glass windows and the floors were polished marble. The lighting was muted and red votive candles caused shadows to dance across the paneled walls. The sanctuary smelled like melting wax. There were no electric votives at St Raphael's. This was old-school Catholicism and most of the parishioners were pretty old-school themselves.

The church was empty except for one young Hispanic woman who sat in the front pew as her fingers flew over her rosary beads. If St Raphael was anything like the Catholic church my family attended on the other side of town, membership had soared in recent years, rising with the Mexican population.

Calvano dipped his fingers into the holy water that shimmered in a basin near the front door and automatically crossed himself, a gesture now found only among older church members. I figured he would head for the side door that led to a small courtyard and the rectory where the priests and nuns lived, but Calvano surprised me. He walked about halfway down the middle aisle, then knelt on one knee, crossed himself, rose, and entered one of the pews. He knelt again and began to pray.

I cannot actually read people's minds. I have had more success with memories. But I can often share in what people are feeling and I found the fallout from Calvano's prayers to be extraordinary. I was sitting in the row behind him when I felt a blanket of cool, comforting air settle in around me. I felt compelled to look up and, as I did so, the light from the votive candles seemed to dance across the jewel tones of the stained-glass windows, sending droplets of fiery red, golden yellow and sapphire blue spinning over the white marble floor. My whole being filled with a warm, comforting liquid, a feeling I had not experienced since I was a young child and my grandmother held me in her lap. I felt a glow somewhere deep inside me and my greatest fear – that I might

never be able to leave this plane – disappeared under its power.
It was as if infinite possibilities had been offered to me and all I
had to do to obtain them was to believe. I was rocked by the sensation. I felt comforted and exalted and powerful all at the same time.
I felt renewed and humbled and honored.

I do not think Calvano felt what I did. I think that only someone
in my state of being could experience what I had. But I was deeply
grateful to know that being the way I was, trapped between the
living and the dead, in an existence which brought so much loneliness, also had its advantages.

Calvano finished his prayers and rose. Reluctantly I went with
him. I'd felt a glimpse of something greater waiting for me one
day. It made leaving behind what I had felt all that much harder,
but what choice did I have? My afterlife is apparently among the
living.

I knew the rectory at St Raphael's would be much the same as
the one so familiar to me from attending St Michael's. I was right.
Behind the church, surrounded by a parking lot, sprawled a low,
unremarkable building that housed the living quarters of the priests
and a handful of nuns who served the church. There was nothing
colorful or stylish about their rooms. Yet somehow, there was a
relief in the sparseness of the outdated furniture and bare walls.
This was not a place of material excess.

An old priest was fast asleep in a leather armchair by a window,
his snores filling a tiny library next to the kitchen. I looked around
to see where everyone else had gone.

Calvano had been met by an older nun who was leading him
back to Father Sojak with a friendliness that was a little too effu-
sive to be genuine. The priest was sitting at the kitchen table with
a cup of tea in front of him. The room was filled with melancholy.
He did not look surprised to see Calvano. He merely shrugged
and Calvano sat next to him with a poise I was not used to seeing
in him.

'Where's Danny?' Calvano asked.

The priest nodded toward the doorway. 'He's putting his things
away in his room. Can't you do something about the situation at
his house? It's not good for him to stay here. He's afraid that his
wife may try to come home and that he won't be there. Or that
someone may call and ask for money for her and he won't be
there to answer it.'

He wanted Calvano to control the media besieging Danny's farm. Calvano knew the task was impossible. 'His home and cellphones are already being routed to the department in case someone calls about his wife, and I'll see if the commander will put a couple of patrol cars on the farm,' he promised. 'But Father, are you sure you want to get involved?'

The priest understood the real meaning behind Calvano's words. He was warning him that Danny Gallagher could well be guilty. And if he was, that he could pull Father Sojak, or even all of St Raphael's, down with him.

Father Sojak glanced at the hallway and lowered his voice. 'I won't pretend that Danny is a faithful member of this church. He only comes to make his wife happy. It's Arcelia that loves St Raphael's. She is the light of our lives here. But he is a good husband to her and I can assure you that he loves her deeply. He would never harm her. She is everything to him. His love for her has no limit, from what I can tell.'

There was a trace of regret in the priest's words, and I wondered how much Arcelia Gallagher had meant to him. As I speculated on their relationship, I realized that the tiny rectory did not have the same glorious feeling that the church itself had. There was human emotion at war within the rectory's walls. I could feel anxiousness flavoring the air around me and something else, too – it felt like an ocean of everything from hope and desire to sorrow, fear, love and utter devotion, all roiling together in such a way that I could not pinpoint who or where it was coming from.

Was it possible that I was simply picking up on what the people Father Sojak counseled had left behind? I did not think the turmoil came from him.

Someone passed by me in the hallway, startling me. She was nearly as quiet and invisible as I was. It was the old nun who had led Calvano to Father Sojak. She had returned to the hallway outside the kitchen to eavesdrop. She was clutching a rosary anxiously and smelled of baby powder. Her cheeks were flushed, as if she were ashamed of herself for spying but could not help herself.

Danny Gallagher was behind one of the doors that lined the hallway, but I did not think that the nun was concerned about him. Was it Father Sojak she worried for? No, her gaze did not linger on him. She seemed concerned with Calvano.

'You'd be surprised at what a devoted husband can do,' Calvano told the priest. 'Are you sure you really know Danny Gallagher?'

'Not as well as you, apparently,' Father Sojak said calmly. Either he was a very smart man or he really did have powers beyond what most people can understand. He was staring at Calvano thoughtfully. 'People can change, you know. I see it all the time. They come to me desperate to change and then they do. I know you have a history with him, but I have never known him to be anything but a devoted and loving husband.'

'And yet, I can't shake the feeling that you are hiding something,' Calvano said. 'I'm a good Catholic boy, father. I like priests. None of you are very good at hiding guilt.'

The priest turned his deep blue eyes toward Calvano. I felt a connection strengthen between them and I wondered if Father Sojak had the same power I did to rifle through, or at least feel, the memories that others held in their minds. Calvano was not intimidated. He was on familiar ground. But the nun hiding in the hallway grew visibly more nervous. Her hands were trembling and sweat gleamed on her forehead.

'I assure you that I am telling you absolutely everything I know about Danny Gallagher,' the priest said firmly.

'But not everything about Arcelia Gallagher, are you?' Calvano asked.

Father Sojak sat quietly, looking at his hands. They were long and graceful and I could understand why some might feel as if they had held the power to heal.

He remained mute, trying to decide how much he could trust Calvano. The clock on the wall ticked loudly in the silence.

The nun was trembling. I moved closer to her, brushing up against her with my essence. She did not even notice.

'Arcelia helps the newest immigrants,' Father Sojak said in a near whisper. 'People from her country, fleeing the drug wars as she was forced to do. Her husband does not know about it. They come here, frightened and far from home, and she calms them. She understands what they are running away from and why they feel they must come here for a better life. Because of what she has been through, she speaks with conviction and from the heart. They respond to her. She has helped many families reunite and many lonely people find their way to a new beginning. I don't know what these people are going to do without her. We have nuns who understand what they are saying, but only Arcelia under-stands what they are feeling.'

'And none of these people have their papers, do they?' Calvano asked, although he knew the answer already.

The priest shook his head.

'I'm not with Immigration,' Calvano told him. 'I don't care if they're here illegally or not. But I need to talk to them. They may have seen something. They may know something. You must under-stand how important this is?'

'I don't think any of them will agree to talk to you,' the priest said. 'I will do my best to convince them. But where they come from, the men who have badges are often the ones they fear the most. But I will see what I can do.'

'What about you?' Calvano asked. 'When is the last time you actually *saw* Arcelia Gallagher?'

'She came here the day before she disappeared,' Father Sojak confessed. 'She wanted to talk to one of our other parishioners. I did not know where he was and I could not help her. She left and I do not know where she went.'

'How about if I talk to that parishioner?' Calvano asked.

'I had not seen him in a week when she came looking for him and I still do not know where he is,' Father Sojak said firmly.

Calvano understood. The parishioner was an illegal immigrant and Father Sojak had no intention of telling Calvano where he might be. He rose to go. The nun, visibly relieved that the ques-tioning was over, backed slowly down the hall. When she reached a smaller doorway at the other end of it, she glanced at it. I could feel her anxiousness radiating toward whatever was behind that door. Interesting.

Calvano and the priest were exchanging goodbyes and I could have followed the old nun as she scurried away down the corridor. But I was a much better detective than I had been when I was alive – and I knew that at least one clue as to where Arcelia Gallagher might be lay behind that door.

As I approached it, I could feel the emotions I had sensed earlier rising in me, growing a hundredfold in strength. I suddenly knew, with an unshakeable certainty, that behind that door lay lifetimes worth of hopes and dreams, an endless plane of happiness and misery entangled together – the essence that connects all human beings. I passed through the door.

A narrow stairway led down into the darkness on the other side. As I drew near the end of the steps, I begin to hear a hum that grew louder and separated into individual voices. I made my way along a narrow, dimly lit hallway that wound back beneath the rectory and under the parking lot to the basement of the church itself.

As I approached a set of double doors at the far end of the underground corridor, the voices grew louder. I could distinguish the deep tones of men from the higher cadences of women and the shrieks of children at play. The sea of emotions I was feeling burbled and boiled, filling me with a strange affection for what I might find on the other side of the double doors. Light leaked out from the crack between them and I followed it like a beacon.

Inside that basement room, I discovered a secret world. A vast space stretched out as far as I could see. It was filled with row after row of neatly made beds, some separated from the others by screens for privacy. Everywhere I looked, people sat in clusters, talking, holding their children, reading books, lying on their beds sleeping, clustered around small television sets or eating at a long, narrow table pushed up against a wall. Every single one of them had the dark skin tones and distinctive features of Mexicans who come from Aztec stock. There must have been a hundred or more people in that basement, not counting the children who chased one another between the rows of beds.

Two nuns walked calmly among the rows of beds, handing out towels and pillows to their weary-looking guests. Some of the people seeking sanctuary at St Raphael's were old, some were young, some were yet to be born. Many looked tired, but all seemed grateful. Relief pervaded the room. I was staring at a refugee camp.

I would never have pegged Father Sojak and the old nun in the hallway as people who would blatantly break the law. I would not have thought the two young nuns helping people settle down for the night could be so cheerful about being part of it. But you did not build a haven this large, or filled with so many beds and other supplies, without knowing exactly what the consequences could be. They had created a sanctuary for illegal immigrants below the very marble floors of St Raphael's. They had to know the chances they were taking.

I became aware of a burning sensation and I knew what that meant – it is the feeling I get when someone on the other side, the side of the living, can see me. I looked around the room and saw an impossibly old woman with a shrunken face collapsed in on itself staring at me as her fingers flew over her rosary. Her nearly toothless mouth was contorted in silent prayer. Her eyes filled with fear as she stared at me standing in the doorway. I nodded at her and she nodded back.

I backed from the room, my eyes never leaving hers. I was not Death, but I knew Death would visit her soon. That always happened to people who could see me.

NINE

D espite my side trip to the basement, I still beat Calvano to the car. He had lingered to talk theology with Father Sojak. I was glad Calvano was not there to witness what I saw before he arrived: Maggie screaming into her cellphone, as angry as I had ever seen her.

'How did you get this number?' She sounded furious. 'Don't ever call me again. You are not going to get anything from me and you should have known better than to try.'

Calvano reached the car and she hurriedly disconnected, setting her phone to silent and storing it away. By the time he slid into the front seat next to her, her anger was under control. 'Find out anything useful?' she asked him.

Calvano nodded. 'Apparently, Arcelia Gallagher is a major stop on the Mexican Underground Railroad.'

Maggie looked confused.

'Seriously? You don't know what the Underground Railroad is? The network of hiding spaces people used to hide slaves in who were leaving the South and fleeing to freedom in the North during the Civil War?' Calvano looked at her impatiently. 'Our town used to be a stop on it. Slaves hid here until they could make the final dash to Philadelphia. It's all we learned about in school.'

Maggie was barely listening. Her mind was still on the conversation she had just had. 'Of course I know about it,' she said. 'But you aren't being serious, right?'

'I'm being completely serious. Father Sojak says Arcelia

Gallagher counsels illegal immigrants who come through St Raphael's for help starting new lives here in America. He made it sound like it was just a couple of them, but when's the last time you only saw a few illegal immigrants together?'

'We need to talk to them,' Maggie said.

'I know. I'm on it. He's going to get back to me.'

Maggie looked at him skeptically.

'I said I was on it. What's next?'

'Gonzales called us back to the office.' Her tone made it clear that this was the last thing she wanted to do. 'We are under orders to come in the front door.'

'Seriously?' Calvano sounded pissed, but he was still Calvano: he looked in the car mirror and started arranging his hair. He knew he'd be on every major network by nightfall tomorrow.

'Yes, seriously. He wants the whole world to know that the best detectives in town are on the case,' Maggie said sourly.

'Hey, it's kind of a compliment, right?' Calvano asked.

'It's kind of a pain in the ass,' she answered.

It may have been a pain in the ass for them to push through the cluster of reporters and cameramen waiting to ambush them when they reached the station house, but for me it was kind of a hoot. I kept walking in front of the cameras, blocking their view, hoping that I might at least create some static and ruin a shot or two. A ghostly figure would have been way more dramatic and, for a brief shining moment, I had a vision of becoming a legend around the station house after all. But I knew it was just a fantasy. I was pretty sure I was destined to remain as unknown as I had been while alive.

As always, the leader of the media pack seemed to be Lindsey Stanford, the stocky woman in a crap-colored pantsuit and a bad haircut who had a bigger entourage than most of the other reporters competing with her. Two cameramen, a sound man, some Type-A skinny blond producer and a terrified-looking intern followed her as she barreled through the crowd, making a beeline for Maggie and Calvano. Maggie must have been under orders from Gonzales to talk to her, because she slowed reluctantly and waited until the reporter reached her. Lindsey Stanford was a legend to some, but she was one of those popular culture figures whose rise to fame I had missed, due to being in an alcoholic haze for the past ten years.

Lindsey Stanford had nerve, I had to give her that. She sent a tiny blond reporter careening off another competitor with one bump from her hip and then planted herself firmly in front of Maggie. Instead of sticking her microphone in Maggie's face, she held it up to her own and launched into a long and well-written introduction about Arcelia Gallagher, the beloved mother-to-be and kindergarten teacher who had surely met with foul play. She fully expected Maggie and Calvano to stand there while she hogged the camera time, and stand there they did. As she was talking, somehow making the disappearance of Arcelia all about her, I saw Maggie's ex-husband inching his way through the crowd, trying to catch Stanford's eye. I wondered what Maggie would do when she realized that her ex-husband was working with the most obnoxious reporter in a field of highly obnoxious candidates.

Stanford was wrapping up her endless intro with a sensationalized account of Maggie's career to date, no doubt fed to her by some public relations flack Gonzales had assigned to the case. It was all Calvano could do to keep from laughing as he listened. Apparently, the fact that he was invisible to both Gonzales, and now the public, did not bother him a bit. For once, being a screwup had its advantages.

'Detective Gunn,' Stanford finally asked Maggie. 'What news do you have in this sad case of a missing, beloved community figure?'

Maggie stared at the reporter like Stanford was some streetwalker she had been caught in the act, and it was not until Calvano gave her a discreet push that she answered. 'We cannot comment on the case, but we can assure the public that we are doing everything possible to bring home this beloved mother-to-be and kindergarten teacher.'

Maggie had nicely regurgitated Stanford's own words but also managed to look like she wanted to throw up a little more.

By then, Maggie's ex-husband, Skip Bostwick, had reached the center of the crowd and was whispering to one of Stanford's cameramen. The cameraman nodded and gave his boss a signal. She caught it out of the corner of her eye and, sensing that Maggie was not going to be the interviewee she had hoped, she smoothly changed tack. Turning to Maggie's ex-husband, she announced to the camera, 'We have a forensic expert straight from the state of Delaware's famed crime laboratory who is prepared to give us insider information on results of sensational tests that call the husband's innocence into question.'

Maggie's mouth fell open, fortunately off-camera, and Calvano tugged her away before she could lunge at Skip Bostwick and start swinging. Calvano hustled her in through the doors of the station house, where four policemen were standing guard to keep outsiders out. He did not say anything until they were near the elevators, but he did not let up on his pressure either. He was going to get Maggie as far away from the news crews and her ex-husband as he could before she exploded. Calvano was a dumb-ass, but he knew women and he could feel the fury sparking off Maggie as surely as I could.

'Inside,' he commanded her as the elevator arrived. She was still looking over her shoulder, but Calvano shooed her inside the car and I hurried in after them. The door closed and at last Calvano could speak. 'You know that he doesn't have anything that's really a clue,' he told her. 'It's just bullshit for the ratings. The lab is not going to give him any meaningful results.'

'You don't know Skip,' Maggie said quietly. 'He has friends everywhere. He could be out there divulging some important piece of evidence right now.'

'No way,' Calvano said shaking his head. 'Gonzales is too smart for that. He's either sending them on a wild goose chase, or just telling them what they want to hear so we can work the real evidence.'

'I hate that man with every fiber of my being,' Maggie suddenly declared, and I knew she wasn't talking about Gonzales. 'Is it just me or does obnoxiousness leak from every one of his pores?'

'You won't have any argument from me on that point,' Calvano admitted.

The elevator doors opened and Gonzales was waiting for them, smartphone in hand, watching the tail end of a live streaming video of their encounter with Lindsey Stanford. God, that was creepy. He had been four floors above them and yet had seen every move they made. 'Nice quote,' he said to Maggie, pointedly ignoring Calvano.

'Sir,' she muttered. 'We need to talk.'

Whatever Maggie had hoped Gonzales might do to help them block the press from access to their investigation, her worst fears were realized when he informed her that he knew that Lindsey

Stanford's technical consultant was her ex-husband and he expected her to make the most of the situation.

'You want me to suck up to him?' Maggie asked in a tone of voice I had never heard from her before. 'Sir, do I have to tell you what it was like?'

'I know what it was like, Maggie,' Gonzales said, using her first name. I had never heard him call her anything but 'Gunn' before. 'But we have to keep the press under control and out of our way, and the best way for you to do that is to suck up to him. I don't care what you're feeding him. I don't care if it's fake information or unimportant information, just use your relationship with him to keep him off the trail.'

'He's already down there claiming he has sensational evidence. Mind telling us what that's about?'

Gonzales waved his hand. 'It's nothing. I reached out to all drug enforcement – the FBI, ATF the state boys, you name it – and none of them have any intelligence leading them to believe a drug cartel has been anywhere near our town in the last three years. They moved the trafficking corridor further east a long time ago and there's no chatter at all about a kidnapping. None. I let Bostwick know that.'

'Well, he's taking that as confirmation Danny Gallagher did it,' Maggie said. 'Which could be a problem.'

Gonzales was losing patience. 'Let me throw them the big bones. You just keep your ex-husband distracted.'

'What about him?' Maggie said suddenly, pointing to Calvano. 'Tell him that he has to suck up to Lindsey Stanford.'

'Hey,' Calvano protested. 'Don't drag me into this. I'm the only one in this room who's been smart enough to avoid getting married. Why should I have to pay the price?'

'Lindsey Stanford doesn't need anyone else to suck up to her,' Gonzales said neutrally. He hesitated, as if wondering if he should say anything at all, but in the end decided it was probably better if Maggie heard it from him. 'Gunn,' he added. 'I think your ex-husband is doing a good enough job of that for us all.'

Calvano looked as horrified as Maggie at the thought, but Maggie was the one to ask Gonzales, 'Please don't tell me he's sleeping with that woman?'

'It's just gossip,' Gonzales admitted.

'Oh, it's true,' Maggie assured him. 'Skip is incapable of not using his looks to get his way and I can tell you right now he is probably dying for a network job. His idea of heaven would be for a camera to be focused on him twenty-four hours a day.'

'Good. Use that against him,' Gonzales said. 'Now what can you tell me about Danny Gallagher?'

'The priest picked him up at the hospital and tried to take him home, but the media has the front entrance to his farm blocked,' Maggie said.

'The priest wants us to put a couple of men on it, so that Danny can go home,' Calvano added. 'He's afraid Danny is going to lose it if he can't be there, waiting for his wife to show.'

'Done,' Gonzales said. 'What do you think about the probability he killed her?'

'I don't think he did it,' Maggie said.

'I don't either,' Calvano added reluctantly.

'Got any other leads to go on?' Gonzales asked.

Maggie left it to Calvano to explain. 'It turns out Arcelia Gallagher counsels illegal immigrants on the sly,' Calvano said. He looked a bit uncomfortable. He was acutely aware he was talking about people who shared an ethnic background with the commander and he did not want to offend him.

Gonzales looked thoughtful. 'That fits in with what I'm hearing,' he said.

'What do you mean?' Maggie asked.

'We set up a hotline for tips,' Gonzales explained, ignoring their groans. Both Maggie and Calvano knew that a hotline would bring in nothing but false leads to waste their time. 'We set up a Spanish-language hotline,' Gonzales added, looking pleased at his cleverness. 'We've gotten a couple of calls from people who say Arcelia Gallagher visited the Delmonte House several times over the past week to talk to some illegals working out there.'

'Seriously?' Maggie asked. 'Are these credible reports?'

Gonzales nodded. 'My guess is that there are more than a few illegal immigrants working at the Delmonte House. It's entirely possible she went out there to talk to someone.'

'We should question the owners and the staff just in case,' Calvano suggested eagerly.

'This wouldn't have anything to do with the fact that Dakota Wylie lives there, would it Adrian?' Maggie's tone was dry. She, like everyone else in town, knew that the Delmonte House had been bought by a once hugely popular television star named Enrique Romero who, now ageing, had bought it for a new wife nearly four decades younger than he was. He had married her at the peak of her popularity as the star of a television series featuring, from what I had been able to tell when watching the show from a bar stool, a lot of scantily clad girls running around a college campus. When the two stars had married a little over a year ago, they had landed on the cover of every magazine devoted to entertainment on both sides of the Atlantic. The husband, Enrique Romero, liked to call himself the first mainstream Latin leading man in America, which did not explain why he had married the whitest leading woman in America. He had purchased the Delmonte House, a massive mansion on the edge of our town, as a gift to his wife, he claimed, because she was a simple country girl at heart and he knew she would never be happy in a place like Beverly Hills. It had to be a bunch of crap, but it had proved a boon for my community when tourists started arriving, hoping for a glimpse of either star, toting their hungry children and credit cards with them.

As for the owners of the Delmonte House before the two stars, they had to have been ecstatic. It had been the scene of a society murder in 1926 and a less highbrow one in the late sixties, when two vagrants sleeping in an apple orchard got in a fight over a bottle of cheap wine. Two murders in one mansion had been enough to win the Delmonte House haunted house status ever since. It had even ended up on some cheesy paranormal television show featuring a lot of black lights and night goggles, but not a lot of ghosts, and I ought to know. Eventually, the mansion had fallen into disarray. Supposedly, the ageing Latin heart-throb had restored it to its former glory for his young wife.

Calvano, of course, was mostly interested in the glory of the young wife. Dakota Wylie had broken into television at the age of fourteen and, within three years, was an inescapable presence on Most Beautiful lists, little girl's tee shirts and all the other crap that people obsess about instead of looking at their own lives. She was probably close to thirty years old now, meaning her incredible body and heart-stopping face would be showing little signs of wear. I had given up any sort of interest in the opposite sex long before I died, my libido doused by too many nights at the bar, but there was probably not a man in America who had not fantasized about Dakota Wylie at least once.

'I'm just trying to do my job,' Calvano told Maggie, a smile spreading over his face.

'Then go do it,' Gonzales ordered them. He looked at his watch. 'The husband claims he has some meeting in Los Angeles tomorrow night so if you don't talk to him first thing in the morning, he'll be gone. I want you two to talk to him personally. I don't trust him. He's too slick and I don't like the way he rode into town thinking he could buy us all with his money.'

Uh oh. Gonzales had a habit of feuding with any powerful man that might rival his standing as top Latino dog. It figures he would see Enrique Romero as a rival, even though the guy was one million times more famous than Gonzales.

'If the media gets wind of this, it is going to be insane,' Maggie predicted. 'If there are any leaks . . .'

'I'll handle the leaks,' Gonzales said. 'I know what I'm doing. You two go home, get some sleep and get out there by eight tomorrow morning. Goodnight.'

Maggie and Calvano were both smart enough to leave without another word.

TEN

I had always wondered why Calvano had so many girlfriends. There were certain neighborhoods in town where I could not go without running into him having dinner with some divorcée who saw him as her next husband. He had also long since gone through the available roster of women on the force – with the exception of Maggie, who was off-limits as his partner, not to mention because of her good sense. But, from what I could tell, he never stayed with a woman for more than two months.

I'd always figured he just couldn't find the right woman, or he'd had a terrifying mother waiting to pounce on anyone he brought home to meet her. But listening to him go on and on about Dakota Wylie on the way to the Delmonte House the next morning made me think that Calvano was one of those annoying people who always thinks they can do better, the kind of person who is always shopping for a newer girlfriend or wife, even when the one he has is right there on his arm.

I had never been like that, though I had been casually faithless and indifferent, which was arguably worse. But even in my darkest hours, part of me understood that I had hit pay dirt when I married Connie. She had been the perfect woman for me. I'd just been the wrong man for her.

For Calvano, Dakota Wylie was clearly the perfect woman, never mind that the Dakota Wylie he knew was a fictional creation of some sitcom writer. He filled Maggie in on the reasons why she was perfect for most of the ride to the Delmonte House. Finally, Maggie had enough.

'Will you shut up about her for one minute?' she complained. 'You are going to have to interrogate her and it would be good if you managed to do it without drooling.'

Calvano had the decency to look embarrassed, but he still did not shut up. 'Oh, is that how it's going to be? Let's see how calm and collected you are when you meet her husband.'

'Seriously?' Maggie asked. 'That guy is, what, seventy years old? It's gross enough that he had to marry someone forty years younger than him. I feel certain I can resist his charms.'

'Don't be so sure. Enrique Romero is a legend. He looks better than men one third his age. Not me, of course.' Calvano smiled. 'But when you're born a ladies' man, you die a ladies' man.'

'You're going to die a ladies' man a lot sooner than you planned if you don't shut up,' Maggie promised him.

Since Maggie drove like a bat out of hell, we soon reached the entrance to the Delmonte House. It was located west of town and was the only structure you could see in either direction for a good half mile. It was only two stories high, but it had that long sprawling architecture that reminds you of Thomas Jefferson's home, with lots of white columns and unbelievably green lawns that stretched everywhere you could see. Because it was June, flowers bloomed everywhere, their fragrance filling the air.

It was quite a sight. As the wrought-iron bars of the front gate swung inward to admit us, I gaped at the sheer perfection of the grounds and house. It had definitely been restored to its former glory. Someone had money, a lot of money.

And yet, as we approached the front door to the mansion itself, an odd sensation overcame me. I felt deeply unhappy, without warning, followed by something close to fear. I found, quite suddenly, that I did not want to go any closer.

I hung back, waiting as Maggie and Calvano rang the doorbell and an honest-to-god butler admitted them after checking their credentials. He seemed at least as old as the house.

Yes, I realized as the atmosphere from inside the house rolled over me, something dark and unhappy lived inside the house. Something I did not understand, except to know that I did not want to meet it.

As if to answer my thoughts, the hands of a framed antique compass decorating one foyer wall began to spin wildly in its casing. I stared at it, certain I was not imagining the movement of the tiny metal hands inside the shadow box. No one else noticed it at all. They were too busy being lectured by the butler on how not to mar the marble floors.

I was not the only invisible company at that house.

I left the foyer and followed Maggie and Calvano down a hallway past opulent rooms filled with furniture that cost more per piece than my entire yearly salary had been. French windows stretched from floor to ceiling everywhere and light bounced off the marble and polished wood floors. Still, I felt filled with darkness. So much unhappiness and then – like a lightning flash before my eyes – I caught a glimpse of arms flailing in blood, screaming, hatred blooming. Pain hit me so intensely I could not move.

Just like that, it was gone.

I tried to regain my thoughts. I did not want to be in the house. It was not safe for me. Something lived in this house, something in my plane. I could not shake my feeling of fear.

It took the old butler forever to lead Maggie and Calvano to a library so perfect it might as well have been a movie set. Perhaps it was. Three men sat in various leather chairs and on leather couches, watching a fourth man who was standing with his back to the others, gazing out a window at the landscaped grounds. They all turned as one to stare when the butler entered the room and introduced Maggie and Calvano.

A tall man with a deep tan and silver hair stepped forward. 'I'm Philip Stein, Mr Romero's agent and manager,' he said. He shook Calvano's hand and gave Maggie the once-over. She didn't even blink. She took out her badge and flashed it at him. When the man recovered and held his hand out to her, she ignored it and turned to the rest of the room.

'Which one of you is Enrique Romero?' she asked. The men look startled but the man at the window whirled around with theatrical poise. He may have been in his early seventies, but he looked more like fifty to me. He wasn't particularly tall and he was starting to put on weight, but he had the classically handsome face of a Latin heart-throb and lots of hair for the ladies to run their fingers through. He, too, had a deep tan, although he was slightly orange and, I suspected, sprayed it on to avoid chancing more wrinkles on his obviously surgically enhanced face. His skin was pulled unnaturally taut and his mouth stretched a hair too wide.

'I'm Enrique Romero,' the man said. He had better manners than his agent and strode over to where Maggie stood. He took her hands in his and held them a little too long.

If he thought that was going to charm Maggie, he was barking up the wrong tree. She wasted no time getting to the point. 'Who are these other two men?' she asked, glancing at a pair of nearly identically dressed middle-aged men perched on the couch.

'Those are Mr Romero's lawyers,' the agent said. He was impervious to Maggie's glare.

'I would prefer that Mr Romero speak for himself,' Maggie said calmly. 'Why don't we sit over there?' She nodded toward two chairs flanking a chess table that looked straight out of a high-end catalog. The pieces were made of real ebony and ivory, I suspected, but I was certain no one had ever actually played a game with them.

'Mr Romero would like counsel present when he is questioned,' the agent said quickly.

'Fine,' Maggie conceded. 'You can all watch, if it floats your boat.'

Calvano kept looking around the library, as if hoping to discover Dakota Wylie lurking in a corner. All he would've found was me. She was nowhere to be seen. I wondered if some of the unhappiness I felt in the house came from her.

Enrique Romero had not become a Hollywood star by being stupid. He pulled a chair out for Maggie to sit in and gestured for his legal team to keep their distance. Sitting across from her, he leaned over with a look of absolute openness and asked, 'What exactly is this about? My lawyers received a phone call from someone whom I understand is high up in local law enforcement asking for my cooperation. Of course, I am glad to give it. But I am unsure as to what this is all about.'

He was a good actor, I gave him that. Or maybe he wasn't acting at all. It was hard to tell. I think he was one of those people who is always on stage, so there's no way to know whether they are being genuine or not.

Maggie had three photos of Arcelia Gallagher ready to show him. She spread them out across the game board.

'A beautiful woman,' Enrique Romero said. He looked up at Maggie, waiting.

'She's missing. She disappeared on the way to work yesterday and she's nine months pregnant. People say they saw her driving out here, to your house, last week. We're sure the information is accurate.'

'Mr Romero employs a number of people at the house,' his agent interrupted. 'Perhaps she is friends with one of his staff?'

'I don't know her,' Romero told Maggie, glancing at his watch. 'I think I would remember a woman as beautiful as that.'

I believed him. Apparently, so did Maggie. She looked around the library. 'Where is your wife? I understood we would be able to talk to you both.'

'Why don't you talk to the staff instead?' the agent suggested. 'Mr Romero's wife is indisposed at the moment.' He, too, looked at his watch. I guess they had allotted enough time for the riff-raff and were eager to get on with their high-powered deals and exciting lives.

'Why don't you tell us where your wife is?' Calvano said, speaking up for the first time. 'We need to talk to her and we need to talk to her today.'

For the first time, Enrique Romero lost a little of his cool. 'My wife is not feeling well. She's pregnant and having a difficult time of it. She suffers from headaches and a number of other conditions.' He looked to his agent for help.

'I'm sure we can arrange for Ms Wylie to speak to you at a later date.'

'Why don't you arrange for us to speak to the staff, and while we're doing that, you can go do whatever is necessary to enable Ms Wylie to speak to us today,' Maggie suggested.

The men in the room froze. They were not used to someone evading their deflections. The lawyers stared at one another and then at the agent. He looked toward his client for help.

'Of course,' Romero said smoothly. 'I will tell the housekeeper to see that she wakes up and gets ready to speak to you. Now, if you will excuse me, I must leave for the airport. I have an extraordinarily important meeting I must prepare for. I'm sure you understand.'

It would have been a good exit line, but Romero's timing was spoiled when a small but stocky man barged into the library and said, without bothering to gauge the mood in the room or caring that he was interrupting, 'Enrique, you and I need to talk.'

The silence in the room was eloquent. Romero was staring at the newcomer like he was dirt on the bottom of his shoe while his advisers had openly contemptuous looks on their faces. I could not quite understand their scorn. The new man was dressed in an expensively tailored black silk shirt and gray flannel pants and his blond hair was expertly cut. Clearly, he spent a lot of time on his personal grooming and he even sported the requisite deep tan. But I guess appearances were not enough. The men in the room considered him an outsider.

'This is neither the time nor the place for this discussion,' Romero's agent snapped. He yawned and held it a little too long for it to have been genuine. 'I will touch base with you when we get back.'

'No,' the new man said abruptly. 'I've waited long enough. Are you going to do the joint project or not?'

'Not,' the agent snapped back before Romero could answer.

'But she's your client, too,' the new man protested.

'That is why I am saying no,' the agent said smoothly. 'She is not ready. One look at her should tell you why.' He turned to Romero. 'We need to get going. I have a few business items to go over with you before the car gets here and you still haven't packed.'

Romero dropped all pretense at charm and simply left the room, without waiting for Maggie and Calvano's permission. The man who had interrupted them followed Romero out like a puppy dog. His agent look anxious and I wondered at his reaction. What was it that made him so nervous?

'Why don't you ask the staff members to come in here?' Maggie suggested. She selected the largest chair – a huge, overblown leather affair – and settled back in it, crossing her legs. 'We'd be glad to wait.'

The lawyers glanced at one another and then stood as one. Tweedledee and Tweedledumber. 'We'll be on our way,' one of them said. They both stuck their hands out to shake the agent's before they left, but Maggie and Calvano merited no recognition. Maybe they were getting paid by the word.

'I'll ask the butler to arrange for the staff to come in,' the agent said through clenched teeth. He acted as if Maggie and Calvano had made him look bad, which I couldn't see. He was one uptight guy and I had a feeling there was no love lost between him and Dakota Wylie, or him and the staff and, possibly, him and the world.

As the agent turned to go, Calvano snagged a prime seat on the couch and gave Maggie a skeptical look. Neither one of them had been bowled over by Enrique Romero's charm and neither one of them trusted the agent any farther than they could throw him.

I decided to follow the agent out to check out what he really said to the butler. We walked down a hallway that led toward the rear of the house. Once again, I could feel despair and unhappiness rushing at me. Two things startled me as we rounded a corner. One, I caught a flash of yellow and turned around just in time to see the man who had barged into the library slowly closing the door to another room. He had been waiting to see who left the room. Almost immediately after that, I felt a sharp pain near my right ear. There was a sound like a clap. The air pressure around me dropped. I felt rocked by the sensation. I looked around and saw no one.

Curious. Where had it come from? The other presence was near and it was growing impatient with me. I was missing something.

The air around me had grown cold and, yet, almost instantly, I stepped out of it into the warmth of the hallway. I looked around but could see nothing, though I felt the presence near. Ahead of me, the agent had disappeared into a large kitchen where he was giving an older woman orders to bring the servants together. She was in her early seventies, with gray hair pulled back in a bun and a face that had once probably been quite beautiful.

'Send them all into the library at fifteen minute intervals,' the agent told her. He checked his watch. 'I'll be leaving in a few minutes for the airport so make sure you follow through. I don't want anyone saying he would not cooperate.'

The housekeeper held a potato peeler in one hand and a partially peeled apple in the other. She was staring at the agent with a blank look on her face.

'Did you hear what I said?' the agent asked impatiently.

The old butler hustled through the door and put his hands on the housekeeper's shoulders. He turned her around and led her to the sink where a mound of apples waited to be peeled. 'I'll take care of it, sir,' he told the agent.

The agent was staring thoughtfully at the old woman, looking her up and down as if she were livestock that he was contemplating buying. Then he glanced at the old man, shrugged and walked from the room.

As soon as he was gone, the woman grabbed the butler's arm and asked him in a frightened voice, 'Who was he? Is he here to take me away?'

'Just peel the apples, Muriel,' the old man said wearily. 'It's OK. I'm right here and I will take care of it.' He gently picked up her hand holding the potato peeler and helped her get back into the rhythm of the task. She fell to peeling automatically until she did not even seem to notice him any more. I felt no emotion from her at all once the flare-up of fear had passed. In fact, I felt very little from her other than a sort of humming that came from where most people held their memories.

She would be of little help to Maggie or Calvano. Her mind was going and the old man was fighting a losing battle to disguise it.

ELEVEN

I returned to the library, where Maggie and Calvano were talking to a nervous-looking Mexican man who sat on the edge of an armchair and wrung his hands as he answered their questions. Apparently, his name was Rodrigo Flores and he was head gardener, a position that came with room and board, including a private bathroom at the rear of the house.

'Do you know her?' Maggie asked, showing him the photos of Arcelia Gallagher.

The man nodded rapidly, fearful of the police and nervous because of it. 'Yes,' he said. 'Yes, I know her. She is from my church.'

Calvano tried to put the poor man at ease. 'St Raphael's?' Calvano asked. 'I know it. I go there sometimes for late mass. It's a very beautiful church.'

The man gulped and nodded.

'Look,' Calvano said. 'We're not Immigration. We're not asking to see your papers.'

I thought the man might faint. 'Papers? I have my papers,' he said quickly, pulling documents from his jacket pocket.

Maggie held up her hand. 'No, no. We're not asking for papers. No. We just want to know if Arcelia Gallagher was here last week.'

The man nodded reluctantly.

'Why?' Calvano asked.

The man looked away, as if he found the books on the shelves fascinating.

'You do know she is missing?' Maggie asked the man.

The gardener looked up in surprise. He had not known Arcelia Gallagher was missing. 'Missing?' His eyes darted from Maggie to Calvano.

'For over a day now,' Calvano explained. 'We need to know why she was here. It may be related.'

The man shook his head vigorously. 'No, not related,' he said. 'Not related at all.'

'Well, what was it? Why was she here?' Maggie asked. Her voice had hardened. She was not above using intimidation to find out what she needed to know.

'I cannot tell you,' he stammered. 'You must ask the priest. I cannot tell you.'

Calvano and Maggie looked resigned. They both knew what priest the gardener meant – and Father Sojak had said nothing about Delmonte House.

'Did you talk to her while she was out here?'

The gardener nodded solemnly. 'Yes. But she was fine when she left. It was last Thursday. She drove herself out here even though her child is not far off. I saw her leave myself.'

'You saw her leave after she did what out here?' Maggie tried again.

Rodrigo looked even more uncomfortable. 'It was something

to do with religious matters. It is a private matter that I do not wish to speak about.'

'And you know nothing else that might help us find her?' Maggie asked.

'I am sorry, I do not,' the man said mournfully. I think he really wanted to help them.

'Do you know of other people we could talk to about her?' Calvano asked. 'Perhaps some people she is counseling?'

The gardener looked nervously at the door. 'I think maybe you should talk to Father Sojak about these things.'

Maggie sighed. She was losing patience with him. 'Is there anybody else here who might know something?'

The man shook his head vigorously. 'We have only the old man and the old woman who look after the house and kitchen,' he explained. 'And a girl who comes in to help Mr Romero's wife. Ms Wylie is with child, you know. And sometimes people are hired to help me with the grounds.'

'Why don't you send in the maid?' Maggie said calmly. 'You can go.' She was determined to get through the questioning without losing her cool.

As the gardener left the library, Maggie gave Calvano the kind of stare he had not seen in at least half a year. 'I thought you talked to the priest?' she said sarcastically.

'I told you I thought he was hiding something.'

'There is no way that one gardener is taking care of the grounds on his own, so we know there's at least one other person working here and we're never going to get to talk to him unless Father Sojak makes it happen.'

'Let's just see what everyone else has to say and then we can talk about the priest.'

Maggie looked skeptical and I couldn't figure out if it was his faith or his incompetence she was holding against him. Apparently, neither could she. 'You believe in some odd things for a grown man,' she finally said. 'I can't decide if I envy you or pity you, Adrian.'

The air in the library grew suddenly cold and there was an odd smell lingering in the corners, like the Easter egg I hid behind the washer one year when I was a boy. My brother discovered it six months later and when we opened it up, it stunk up the house for days. Now, the same smell permeated the library. The flowers in a vase on a table behind Maggie and Calvano fluttered, as if a wind was passing through them. I was the only one to notice.

Calvano was trying to be gentlemanly but he had smelled the odor, too. He glanced at Maggie.

'Don't look at me,' Maggie said grimly, shooting him a glare.

'That's not me,' Calvano said, looking mortified.

While neither had seen the flowers, they could not miss what happened next. As if in slow motion, a book high up on a shelf, nearly to the ceiling, tumbled off and spiraled downwards to the floor, hitting it with a crack as loud as a gunshot.

Maggie and Calvano were instantly on their feet, hands on their guns.

'What the hell was that?' Maggie said. 'This place gives me the creeps.'

'That is because it is full of bad spirits,' a voice said timidly from the doorway. 'I say over and over that something lives here, but no one will believe me.' A young Mexican girl no more than twenty entered the room, clutching papers in her hand.

Maggie could barely hide her skepticism as she settled back into her chair, but Calvano was too busy gawking at the maid to respond. I didn't blame him. She was absolutely beautiful, with thick black hair that framed her oval face and hung straight to her waist. Her skin was the color of caramel.

Calvano decided to be a gentleman. He led her to the chair across from him and took her papers, bringing them back to Maggie to examine.

'I am in this country legally,' the girl said. 'My papers prove it.'

'I'm sure you are,' Maggie agreed. 'If you weren't, we would not be looking at you right now. I find it curious that so few of you manage to take care of this huge house.'

The girl did not blink. 'We work very hard,' she said.

Her name was Lupe and, apparently, her sole job in the household was to help the lady of the house, Dakota Wylie, dress each day. Which wasn't hard, from what I could tell, because it sounded like the lady of the house never actually got out of bed to get dressed.

'That's it?' Maggie asked incredulously.

Lupe hesitated. 'She is a very lonely person,' the girl said. 'I keep her company and I listen to her talk and, when she will eat, I bring her healthy things to eat.'

'Really?' Calvano said, unable to help himself. 'What does she like to eat?'

'Adrian – really?' Maggie stared at him until he had the decency to look ashamed.

Lupe, who probably had no concept of what a star-struck American would look and act like, took his question at face value. 'She will eat things that are bad for her unless you tell her not to,' she said. 'She likes the junky food. But Mr Romero would fire me if I brought her those things. I am only allowed to bring her fruit if she wants something sweet. So even when she tells me to bring her the Twinkie or I am fired, I bring her the fruit.'

'Her husband tells her what to eat?' Maggie sounded disgusted. Her sturdy body was a machine of strength. She ate like a lion: mostly red meat and more red meat. But she also ate only ruthlessly healthy foods, ran every day and lifted weights five times a week. She was an animal and her body showed it.

'Ms Wylie says that Mr Romero only wants her to stay beautiful so that she will be a star for a long, long time,' Lupe explained.

Maggie had had enough of talking about the lady of the house. Until she could question her for herself, she had no use for Dakota Wylie.

'Do you know this woman?' Maggie asked her, handing Lupe a photo of Arcelia Gallagher.

'This is the woman who is missing,' the maid said softly. She crossed herself. 'Everyone knows what she looks like. Everyone is praying for her to be brought back home safely.'

'But have you ever seen her here?' Calvano asked.

The young girl nodded solemnly. 'She was here last week.'

'Here? In this house?' Maggie asked. 'Because everyone else is telling us she's never been here.'

'Maybe they did not see her?' She had picked up on Calvano's glances and was starting to return them with a shy yet confident flirtatiousness that told me she was used to men admiring her. Oh boy, if he kept that up, Maggie was going to grab the girl's immigration papers and beat Calvano over the head with them like a bad dog. She was all business in these kinds of situations.

'Tell me exactly how and when you saw her,' Maggie said. 'Who was she talking to?'

'She was out on the lawn, talking to the gardener,' the girl explained. 'I was standing at the window of Ms Wylie's bedroom upstairs, looking out at the flowers. It was a very beautiful day and I was sad to be inside. Ms Wylie always stays inside. The shades and blinds are always drawn in her room. It is a sad place to be on a beautiful day.'

No kidding. It was depressing me just to hear about it.

'I saw the missing lady pointing to the windows of this house and the gardener nodding. She took something from her pocketbook and gave it to him. Then they looked like they were having an angry talk.'

'Angry at each other?' Maggie asked.

The maid nodded. 'I think they were yelling. I could not hear, but Rodrigo looked angry and she was waving her hands at him. But then it looked as if he was thanking her. She held his hand in hers for a moment and then she left.'

'How can you be sure it was her?' Calvano asked. 'How far away were you?'

'Close enough to know it was her. She teaches my nephew Arturo. He is half in love with her. He says he wants to marry her one day and my brother tells me all Arturo does is cry, now that she's gone. You must find her and bring her back.'

Maggie and Calvano looked discouraged. They'd heard the same plea ten times already from various people and were getting nowhere in finding Arcelia Gallagher.

The maid had nothing else to offer and Maggie lost interest.

'You can go,' Maggie told her. 'But we need to talk to Ms Wylie. And we're not leaving until we do. I get the feeling that people do not want us to talk to her.'

The maid's eyes grew big. For the first time, I had the sense that she was not being completely honest with Maggie and Calvano. 'She's very shy,' the maid said softly. 'She is not very strong and she does not like company. She is not feeling well because of her pregnancy but I will explain to her that she has no choice, that she must speak to you.'

'You do that,' Maggie told her, watching in disgust as she gave Calvano a final parting glance and he beamed back at her.

'Really, Adrian,' Maggie complained once the girl had left the room. 'You're like a little kid in a candy store.'

Calvano defended himself. 'I was just trying to relax her,' he protested.

'Sure you were,' Maggie said, rolling her eyes.

A discreet cough from the doorway surprised them. The butler stood at the entrance to the library, his hands folded in front of him. He was a tall man with stooped shoulders and a high, rounded head with a smooth dome. He looked like nothing so much as a vulture staring down from a tree at them.

'I am here to be interrogated,' he said in a clipped voice. I felt something at odds with his dignity swirling about him. Sorrow or apprehension, perhaps? I wondered what he was hiding.

Maggie waved at him to sit and wasted no time in establishing that the old man had been at the mansion since well before the current residents. For forty years, in fact, as had his wife, the housekeeper.

'I remember you,' Calvano said. 'You found the dead guy in the orchard back when I was a kid.'

The butler appraised Calvano. 'I called the police immediately. Am I to understand that I am *still* under suspicion?'

Either he had the world's driest sense of humor or he had no sense of humor at all.

Maggie laughed, though more at Calvano than at the butler's remarks. 'No, we want to know if you have ever seen this woman,' she said. 'And we also would like to know why some of your staff are lying about it.'

The butler glanced at the picture of Arcelia Gallagher. 'She was here last week talking to Rodrigo, the gardener,' he said carefully. 'That is the only time I've seen her here.'

'Talking about what?' Maggie asked.

The butler made a face of disapproval. 'Something religious,' he said. 'I am not in the habit of eavesdropping. But Rodrigo had a vial of holy water and some objects that he tried to conceal from me when he came in through the kitchen door after meeting with her.'

'Well, what do you think it was about?' Maggie asked. 'Come on. You run this household. You see everything. Why would Rodrigo want holy water?'

'I imagine he was attempting an exorcism of some sort,' the butler replied stiffly.

'An exorcism?' Calvano asked. His eyes lit up. 'Who exactly is possessed?'

The butler looked at him scornfully. 'The house. I assure you it is not a joke. Ever since I have worked here, there has been a presence here. We hear things at night. Someone running up and down the steps. Books fall off the shelves without warning. Sometimes the lights go on and off. I have felt cold patches appear without warning in the halls and heard whispering at all hours of the day, right behind me, only to turn around and see no one there. You may not believe in such things, but I live with them.'

'And Rodrigo was bothered enough to want to do something about them?' Maggie asked.

The butler shrugged. 'Rodrigo is very superstitious. I tried to tell him that the spirit had lived here as long as I had, but it was upsetting to him nonetheless. He claims that one night the spirit tried to smother him in bed. That just as he was about to fall asleep, something heavy pressed down on him and tried to suck the air out of his lungs, he claims. He has not slept well since that night.'

'Can't say I blame him,' Maggie said. She looked at Calvano, mystified. 'I think we would like to speak to Rodrigo again,' she said firmly. 'And after that, we need to speak to your wife.'

There it was again – a wave of apprehension swept over the old man. He struggled to keep his voice under control. 'I am afraid you will not find an interview with my wife useful,' he said formally. He cowered slightly as he said it, as if he feared they might hit him.

'Why don't we decide that?' Maggie said mildly. She was staring at the butler. She, too, could feel that he was hiding something.

But Calvano, seldom the sensitive one, had seen something on his way into the mansion that led him to say, 'Is there something the matter with your wife?'

The butler stood stiffly, saying nothing.

Calvano tried again. 'Sir, if there is anything that prevents her from talking to us, you need to tell us. We cannot leave until we establish that fact.'

The butler sat stoically, saying nothing. The clock in the corner seemed to tick even louder and I could suddenly feel the presence in the room, the same cold thickness of air I had walked through in the hallway. It seemed to be roaming the room. There was definitely someone there like me. I peered around, checking every corner and high up on the shelves. I could see nothing. I wondered if it could see me.

'Sir,' Calvano said more kindly. 'Whatever you say will be kept in confidence.'

It was painful to watch the butler struggling between his dignity and what he knew he must do. 'My wife is suffering from dementia,' he finally said, his voice unconsciously dropping to a near whisper. 'Mr Romero does not know. If he or his advisors find out, they will let her go. I do not have the money to pay someone to care for her. I will have to quit my job to care for her and then we will have nowhere to live. And no money to live on.'

'Surely Mr Romero would never throw you out on the street,' Maggie said.

'I would not be so sure,' the butler said. 'Mr Romero has a habit of viewing people as disposable. He is particularly bad about it when his agent is involved in the decision.'

'Then there is no need for us to talk to your wife, but we do need to talk to the gardener again. Anything you can do to convince him to be more forthright with us would be best for everyone,' Maggie said.

'I will inform him,' the butler promised, hiding his gratitude to them behind a façade of formality. As he left the room, I felt the presence pass in front of me. Ouch. There it was again – a sharp pain, as if I were still alive and someone had bounced a slap off my head. What the hell? There was definitely someone else in this house, someone more like me than like the living. I glared in its direction and could have sworn I heard laughter.

The gardener was nowhere to be found. The butler returned looking shocked and apologetic. Rodrigo had left, apparently upset by the police questioning. There was nothing he could do.

'Sure there is,' Maggie told him. 'You can go upstairs and tell Ms Wylie that she must come down and speak to us.'

The butler risked giving advice. 'If you wish to speak to Ms Wylie, I recommend that you go upstairs to her. I will see that she is ready to receive you.'

Maggie agreed, but I don't think that she, or Calvano, or any of us in the room – seen or unseen – were prepared for how odd that interview would be.

TWELVE

The whole world knew Dakota Wylie as a willowy blonde with a face so sweet that men, literally, had stopped to stare when she passed by, even before she became famous. Her hair was the color of butter and as fine as corn silk. She had based a career on appearing slightly dumb with a goofy, clueless sense of humor. As a result, everyone longed to protect her. Or at least every male. On the television screen, she had seemed forever young, caught on the cusp of womanhood and unaware of her astonishing beauty.

Her bedroom at the mansion felt nothing at all like this public persona. It should have been painted pink with a white frilly bedspread and flowers everywhere. Instead, it was painted an unforgiving white, harsh even in the dimmed lighting. The curtains were blood red and shut against the afternoon sun, creating a permanent twilight in the room. Her bed was a huge canopy affair, with white gauzy curtains all around, creating a barrier between her and any visitors. When Maggie and Calvano entered her room, with me hot on their heels, she was leaning back against a pile of satin pillows behind the bed curtains, her head wrapped up in a blue silk scarf as if she were heading out for a drive in a convertible on a winter's day. Huge sunglasses covered most of her face. All you could see of her fabled beauty were her hands, which she clasped on top of a pillow she had pulled over her lap as if to shield her from bad intentions.

Her maid sat in a chair by her side, looking apprehensive. I got the feeling she was as close to a female friend as Dakota Wylie had ever had.

The starlet did not seem to take any notice of Maggie or Calvano at all. She was staring at her windows, though the heavy curtains made it impossible to see anything outside.

'Has he left yet?' she asked her maid in a whispery voice. That voice had been her trademark. It was three-quarters Marilyn Monroe and one quarter her own – a throaty honey-colored voice with just a trace of southern drawl.

The maid jumped up and scurried over to a window, opening the curtains a crack to peer outside. 'He is leaving for the airport now,' the maid said.

I followed her to the window. Below us, an entire caravan of luxury cars rimmed the circular brick driveway that curved in front of the house. Enrique Romero was sliding into the back seat of a Rolls-Royce as the butler stoically packed the trunk with enough bags for a three-year stay away. His agents and lawyers were each eyeing their own cars, anxious to leave. Rats deserting a sinking ship. For a man with a young and heart-stoppingly beautiful wife, he was curiously willing to leave her to fend for herself.

'I expect he has a plane to catch and is in such a hurry that he forgot to say goodbye,' the star told her maid in a dreamy voice. 'He can be so silly that way.'

'Yes, ma'am,' the maid said dutifully, though she surely knew the truth.

Dakota Wylie knew it, too, if only in her heart of hearts. I could feel the sadness leaking from her, and there was a familiarity in her yearning to not be abandoned. Then I felt a flash of fear from her, followed by memories of hunger and I knew that she had come from humble beginnings. How she had ended up here, in an immense mansion with a Hollywood star husband, was a story I did not know. All I knew was that the ending had not been a happy one. She was no more than a prop to Enrique Romero. She had been his ticket to a few more inches of tabloid fame. He didn't give a crap about her.

'We need to talk to you alone,' Maggie said, addressing Dakota Wylie directly for the first time. It was hard to read Maggie's tone. I think she felt sorry for the woman hiding behind gauze curtains and sunglasses, but she had no patience for her at the same time.

'Mr Romero says she is not to be questioned alone,' the maid said apologetically.

'Then maybe Mr Romero should have stayed with his wife,' Calvano snapped back. He sounded angry and I knew what he was thinking: if she were my wife, I would treasure her. I would never abandon her like this.

'It's OK, Lupe. I will sit with her while they question her,' a familiar voice said from the bedroom door. It was the man who had interrupted their meeting in the library earlier and I realized that he must be Lamont Carter, Dakota's manager. His expensive clothes could not disguise his rough edges or mannerisms. He held himself coiled, as if he were waiting for someone to pick a fight. Judging from how the other men in the library had treated him, it was an understandable attitude.

'But Mr Romero said—' the maid began.

'Leave,' the man said sharply and she scurried from the room.

Maggie did not like him. At all. 'Who are you?' she demanded.

The man responded by sitting in the chair by Dakota Wylie's bed. He crossed his legs as if he were there to stay. He ran a manicured hand through his hair. 'My name is Lamont Carter.' He sounded unconcerned about Maggie's abruptness. 'I am Ms Wylie's manager. I am also her financial advisor, hold power of attorney over her affairs and have been her legal guardian for the past sixteen years.'

'And here I thought Lincoln had freed the slaves,' Maggie snapped. She did not like short men in general, they postured too much for her, and this one she *hated.*

'Ms Wylie started out in the business very early on,' Carter explained, sounding bored and unapologetic, as if he had explained it one too many times before. 'It would have been ridiculously easy to take advantage of her had I not been looking out for her interests. Believe me, people would have tried. Hollywood is full of bottom feeders.'

'You've convinced me of that,' Maggie said, giving him the once-over. The man did not flinch. He shrugged, examined his cuticles and waved toward Dakota Wylie as if giving permission to Maggie to get started.

Maggie decided to ignore him. She looked around, seeking a chair, but Calvano had beat her to it. He was dragging a vanity table chair and an armchair over to the far side of the bed, across from the manager, and had taken the closest one for himself. He was about to see his fantasy in the flesh and he wanted a front row seat, even if there was a curtain between them.

'Ms Wylie,' Calvano asked softly. 'Are you feeling up to answering some questions?'

Instead of answering, she let out a long sigh and tilted her head back against her pillows. The blue scarf wound around her head slipped away from her face, revealing small white butterfly bandages underneath, as if keeping her face in place. She had clearly had some sort of surgery and was in the healing phase, but something was wrong. I had only caught a glimpse, but her face seemed out of kilter. Her famously symmetrical features were gone. She tucked the scarf back around her face, adjusted her sunglasses and turned to Calvano. When she spoke, there it was: the trademark voice. I could feel Calvano surrendering to it.

'I will do the best I can,' she said. She waved her hand over the top of her embroidered covers, a gesture as graceful as water lilies floating in a stream. 'As you can see, I am not feeling well. My pregnancy has proved to be a difficult one. But I am determined to see it through. Enrique wants a family badly.'

I knew what Maggie and Calvano were thinking, because it was the same thing I thinking: if Enrique Romero wanted a family so damn badly, why had he just ditched her and fled to California with a coterie of advisers but not her?

'We won't take up much of your time,' Maggie said. 'May I hand you a photograph?'

The actress nodded and reached languidly through the gauze curtains. She definitely had a flair for the dramatic. Maggie brushed her fingers lightly while Calvano looked on longingly. Boy, he had it bad.

I was less enchanted. I was confused by the emotions tumbling through the room, by the territorial way the manager hunched over in his chair watching every move Dakota Wylie made, no matter how small. His eyes darted back and forth between Maggie and Calvano as if he were certain they were out to harm his client.

It was odd, but he and Dakota Wylie seemed so much in synch they gave off what was almost a single aura, as if they were very nearly the same person. How long had he been protecting her? Perhaps he had been telling the truth. Perhaps, without him, she would have been used and discarded like so many other young actresses. Instead, she was a millionaire married to a multi-millionaire, and the whole world watched to see what she would do next.

Dakota Wylie was studying the photo of Arcelia Gallagher carefully, and though you could see little of her face except for her swollen mouth, she exuded an air of concern. She was an actress of course, and it could all have been for show, but she seemed genuinely distressed about Arcelia Gallagher.

'I'm sorry,' she said in her breathy voice. 'I've never seen her before. I'm sure of it.'

'What about you?' Maggie asked her manager.

Lamont Carter barely looked at the photo and shrugged. 'I can't be expected to remember everyone who works here. They all look alike to me.'

'She didn't work here, asshole,' Calvano interrupted. 'She's a preschool teacher and a lot of people are upset that she's missing. She was spotted here at the mansion. Are you telling me you don't know anything about that?'

Lamont Carter looked surprised at Calvano's anger. I realized that he had little sense of how others saw him. He was one of those people who go out into the world with a determined sense of self – but absolutely no clue as to how others perceive them.

'There's no need to get nasty,' Carter said. 'I just meant that I don't know her and I have never seen her.'

'What do you know about your gardener Rodrigo?' Maggie asked Dakota Wylie.

She shifted slowly in the bed, as if it were taking a long time for Maggie's question to permeate her brain. I wondered if she was on some sort of medication, or if she was acting this way on purpose. I know I was not the only one wondering.

'Ms Wylie does not know anything about the help. That's why she has me, not to mention a butler to manage the staff.' Lamont Carter's voice had taken on a hard edge and I knew with a certainty that he was a man who could not keep his temper in check.

'Are you all right?' Calvano asked Dakota Wylie directly. 'Can I get you a glass of water? You don't look well.'

That was both an understatement and a kindness. Once you got used to the dim lighting of the room, it became more apparent that something terrible had happened to Dakota Wylie's face. Her lips were not only swollen, they were misshapen, and flesh-colored bandages braced her nose on either side. Bruises snaked up from her nose to disappear underneath her huge sunglasses. I didn't want to think about what had caused those marks.

'I would love a glass of nice, cool water,' she told Calvano. She leaned forward and reached through the curtains to briefly stroke his hand. It had an almost magical effect on Calvano. He rose and went to a pitcher of ice water that was sitting on top of a table in one corner of the room, poured her a glass and returned, walking as carefully as if it was plutonium, unaware of the silence as both Maggie and the manager watched him curiously. Calvano parted the curtains, leaned forward and steadied her chin with one hand as he carefully tipped the glass until the water trickled through her swollen lips. She drank as if she were a baby, nodding when she'd had enough.

Calvano sat back down holding the glass of water like it was the Holy Grail. Maggie was staring at him, dumbfounded.

'I believe Ms Wylie has told you everything she knows,' the manager said sharply. He made a big show out of checking his incredibly expensive-looking watch. 'I have some business matters to discuss with her now, if you don't mind.'

Maggie knew it was useless to try to get anything more out of her anyway. She rose and tapped Calvano on the shoulder. He was lost in staring at Dakota Wylie.

'Let's go, Adrian,' she said sharply, hoping to penetrate his hormonal fog.

Calvano nodded, then rose and made a half bow. 'It was a pleasure meeting you, Ms Wylie,' he said. 'If ever you need anything, please do not hesitate to call on me.' Lamont Carter was staring at his nails, bored with the spectacle. He had no doubt witnessed it dozens of times when he was out with Dakota Wylie in public.

'Thank you so much,' Dakota Wylie told Calvano. Her mouth stretched in smile that quickly turned grotesque. *What had she done to herself?* 'You're such a gentleman and it was so nice to meet you.'

Calvano nodded mutely, unable to speak.

I followed Maggie and Calvano out into the long hallway toward the curving grand staircase that led to the ground floor. Once again, we stepped through an icy patch of air and I wondered who or what was holding the mansion hostage. At least this time I felt no pain.

Amateur, I thought to myself. Patches of cold and shoving books around. Sitting on the gardener's face? Big deal. I could do that. I could do something even better than that. If you're going to haunt a house, then, by god, haunt it.

As if my fellow traveler could read my mind, the huge chandelier that anchored the center of the foyer began to tremble. It shook faster and faster until the hanging squares of glass began to clatter against one another.

Well, excuse me.

Maggie and Calvano were staring at the chandelier.

'Was that an earthquake?' Maggie asked after a moment. Calvano shrugged and she did not speak again until they were halfway down the stairs when she turned to Calvano, stopping to emphasize her words, and asked, 'What the hell was that all about up there? Is it just me or was that interview creepy as hell? What was with her face?'

'I think she's had plastic surgery,' Calvano admitted. 'Up close, you can see the scars at the base of her hairline. She can't be more than thirty years old. Why would she feel she has to get plastic surgery?'

'That's not the main question, Adrian,' Maggie pointed out. 'The real question is why anyone would risk getting plastic surgery when they're pregnant? How self-centered is that?'

As if to emphasize her words, a vase of flowers on an entrance table in the foyer below them suddenly tumbled over, spilling water and stems to the floor.

'Let's get the hell out of here,' Calvano suggested.

'I'm right behind you,' Maggie agreed.

THIRTEEN

The rest of the day had been spent on interviewing Arcelia Gallagher's co-workers and neighbors, checking in with the task force and plowing through any open cases that might possibly be connected to Arcelia's disappearance. The only respite from paperwork came when Maggie and Calvano got a call that Danny Gallagher had been assaulted at a local restaurant. They rushed to the scene and understood at once what had happened. Danny had tried to resume some semblance of a routine, at the urging of those who knew him, but routine would not be possible. He had not been in the restaurant for more than a minute, waiting for the owner to come out so he could apologize for the lateness of his produce order, when a pair of elderly patrons had stood up in a huff and stomped out the door without paying, hurling names at Danny as they left. Danny had been too stunned to react, which made him an easy target for the drunk at the bar who decided to punch Danny in the face and teach the wife killer a lesson. Danny refused medical care and fled home. Neither Maggie nor Calvano thought he was likely to venture out again. Not with all the television networks broadcasting his photo and speculating that he killed his wife.

Now, Maggie and Calvano had reported for a briefing with Gonzales. Unfortunately, they had little to offer him and Gonzales was not interested in either strange noises or Hollywood eccentrics. He dismissed their lack of progress at the Delmonte House with a shrug.

'What did you expect?' he asked them. 'They don't live in the real world. They have other people to do that for them. Maybe she's just using pregnancy as an excuse to stay away from the public view while the scars of her plastic surgery heal. If she doesn't come up with the kid, because she won't be the first person to have elective surgery while pregnant, trust me, then she'll announce she's had a miscarriage in a couple of weeks, get a bunch of tabloid headlines, and that will be that. She'll emerge from her so-called tragedy looking ten years younger than she used to and no one will notice.'

'If she emerges looking ten years younger than she used to, then she'll look like she's ten years old,' Calvano said.

'I don't care about Hollywood stars, got it?' Gonzales said. 'Enrique Romero uses our town like it's a set for his press conferences. I won't play into his hands. He probably wants to be accused so he can pull rank and then tell the press we're persecuting him. From what you are telling me, I suggest you take a clue from the gardener and go talk to the priest again. Could he have made it any more plain?'

'OK, sure, we can do that,' Maggie said. 'But you are aware we have to battle an army of reporters every time we come in and out of here just to report to you, right?'

I had never heard her sound more frustrated with Gonzales.

'I am aware of that,' he said. 'And I apologize. Right now, I'm mostly concerned that the majority of this town assumes Danny Gallagher killed his wife and hid the body. People keep calling in asking when we intend to arrest him. So if you two don't find out whether that's true or not, they're going to start gathering their pitchforks and torches, and I don't know that I can keep him safe if they do. I've got officers with him around the clock, and I put a few more men on him after this afternoon, but the threats coming into the station are ugly.'

'It's that woman's fault,' Maggie said. 'She's like a human bulldog. With rabies.'

'Yes, Lindsey Stanford is fanning the flames of guilty as charged,' Gonzales conceded. 'And apparently her ratings are through the roof because of it. Perhaps giving her free rein was a mistake. But at least she is distracting everyone from our investigation. Just work the case. Go back and talk to the priest again.'

Easy for him to say. Maggie and Calvano were only human. They needed to stop for dinner, or shower, or maybe even grab a drink, before they'd be able to keep going. It had been another long day. But I was no longer bound by the constraints of the human body, and so I could take Gonzales's advice to heart. When Maggie and Calvano turned away from St Raphael's in search of dinner first, I split and went in search of Father Sojak and the missing gardener on my own.

I admit I was also in pursuit of that state of grace I had felt, however fleetingly, with Calvano in the church the night before. I did not find it. St Raphael's was empty and felt more like a warehouse than a place of worship. I knew that beneath my feet, a roomful of families, with all of their hopes and dreams, teemed. But up above, amidst all the splendor, I felt cold and alone.

I was not the only one.

I found Father Sojak sitting by himself, hidden away in the confessional chamber, praying as he wrestled with his soul.

There are times when I can go deep into a person's thoughts, uncovering memories or sensing emotions otherwise buried by the external world. When people are in prayer, or meditating, or simply sitting quietly in the sun, it is as if the noises of the present world fall away and the pathway into the past, stored in the deepest recesses of the heart, opens up to me. So it was with Father Sojak. He was huddled alone in the confessional chamber, and I joined him on the other side of the panel, a place I had seldom occupied when I was alive for I'd had far too many sins to confess to ever accompany my family willingly to confession.

I had never noticed how quiet and pleasant it was in the confessional booth. It smelled of cedar and the air seemed dignified and forgiving. I wanted to say, 'Bless me father, for I have not only sinned, I died and then sinned some more.' But, of course, I could not.

On the other side of the partition, I heard Father Sojak murmuring. There were no conflicting emotions about faith in him. He was deep in full-blown, saint-invoking prayer. I stilled my thoughts and tried to feel what he was feeling. He was a complicated man.

He held within him the memories of those who had come to him for help; not just who they were and what they meant to him, but how those poor souls had felt: what they hoped for, what they had feared and, most of all, how they had suffered. Whatever work he had done, and however much I believed – or didn't believe – in his power to heal, I could feel that parts of the people he had helped had transferred themselves to his soul. He carried their sorrows and pain around in him. They weighed him down. It was a gift to some, but to Father Sojak I could not help but feel as if, as the years went by, it would be less of a gift and more of a burden.

Deep within that stew of human sickness and desire, I could feel the spark that was Father Sojak himself. I saw him as a child holding his grandmother's hand and entering a great, soaring Catholic cathedral. I could feel his wonder at its magnificence. I could smell Polish food cooking and hear his parents fighting as he huddled behind the paper-thin walls of his childhood bedroom, clutching a rosary and praying for it all to go away. I could feel him relaxing as a young man in the stark peace of the seminary. And I could also feel a heat in him that, I thought, perhaps, was his faith. It was a flame that burned deep in his center and warmed all that happened in his world.

Yes, Father Sojak was a holy man. His faith was everything to him. He would not risk it for anything as fleeting as carnal desires – but he would risk it for his conscience.

It was his conscience that he was fighting now. A woman was missing and would surely die if she was not found soon. And not just a woman, but an angel among us. Someone who devoted herself to helping others, someone who lived to bring light into the darkness. What kind of a man would he be if he abandoned her, yet what kind of priest would he be if he sacrificed all of the families living below him by revealing their presence to the police?

Almost greedily, I tried to probe every nook and cranny of his soul, hoping for another taste of the glorious sense of grace I had experienced in the church the night before. But he was in too much turmoil to be in harmony with the heavens, so I was out of luck. Grace is, after all, an emotion as finely tuned as a symphony.

At last, he reached a decision. He adjusted his robes and left the confessional as silently as a shadow. I was curious as to where he was going, but I heard car doors slamming outside and I knew that Maggie and Calvano had arrived.

I soon had my answer anyway: the two detectives were still standing in the doorway of the rectory, waiting for someone to answer the door, when Father Sojak appeared from behind a corner of the church with Rodrigo, the gardener at the Delmonte House, beside him.

'I have been expecting you,' Father Sojak said. 'Mr Flores would like to speak to you.'

'About everything?' Rodrigo asked the priest dubiously, his eyes sliding toward the church. Below, I suspected, were his friends and relatives. Their discovery could mean deportation or even death for some.

'If you mean everything about why Mrs Gallagher came out to the house then, yes, tell them everything.' Father Sojak was a smooth one. Rodrigo got the message – he would tell them nothing about the families hidden below – but neither Maggie nor Calvano thought the exchange odd.

The priest led everyone inside to the kitchen, where they all took seats around the table. The old nun awoke and came fluttering in, insisting on making cocoa for them all. I think she just wanted to hear what Rodrigo had to say.

Father Sojak stayed silent as Rodrigo explained that bad spirits lived in the Delmonte House, unhappy souls who had torn through the veil of their world into this one. They were the unsatisfied dead who could move objects, make noises, cool the air and fill the house with unhappiness, he said. It made life difficult for those who lived and worked there. He had sought advice from Father Sojak, but Father Sojak had not been able to help him banish the spirits.

'I wanted to,' Father Sojak said in apology.

'You are forbidden,' the nun interjected sharply. She had been a nearly invisible presence until then. 'You must let others do that kind of work. You are too connected. Just as you can find your way into the thoughts of others, there are things that might find their way into yours.' She turned to Maggie and explained, 'There are some in the Church allowed to deal with such things, but Father Sojak is forbidden. His gifts are too precious to risk.'

Rodrigo crossed himself and Father Sojak looked down at his cocoa.

'So you came to Arcelia Gallagher for help?' Maggie asked, sounding unconvinced.

'She offered to help me,' Rodrigo explained. 'At home in Mexico, her grandmother is known throughout the village as a witch. She is skilled at placating spirits and clearing houses of their sadness. Mrs Gallagher helped her grandmother as a child and knew what to do. She brought me oils and special plants to burn, and she told me to walk through the house and what to say as I did so.'

'What did she tell you to say?' Calvano asked curiously.

Rodrigo began chanting a rapid-fire stream of Spanish incomprehensible to anyone but him. Maggie finally cut it short. 'But you were seen arguing with her,' she said.

'Just about the spirits,' Rodrigo explained. 'She said it was dangerous what I was doing, that she could feel the house and it was unhappy, that I must be careful not to awaken more bad spirits. She wanted me to understand how serious the danger was. But I knew I had to do something. The spirit, it was unhappy and changing the people in the house.'

'You don't mean the housekeeper?' Calvano asked. 'She's not possessed, she has Alzheimer's.'

'She is supposed to have Alzheimer's,' Rodrigo said, 'but sometimes she looks at you like she is someone else and she knows things you do not. And then she speaks and . . .' He shivered. 'It is not good. It is a deep voice and it is not her. It is not holy. I tried to tell Mrs Gallagher this, to explain why I had to try to banish them, but she was worried about me and tried to convince me not to. But we were not fighting. She helps our people. I would never do anything to harm her.'

'And when was this exactly?' Calvano asked.

'She came to see me last Tuesday, about a week ago . . .' Rodrigo's voice trailed off.

'Tell them,' Father Sojak said gently. 'You must tell them.'

Rodrigo reached into his jacket pocket and took out a photo of a man and a woman. The man was chubby with dark skin, tiny eyes and friendly features. He looked a lot, in fact, like Rodrigo.

The woman was plump and happy, her smile beaming at the camera as she caressed the man's cheek with her hands. 'This is my brother Aldo, and this is his wife Carmen.'

'And?' Maggie asked. 'What have they to do with Arcelia Gallagher?'

'Carmen is missing,' Rodrigo explained. 'She is having a child and she is missing. She has been missing since a week before Arcelia Gallagher disappeared.'

The room grew quiet. I had seen both Maggie and Calvano flinch. They did not want to even begin to think what this news might mean.

'You're sure?' Maggie said. 'Are you absolutely certain she did not simply return home to Mexico?'

'I am certain,' Rodrigo said solemnly. 'My brother has looked everywhere for her. He has called everyone he knows in Mexico. He has called all of our relatives. She is nowhere to be found. She was to give birth this week. Now she is gone and he cannot go to the police. He does not have his papers and something bad will happen to him.'

Maggie appealed to Father Sojak. 'We have to talk to his brother,' Maggie said. 'You must help us with this.'

Father Sojak had known this was coming and he had prayed about it before they arrived. 'We are looking for Aldo now. He helps Rodrigo with the grounds of the mansion, but when he heard the police were coming to question everyone, he disappeared. He is afraid of being sent back to Mexico, or locked up so he cannot look for his wife. It may take us a while to find him.'

'You must bring him to us as soon as you can,' Maggie said. She took the photo that Rodrigo had placed on the kitchen table and pulled it toward her. 'She's a beautiful woman,' she said softly, almost to herself. She looked up at Rodrigo. 'Can we take this photo? We need a photo of your sister-in-law if we have any hope of finding her.'

Rodrigo nodded solemnly.

'Why did you not tell us this before?' Calvano asked the priest.

Father Sojak shifted uncomfortably in his chair and could not meet Calvano's eyes. 'You must understand that if you start looking into their world, you will discover many people who are not here in this country legally.'

No kidding. Try one hundred of them right below our feet.

'If you send them back,' Father Sojak continued. 'You are sending some of them to their deaths. Whatever you have seen of Mexico, whatever you have read about it lately, the reality is worse than you can imagine. These people come here because they are terrified. These people come here because they fear for their lives if they stay in Mexico.'

Maggie and Calvano were silent. They did not want to argue with the priest, but neither were they sure they believed him entirely.

Me? I knew he was telling the truth. I had seen the scars on Arcelia Gallagher's body. I had walked through the row of the immigrants. I had felt their emotions and glimpsed their memories, and I knew with a certainty that what Father Sojak said was true.

FOURTEEN

That night, I roamed the streets of my town. I could feel the fury and speculation growing over Arcelia Gallagher's disappearance. People sat in front of their television sets watching as Lindsey Stanford proclaimed Danny Gallagher guilty. Others called their friends to talk about the times they had seen Danny and his wife together and how they had noticed that something was 'off'. Reporters worked frantically to find a new angle on the story to keep it alive. The only person who did not seem energized by the possibility that Arcelia Gallagher had been murdered by her husband was Danny Gallagher himself.

I found myself drawn to the farm, once an oasis surrounded by quiet fields and now a clapboard fortress surrounded by news vans. But there was no way anyone could get through to Danny Gallagher. Gonzales had seen to that. Several patrol cars blocked the entrance and two men were guarding the house at all times. I don't think the protection gave Danny any solace, though. He sat alone in the bedroom he had shared with his wife, sobbing on the edge of his bed. He was holding her yellow sundress and smelling it as he cried. He didn't look much like a killer.

I could feel death all around him. Not the death of a human being, but the slow decay of crops going untended in the fields:

unpicked strawberries rotting; new shoots of corn starting to wither in the dry soil. Danny had become paralyzed by fear and shame that the town he had grown up in now saw him as a murderer.

In the living room, even his own television set blared his guilt. He had been seeking information on his wife and found only condemnation of himself. I watched Lindsey Stanford reigning supreme over the cable airwaves for a few moments. Maggie's ex-husband, Skip Bostwick, sat next to her, looking unnaturally handsome in a tailored suit and crisp white shirt. A forensic expert and psychologist framed them. Everyone looked very earnest and self-satisfied. There was apparently no shortage of people willing to speculate on how Danny Gallagher had gotten away with murder.

It is difficult to get a reading of a person off a television screen. It is the perfect medium for disguising who or what you really are. It is all about appearances and it does not favor substance. But I wanted to find out what the real Lindsey Stanford was like. I wanted to know why she felt compelled to condemn people she did not know, why she could not wait and let the justice system do its job, how she lived with herself after so many instances of being wrong and destroying lives without any evidence at all, with only the motivation of higher ratings to drive her. Did she really believe that she was morally superior or did her self-righteousness come from some sort of void within?

The show ended and I went in search of Lindsey Stanford, needing to know what drove her to destroy Danny Gallagher. There are only two hotels that a person with more than a few bucks to spend would choose when visiting my town. The most expensive is a small hotel built near the interstate with a spa to keep the mob wives happy while their husbands spend time in Atlantic City. I suspected Lindsey Stanford would be there.

I waited in the lobby, watching late-night travelers return to their rooms, tipsy and infatuated with each other. About an hour after midnight, she walked in the door, her stocky frame seeming to demand that others make way for it. She looked exhausted and her heavy television make-up only accentuated her coarse features. She kept her head down and headed straight for the elevator. I hopped in for the ride.

She kept jabbing the floor button until the doors shut – she was not the kind of person who waited patiently for anything. She wanted it all and she wanted it now. Up close, she mostly felt angry, although I could not tell if the anger was directed at herself or at others. Her memories were a kaleidoscope of people who had ignored or offended her, and her emotions tainted by a constant need for revenge. No wonder her face always looked so contorted as she ranted about the need to put a suspected killer to death – her whole being had been poisoned with resentment. Her soul was steeping in it. I would not want to live in her skin, not even for a day, and I was glad when the elevator stopped on the top floor and she barreled out, angry the ride had taken so long.

Of course, she was staying in the penthouse. Lindsey Stanford would never settle for less. She flung open the door and inspected the room, finding disfavor with it although it was immaculate, immense and completely over the top. Her suitcases had been brought up and unpacked for her. She had fresh ice in a bucket, bottled water nearby and a bottle of champagne on ice waiting just in case she wanted it. There was a fruit basket on a desk which she tore open and inspected with the greed of a child, selecting a box of chocolate-covered cherries. She ate them so quickly she barely stopped to chew. This was a woman intent on proving the world wrong about her – but so filled with self-loathing she could not take care of herself.

A stack of newspapers waited on a desk and she flipped through them quickly, hungry for news about herself. Done, she tossed the papers into a trash can and looked around as if there had to be somewhere better she could go. Yes, I thought to myself, this was a woman who was always running away from herself.

A soft knock at the door diverted her attention. She did not seem surprised to hear it. She did not seem excited, either. She glanced briefly in the mirror, rearranged her helmet of hair, then peered out the peephole and opened the door.

Skip Bostwick stood in the hallway holding two bottles of red wine and a box of expensive chocolates. I would have needed two bottles of tequila to do what I was pretty sure he was about to do.

'Heard you like these,' he said, handing her the candy. She took it and stared at him, blatantly evaluating whether he would be worth her time.

He raised the bottles of wine and smiled, revealing perfect teeth. 'It's the new Beaujolais. No one else has it.' God, how had Maggie been able to live with such a self-satisfied twit?

Lindsey Stanford grunted and opened the door wider. I guess

that was her idea of gracious. As old Skippy walked inside, she stared at him from behind, gauging how well he was built.

Now, I am no stranger to seedy encounters. I have had my share of meaningless nights trying to forget myself in the sweaty embrace of an equally frantic stranger. But this? This seemed as passionate as an ATM transaction. He wanted a leg up for his career, she was bored and looking for something to distract her from herself.

I fled. It was the last thing on earth I wanted to see.

FIFTEEN

B ack at the church, a terrible lottery of sorts was being held. Father Sojak was huddled with the nuns in the hallway outside the basement room where the refugees were hidden, whispering. The oldest nun was unhappy with her priest.

'If you send him there, they will arrest him,' she told Father Sojak. 'They don't care about where his wife may be. They're looking for someone to blame.'

Father Sojak looked stricken. 'We have no choice,' he said. 'We have to give them someone or they will come back around here, looking harder, and if they do that then you know they will find all of them.'

'Can't we claim we are giving them sanctuary?' the youngest of the nuns asked. She was so nervous that her voice was shaking.

'Not in this day and age,' the oldest nun said bitterly. 'We'll be lucky we don't all get arrested for it.'

'We knew what we were getting into,' the third nun said. She sounded quite at peace with her conscience. 'I am not afraid of being arrested. We are doing the right thing.'

'No one is getting arrested,' Father Sojak promised. 'Rodrigo assures me that Aldo is willing to go to the police.'

'Only because he is desperate to find his wife and he actually thinks they might help him,' the old nun insisted.

Father Sojak held up his hands for peace. 'It has been decided. There is nothing else we can do. Aldo must go to the police.'

'That's not enough,' the youngest nun said timidly. She flushed when everyone turned to look at her. 'I understand that we must hide the existence of these people from the police, but what if one of them knows something that might help the police? What if one of them might lead them to Arcelia? She is our friend. We must help her. We can't take the chance that anything is overlooked.'

The others, perhaps too old to understand how dear friendship could be to a lonely nun isolated from other women her age, thought about it in silence. At last Father Sojak spoke. 'I suppose we could interview all the refugees ourselves and see if they know anything,' he said. 'If they do, we'll just have to figure out a way to bring it to the attention of the police.'

'All three of us know Spanish,' the old nun agreed, looking at her peers. 'Together, we should be able to question at least thirty to forty people every night. If we hear anything useful, we will let you know.'

Just as the other nuns nodded their agreement, the door to the underground room opened and a small, frightened-looking Mexican man stepped out. Rodrigo, the gardener at the Delmonte House, entered the hallway after him, gently pushing his brother forward toward the waiting nuns. 'My brother's English is bad,' Rodrigo explained. 'I will accompany him to the police station and interpret.'

'I'm sure the police will have an interpreter,' Father Sojak said.

Rodrigo looked at him with calm eyes. 'I will not let my brother go alone.'

'Understood,' Father Sojak acknowledged. 'My car is ready. It is best we go now.'

Although Aldo had yet to say a word, he was shaking and that told me he understood what lay before him. How badly he must have been worried about his wife to risk deportation. His only hope, I knew, was that he somehow had seen or heard something that might lead the police to whoever had taken Arcelia Gallagher and, most probably, his wife. If he proved useful, perhaps they would show him some mercy – or at least keep him around long enough to testify if they caught the culprit.

I had not counted on Gonzales. I should have known that after a lifetime of trying to rise above his heritage and lay claim to power that only white men had enjoyed in our town before him, the commander would be the last person likely to show an illegal immigrant any mercy. Gonzales was determined to prove that he was not one of them and, so, he turned out to be the harshest of them all on Aldo Flores. He stood on the other side of a one-way mirror, in a small room where detectives sometimes gathered to monitor the interrogation sessions on the other side. He was alone in the room, except for me, and I drew no more attention from him than I had when I was alive. Maggie and Calvano sat in the interrogation room on the other side of the window, looking exhausted. Calvano's usually impeccable clothes had started to wilt and Maggie had deep circles under her eyes. Aldo and Rodrigo Flores sat across from them, side by side in solidarity. An interpreter from the department sat at the end of the table and a camera was recording the interview just in case.

'Are you sure your brother does not want a lawyer?' Maggie asked Rodrigo.

'He has agreed to talk now,' Rodrigo said. 'He does not need a lawyer.'

Maggie and Calvano both looked uneasy. They both knew that anyone connected to this case, however remotely, needed a lawyer. The whole town was on a hunt to blame someone for the loss of Arcelia Gallagher and if they could not pin it on her husband, they would find someone else to blame. They could not, of course, turn down Aldo's offer to talk without a lawyer present. No detective could.

Aldo Flores looked as if he might faint dead away at any moment. He was sweating and his right leg would not stop tap-tap-tapping on the floor. His eyes were wide with fear. He clutched a small cloth hat in both hands, wringing it out like it was a washcloth. The guy was absolutely terrified. Calvano tried to put him at ease. He assured him they were not from Immigration and that he should not worry about that. But nothing he, nor anyone else could say, served to calm the man.

His brother was far more confident, and I wondered how accurately Rodrigo translated his brother's stumbling answers. I wondered if he was shading them at all in an attempt to help Aldo, who looked far too frightened to exercise caution. But I did not speak Spanish and I could not tell. The official translator kept a neutral expression on her face at all times and seldom interrupted Rodrigo's translations of his brother's words. It was impossible to tell how she felt about the situation. But what emerged from the conversation did little to either help Aldo establish his innocence or encourage the police to find his wife.

In halting sentences and bursts of information that later had to
be put in proper sequence, the story that emerged was this: Aldo
and his wife had arrived in the States three months before, with
his wife six months pregnant at the time. It had been a difficult
pregnancy. She was frightened and did not like America. It was
too cold, it was too different, it was too far from her family. On
top of that, she was still suffering from sickness each morning
that lasted nearly all day. Worse, Aldo confessed with downcast
eyes, she kept saying that she did not want the child, that she was
afraid she would not know how to take care of it. She had soon
transformed from a loving wife who would take the bus to bring
her husband lunch each day to a woman he scarcely knew. Aldo
had visited the church seeking help and Father Sojak had recom-
mended that Aldo's wife talk to Arcelia Gallagher.

Arcelia had helped his wife so much, Aldo told the police. She
had calmed his wife down and explained that all new mothers
were nervous, but that she would love her child when it came and
find it in herself to be a wonderful mother. Arcelia had promised
the woman that life in America would get better and that there
was no better place for her to raise her child.

Aldo's wife had returned from her visit to Arcelia Gallagher
saying that everything was going to be OK. Aldo had seen great
improvement in her after that. His wife had started to look forward
to their baby's birth and begun discussing names with him. But
then, a little over a week ago, she had left the house one night
– to go to the store, she said, because she wanted a mango, but it
had to be ripe and only she could pick it out. She had returned a
half-hour later, flustered, without any fruit. Aldo had chalked it
up to her being pregnant and changing her mind. But that night,
he felt her tossing and turning all night long. Neither one of them
had gotten much sleep.

He had gone to work the next day. When he returned home that
night, his wife was gone. Unlike Arcelia Gallagher, she had taken
at least one thing with her – a small suitcase filled with a few
articles of clothing. But she had left no note and no clue as to
where she was headed.

It made no sense, Aldo Flores insisted, she was to have a baby
any day now and the doctors had been arranged. There was a clinic
where she could go that did not ask any questions. They had
discussed it at length and were happy their baby would be born

with doctors on hand. Why would she leave under those circumstances? Aldo was sure something terrible had happened to her.

He had not known where to turn for help, Aldo told Maggie
and Calvano. And although his brother hesitated to translate the
words, it became apparent that Aldo had visited Arcelia Gallagher
at school the day after his wife disappeared, asking her for help
in finding his wife. Which meant the little Mexican boy in Arcelia's
class had been right after all – she had been talking at the fence
to a man with hair and skin like his.

'What did she do when you asked her to help you find your
wife?' Maggie asked. Her voice was thick with worry. I knew
why: if Arcelia Gallagher had stumbled on whoever had taken
Aldo's wife, she may have walked into an incredibly dangerous
situation. She may well have put her own life in danger trying to
help someone else.

Aldo looked confused. Eventually, through his brother, he was
able to convey that he did not know what Arcelia Gallagher had
done to help them. She had said she would call him if she found
out anything and, although he had received a phone message from
Arcelia the day before she disappeared, she had not left any details.
She had only said he was not to worry about his wife, that she
would be OK, and would contact him when she could.

'But then I hear that Mrs Gallagher is missing, and my wife
still does not call or come home, and things are twice as bad, not
better,' Aldo added through his brother.

As he told this story, I could feel Gonzales turning against the
man. I understood why, but I could not forgive the commander for
it. Aldo Flores was all that Gonzales feared others would see him
as: someone who did not belong in the community, beaten down by
life, fearful of the authorities, unambitious, content to rake someone
else's leaves, his whole world revolving around family, with no
aspirations to power or vast wealth even envisioned. He had not
learned to speak English and he dressed like a peasant. He was
exactly what Gonzales did not want to be. Even more troubling,
Gonzales could understand every syllable the frightened man uttered
and I am certain he brought his own interpretations to all those stut-
terings and silences. By the time Aldo was done, I knew the absolute
worst possible outcome was all too likely to occur. And it did.

My fears were realized when Maggie excused herself from the
interrogation room and joined Gonzales in the observation chamber.

'It sounds to me like he has a reason to be concerned,' she told Gonzales. 'His wife is missing and you cannot ignore the similarities between her and Arcelia Gallagher. I think we need to start investigating his wife's disappearance as part of this case.'

'Book him,' Gonzales said abruptly. He looked at his watch. 'I've got to go home and get some sleep. We'll talk more in the morning.'

Maggie stared at him incredulously. 'Book him? I can't do that. What reason do we have? You can't throw him in a jail cell. Look at him – he's terrified. His wife is missing. Think of how frightened he must be.'

Gonzales would not look her in the eye. 'Think of something and book him. I don't want him leaving this town and I don't want him leaving this country. There's something off about him. And by his own words, he's connected to both missing women. Book him, put him in a holding cell for now and then lose the key.'

'Sir,' Maggie said, shocked. She was at a loss for more to say.

Gonzales brushed past her, eager to get out the door. 'We have to have someone to show for the last two days, Gunn. If we don't arrest someone soon, this town is going to lynch Danny Gallagher. Just book him and we'll sort it out later.'

He had disappeared down the hall but Maggie still could not move. She stared after Gonzales, her innate sense of fairness in chaos. Calvano grew curious at her long absence and poked his head out into the hallway. Seeing her standing there, he gave her a quizzical look and mouthed the word 'What?'

'You don't want to know,' Maggie said. She reached for the door to the interrogation room. Her face was grim. 'And you're not going to like what I have to tell you.'

SIXTEEN

To say that Calvano didn't like the orders Gonzales had given them was an understatement. He flat out refused to do it. He left Maggie to process Aldo Flores and to handle his outraged brother. It was not like Calvano to walk out on Maggie and so I followed him, curious to see where he was going.

It was well after midnight and the streets were empty. All the reporters were, thankfully, back at their hotels, downing drinks and telling themselves they performed a valuable service by exposing dangerous killers like Danny Gallagher.

Calvano looked up at the clear, starry skies and began to walk west until he reached a seedy coffee shop frequented by prostitutes and drug dealers. Most of the booths were filled, but the waitress quickly cleared one for Calvano. Like everyone else in the coffee shop, she knew he was a cop and she didn't want any trouble on her shift.

I sat across from him, drinking in the aroma of his coffee as I tried to figure out the enigma that was Adrian Calvano. Not so long ago, he had been a swaggering ladies man and a useless detective. Then he had met Maggie and, with nothing between them but professional respect, she had made him both a better man and a better detective. I think something had been awakened in him, perhaps even a conscience. He was finding it harder to accept some of the things Gonzales asked him to do now that he was thinking for himself. I had never taken that step as I had never made it that far. I admired him for it.

He sat there for nearly an hour, drinking coffee and staring at the place mat, his thoughts unreadable and his mood inscrutable. It was close to three o'clock in the morning when the coffee shop door opened and Maggie stuck her head inside. She spotted Calvano and slid into the booth across from him, causing me to scramble to one corner to avoid that somersaulting feeling I get when someone occupies the same space as me.

'I figured you'd be here,' Maggie said. 'I processed him. His brother Rodrigo is getting him a lawyer.'

Calvano was not going to thank her for doing Gonzales's dirty work. Nor was he going to apologize for abandoning his duty. 'Gonzales is a douche bag,' he told Maggie. 'I don't care if he's your godfather or not. I don't trust him. And what he's doing right now? There's no excuse for it. It's not right.'

'Aldo is connected to both missing women,' Maggie pointed out. 'Would you rather we were still focusing on Danny Gallagher?'

'It's times like these when I wish I smoked,' Calvano said. He stared longingly at a couple of streetwalkers who were eating chocolate sundaes and smoking cigarettes in defiance of town ordinances banning smoking in restaurants. He turned back to

Maggie. 'You know, Aldo Flores and Danny Gallagher aren't the only people who had contact with both women. It doesn't have to be a choice between the husband and some poor beaner, who has no idea what hit him and who only wants to find his wife and kid.'

'Like who?' Maggie asked, gently sliding Calvano's coffee out of his reach. He had clearly had enough for the night.

'Like Father Sojak,' Calvano said reluctantly. 'And we both know that Aldo helped his brother out at the Delmonte House. That means his wife took the bus to bring him lunch there. Which means there are people at that house who came in contact with both her and Arcelia Gallagher. For all we know, Enrique Romero is behind this all.'

Maggie laughed. 'Now you sound like Gonzales. Look, I don't like Romero any more than you do. That Hollywood routine wears me out in about ten seconds. But he has no reason whatsoever to have anything to do with either woman. You're just angry because he's a lousy husband.'

'I still say we're not done out there,' Calvano said stubbornly. 'There are too many roads that lead to that house.'

'I hear you,' Maggie said. 'It bothers me as well. But Gonzales wants us to focus on making a case against Aldo Flores.'

'Then let him think that's what we're doing.' Calvano said flatly. 'But me? I want to find Arcelia Gallagher, not chase dead ends. And I'm telling you, there's something that connects her to that house and it's not just that exorcism she helped with or whatever the hell it was.'

'OK,' Maggie conceded. 'I'll make a deal with you. If you can still sleep after all that coffee, let's each grab a few hours and then we'll head out there again in the morning.'

'For real?' Calvano asked.

Maggie nodded. 'For real.'

Because I was facing the plate glass window of the coffee shop, I saw Skip Bostwick approaching before anyone else did. I knew immediately it would not end well. Maggie's ex was bopping down the street in that annoying way of his, in search of local color for his story. Or maybe he was looking for a hooker to erase the memory of Lindsey Stanford. Whatever he was up to, it had not taken him long to make Stanford happy and, judging from the spring in his step, he thought it had done him some good.

Son of a bitch – he had been following Maggie. That's what had brought him to this street. He kept peering into alleys and looking at the cars parked along the street, wondering where she had gone. I shot him the bird in a burst of solidarity with my living partners, but he probably wouldn't have noticed had I been visible. The guy was that into himself. He spotted the brightly lit coffee shop from down the street and hurried toward it. I saw him recognize Maggie's car parked a few doors down. Then he saw Maggie and Calvano, heads bent together over coffee, and I am sure he leapt right to the wrong conclusion. Like the jerk he was, he acted like he still owned her. He came inside looking for a fight.

Some people are capable of opening a door and simply walking through it. Others have to fling it open with the bang to announce to the world that they are there. Naturally Skip Bostwick fell into this category. All eyes turned to him and not a single person in that coffee shop gave a crap that he was handsome. They were street people. They had been around enough to know an asshole when they saw one. I think everyone, down to the harried waitress, pegged him for what he really was within three seconds of seeing him.

He was oblivious to the impression he made and sauntered over to Maggie and Calvano's booth with his customary cockiness. 'Well, well, well,' he said. 'What have we here? I guess you two are part of the very tiny city that never sleeps. Working on a new lead in the case?'

With monumental effort, Maggie kept her cool. 'Go away, Skip. You're the last person on earth we would tell anything to.'

Calvano entered the fray. '*Skip?*' he asked. 'What kind of name is that for a grown man?'

'You tell me, *Adrian*,' Skip shot back. 'Yo, Adrian!'

How mature. They were fighting over their names. The two little boys in Arcelia Gallagher's class had shown more maturity than these two.

Calvano stood up and, I had to admit, he could be very intimidating. I think it's the combination of his prissy hygiene and the slightly crazy look he gets in his eyes that is one hundred percent Italian.

The street whores appreciated Calvano way more than they admired ole Skippy's fake good looks. They squealed in anticipation as the two men squared off. The waitress hurried over, took a closer look at them and decided to wait by the cash register until it was over.

'Mano-a-mano!' one of the prostitutes announced, making it apparent that she was a he.

'Come on guys,' Maggie pleaded. Her worst fear had just arrived. But she may as well have been spitting into the wind. There was only one way this was going to go down.

'What's it like working with my ex-wife?' Bostwick asked Calvano. 'You get off on how bossy she is?'

There were a lot of things Calvano could have said in reply. But he decided to get right to the point. He landed one of the best right hooks I have ever seen – and we're talking about many drunken nights at a bar staring bleary-eyed at televised fights – right in the center of Skip Bostwick's nose. The man dropped like a rock as blood gushed out in rivers. Calvano pulled his fist back and stared at it, astonished. I'm not sure he had ever connected so thoroughly before.

The coffee shop was dead quiet. Not a person moved. Even Maggie was speechless.

I was euphoric. I was, in fact, dancing on the tabletop, although no one could appreciate it. Oh, how many times I had wanted to do what Calvano had just done – to haul off and slug someone who richly deserved it and let my fists do the talking. It felt good to see Skip Bostwick go down. And it was pure heaven to see him writhing on a dirty coffee shop floor.

If Calvano agreed with me, he hid it well. 'I'm sorry,' he said to Maggie. 'I didn't know I could do that.'

Skip Bostwick had begun to groan. He held his nose in both hands and rocked from side-to-side, mumbling something that sounded like 'my node, my node', as blood ran over his hands. Maggie gestured for the waitress to bring over some napkins. When she hurried over with a fistful of them, Maggie grabbed a handful and bent over Skip. She started to dab the blood from his face and then thought better of it. She ended up dropping the wad of paper on his chest. 'Be a man and mop it up yourself,' she said, sliding back into her booth. She had decided she was going to simply watch and see what unfolded next.

If Bostwick had hoped for help for his injuries, he gave up the tactic quickly. Struggling to sit up, he glared at Maggie and

Calvano, his hands cupped under his nose to catch the blood flowing from it. 'I'm going to sue the shit out of both of you and the department,' he told him. 'That was assault. There were witnesses.'

'Don't look at us,' one of the prostitutes told him. The others nodded their agreement. 'You're looking at Miss Hear No Evil, See No Evil and our little sister Speak No Evil.' Amid a chorus of 'uh-huhs' she turned her back on Bostwick.

Maggie had decided that she was backing her partner on this one. She leaned over until she was only a few inches from her ex-husband's face and whispered to him, 'So help me God, Skip, if you even so much as *tell* anyone how you got that, I will make sure that no one on the force ever talks to you again. And trust me, there are way more people who like me at this point. I will make sure that no one in this town gives you the slightest scrap of information to help you with your story. Walk away or your so-called career as a crime reporter is over before it starts.'

Holy crap. I had never heard Maggie sound so mean before. She sounded like she was going to rip off his head and breathe fire down his neck. I think she meant every word of it.

Calvano had watched the interchange without speaking. He raised a finger in the air and said to the waitress with exaggerated politeness, 'Check, please.'

The waitress approached warily, proffering the slip of paper. Without even looking at it, Calvano gave her a ten and told her to keep the change. That locked in her loyalty.

As Calvano and Maggie scrambled from the booth and headed out the door, the waitress bent over Skip Bostwick and surveyed his injuries.

'You're gonna have to get up off the floor,' she finally said, with a snap of her gum. 'You're in my way, you're drippin' blood on the floor and I've got customers to serve. If you want a booth, there's a five dollar minimum.'

SEVENTEEN

Maggie had offered to drop Calvano off at home, but once she reached his apartment, neither one of them wanted to stop talking about Calvano's punch.

'Does your hand hurt?' Maggie asked.

'Hell yeah, my hand hurts,' Calvano complained. He examined his knuckles. 'It's none of my business, Gunn, but I just got to ask – how did you end up married to that guy?'

The question bothered Maggie. For a moment, she did not answer. But when Calvano started to apologize for asking, she interrupted him. 'No, it's OK. It's a fair question. I just hate admitting it when I make a mistake.' She stared out the front of the windshield, deciding how to explain. Before long, night would give way to dawn. They had nearly worked through the night. 'The best way to explain it is to say I was overcome by a temporary madness.'

Calvano laughed. 'That's the first time I've heard love described that way, but it fits.'

'I'm not sure it was love exactly,' Maggie admitted. 'But the truth is even more pathetic. He was the guy that everyone wanted. We went through the Academy together. There was a huge class of women that year because of some new EEOC guidelines. Everyone was crazy over him. Skip wasn't so full of himself back then. I'd known him since I was a kid, so I had the edge. Our fathers were friends from when they were both on the Wilmington force so we would visit their family a couple times a year and sometimes even share a beach house in the summer. Skip and I were just buddies growing up, but that year, when we started the Academy, everything changed.'

She seemed ashamed of what she was about to say and Calvano gave her room to collect her thoughts. 'I'm listening,' was all he said.

'Skip was still really insecure, I guess. I can't think of any other reason why he would pay me so much attention. But he already knew me, and maybe all the other women coming after him as hard as they were scared him. I'm not sure. Trust me, I was no prize.' She smiled. 'I had the best times of any woman in the class and my scores on the range were off the charts, but that was the extent of my attraction.'

'Don't say that, Gunn,' Calvano told her. 'Never sell yourself short. It just opens the door for jerks like him to do the same thing.'

Maggie smiled her gratitude. 'He swept me off my feet. I admit it. He'd gone from being geeky the last time I saw him to being, well, you know what he looks like now. Television handsome. I fell for his outside. I didn't understand his inside had changed, too. The kid I used to sit with on the dunes and talk to for hours at a time was gone. But we were already married when I realized he had turned out to be incredibly self-centered and ambitious. That the only person he would ever be capable of loving was himself.' She shook her head, disgusted at herself. 'Honestly, Adrian, I was so competitive. I know this sounds horrible, but I think I just married him so that the other women couldn't. I'm not sure I ever felt that much for him. God knows, it was easy to walk away from him once I figured it out. I'm not sure I *can* feel a lot for someone. I'm not sure I have that left in me after days like this one.'

Calvano was nodding his head. 'I've gone out with women for even worse reasons, trust me. This job takes a lot out of you, Gunn. We can look for one million excuses not to fall in love and then, when we do, against all of our best intentions, we look for something else to call it. We've done a lot of dangerous things to get our shields, but sometimes I think letting ourselves have a private life feels like the most dangerous of all.'

Maggie looked surprised. 'That was pretty perceptive, Adrian. Have you been watching *Oprah* re-runs again?'

The mood was broken. Calvano punched Maggie on the shoulder and climbed out of the car, leaning in for a final parting shot. 'Do what I do, Gunn. Just go out with so many of them, no one ever has a chance to stick.'

Maggie sat in the darkness for a moment before she pulled away. When she did, I knew that they would not talk of this conversation again.

The next morning proved me right. She picked him up as if their talk the night before had never happened. A few hours of sleep had done them both good. Both Maggie and Calvano looked as if they might survive the week after all.

They arrived at the station house before either Gonzales or the media showed, checked in with their other teams and left after Calvano looked in on Aldo Flores. He came away with the information that Aldo had indeed worked at the Delmonte House with Rodrigo and that Aldo's wife had taken the bus out there several times at lunch. That meant anyone at the house could have had contact with both her and Arcelia Gallagher. Now they were on their way to the mansion again.

Calvano was in a subdued mood after his visit with Aldo Flores. 'That poor bastard. He has no idea what's happening to him. I had to pull another prisoner over to translate and I'm not sure I got everything, but he pretty much thinks his world has collapsed around him. He's convinced he's going to be shipped to some deportation center next.'

'I hate to tell you, but he probably is,' Maggie said.

'It doesn't seem fair. The guy just wants a decent life.'

'Tell that to your congressman,' Maggie suggested. 'And don't count on Gonzales to back you on it.'

'Yeah, what's up with that?' Calvano asked. 'He hates Enrique Romero for being more important than him and he hates Aldo Flores for being less important than him. You think he'd be a little more sympathetic.'

'Since when has the city mouse ever wanted to hang with the country mouse?' Maggie asked. She pulled up in front of the gate of the Delmonte House, pressed a button and waited several centuries until the old butler buzzed them in. When she reached the top of the circular driveway in front of the mansion, she pulled to a halt. The three of us sat in the car, staring at the house. I know they were thinking about ghosts haunting the halls and wondering what freaky reception awaited them this time. I enjoyed the irony of being the ghost in the back seat, less than two feet away, worrying about the same thing. But I was also thinking of the unhappiness I had felt so acutely in the house on our prior visit – all the despair and the bleakness and that horrible moment when I had experienced the feeling of being attacked with a sword.

Something very bad had happened in that house and moments of it still lingered. I wondered what it had to do with Arcelia Gallagher, if anything.

'What's our approach?' Calvano asked Maggie. 'You think Romero is back from Hollywood yet?'

'You know what I think?' Maggie said. 'I think the husband is never coming back from Hollywood. I think he's gotten as much good publicity from his marriage as he can and he's going to run as far away as possible, as fast as he can, from the bad publicity that's left.'

Calvano thought it over. 'So, let's go after the butler?' he suggested. 'Let's see what we can get out of him. The guy owes us a favor. We were easy on him and we left his wife alone. Maybe he knows more than he's telling?'

Maggie nodded her approval. 'That's a good approach. Though I feel certain we won't get anything from him that he isn't fully prepared to give.'

'Maybe the butler did it?' Calvano suggested hopefully.

'Not this one,' Maggie said. 'The only thing he's hiding is his wife's condition. And wouldn't you rather live here than in some state-run nursing home?'

'I'm not so sure about that,' Calvano said. He checked his gun and climbed out of the car. 'This place gives me the creeps.'

'Me, too,' I wanted to say, but my thoughts were distracted by what I saw in an upper window staring down at us. It was a lopsided face with the right cheek off-kilter, where it had been augmented too far toward the hairline. The eyes were stretched so tight they did not look like they could close and the corners of the swollen lips drooped down, as if the mouth was melting. I realized with a start that the face belonged to the girl once called 'the most beautiful person in the world.' Dakota Wylie was watching us, her face bare of bandages, scarves and sunglasses, revealed for what it was. Ruined. She was staring down at Calvano.

Maggie and Calvano were juggling cups of coffee and keys, too busy to notice what I had seen. They were also too busy to notice the amazing morning coalescing around us – but I could not ignore it. It was moments like these, when I see what others overlook, that I feel most alive. And I cannot seem to pass these moments by. Dew still gleamed on the new shoots of grass and the flowers were opening to the sun above. Birds flew from lawn to lawn in search of food for their young. The breeze sweeping in from the surrounding fields smelled of green.

I turned my back on the mansion, with all of its unhappiness,

and visited the edge of the lawn, unable to resist an immense bed
of flowers rioting next to new roses that were just beginning to
bud. I looked out over a sloping lawn surrounding a marble statue
of a woman dressed in Grecian robes. She was looking pensively
down at granite waters swirling about her feet. Her face reminded
me of the missing woman, Arcelia Gallagher. It seemed so tranquil,
yet also as if it were hiding a hint of sadness.

As I stood there, thinking of her, wondering if she was still
alive, the wind shifted and I realized that I felt *her* – I felt Arcelia
Gallagher as surely as if she had been standing right beside me.
I was certain of it. It was her essence, her unique combination of
joy at being alive tinged with sorrow at the past. It was her smell,
her being, her smile and her beauty all wrapped up into one feeling,
a feeling that washed over me as surely as the sunshine spilling
through the trees from above.

She was near and she was alive. I knew it with every fiber of
my being.

I looked around and saw no one, not even the gardener, tending
to the lawn. Behind me, Maggie and Calvano were trudging to
the front door, preparing to get what they could out of the elderly
butler. I moved over the lawn and the flower beds, searching to
see if she was there somewhere. Nothing. I searched some more.
Nothing still. Eventually, I turned back to the house, ready to
follow Maggie and Calvano inside, my confidence starting to erode.
Perhaps I had just imagined it? Perhaps the statue had triggered
a memory of her so acute that I felt as if I were in her presence?
Perhaps I only hoped that she was still alive.

The butler had opened the door with resignation and ungra-
ciously welcomed Maggie and Calvano inside. Their politeness
did not soften him, but he gestured for them to follow and tromped
resolutely toward the kitchen. We formed a curious parade through
the halls. The old butler, once king of a long-lost era and now an
old man, Maggie and Calvano, burdened with their failure to find
any leads, and me, an aimless ghost who lived neither here nor
there and who glanced around fearfully, afraid of another ghost I
could not see.

The house seemed particularly empty that morning. Their footsteps echoed in the hall and the air smelled dusty and dry. It was
in the stillness that I felt someone watching us. I looked around
but saw no one. But the heat of that gaze was almost palpable

and I knew that someone – or something – was spying on our parade.

As we neared the end of the long hallway, the bright lights of the kitchen called to us. I could smell fruit cooking on the stove and felt something, perhaps happiness, perhaps contentment, sending out tendrils of welcome. The old butler quickened his step and seemed almost to flee to its warm embrace.

There was someone behind me. I felt it.

I whirled around and found nothing there.

I turned back toward the kitchen and there it was again: a brush against my back, a breath down my neck, the barest of touches from another being.

I turned around again and, this time, heard laughter. I looked at the others. Maggie and Calvano did not seem to have noticed. With a glance over my shoulder, I caught up with them. Whatever lived in this house, it was trying to make contact with *me.*

The kitchen was warm and steamy. Pots bubbled and boiled on the stove, sending fragrant wisps into the air. Sunlight poured through the French windows, transforming it into a whole different room compared to how it felt at night. Every countertop was scrupulously clean and gleamed in the sunlight. The floor was immaculate white tile. An old oak table took up a corner of the kitchen and the butler's wife sat at one end of it, green beans spread out in front of her. She methodically snapped one in half, pulled off the string and deposited what was left into a bowl. She was humming and her eyes sparkled as she looked up at the newcomers, smiling.

I realized with a start that she was looking at me. Her eyes were dark and intense. I did not remember them looking like that before. Could she really see me? I raised my right arm. She raised hers, mimicking me. I cocked an eyebrow. She cocked hers. I smiled and she smiled back.

No one else had noticed our exchange. Maggie and Calvano were telling the butler about their lack of progress in the case and the old man's wife had been forgotten.

The old woman was staring at me even more intensely. I felt myself drawn to her dark eyes. As I stared into them, I could feel the light around me shrink, as if I stood at the center of an aperture closing on me. It felt as if all the air left the room and that its very walls were shrinking in around me. For just a few seconds,

I looked about and saw nothing but clay walls pressing in on me. I was trapped in the darkness. I smelled sweat and felt terror.

I felt Arcelia Gallagher.

Abruptly, I was back in the kitchen with the others.

'Hello,' Maggie was saying cheerfully to the butler's wife. Maggie pulled out a chair and reached for a handful of beans. She automatically joined the old woman in her task, as she had no doubt done many times with her own mother. The butler's wife smiled at Maggie with calm, green eyes. Though it was clear that she did not remember Maggie or, perhaps, even remember her husband, she knew that she was safe, and that when she was in her kitchen, she was home. She was happy. The old woman who had stared at me was gone.

My friend, I thought. My fellow traveler. He was able to use her somehow.

The butler moved protectively to his wife and put a hand on her shoulder, patting it gently. It was a small gesture but so at odds with his formal demeanor that it made me like him just a little bit more.

'I'm not sure there is anything I can tell you,' the butler said as he finished polishing a coffee urn and began to fuss with the settings. Calvano hurried to help him. It was a cozy sight – the two women sitting at the sunlit kitchen table and the two men making coffee. I knew that Maggie and Calvano had planned to approach the butler gently. But I also think that their actions were genuine. They had been seduced by the kitchen's embrace and were basking in its warmth. It was impossible to resist. This had been a refuge for the butler and his wife for over forty years, I realized; the one place that was theirs, where whatever troubles occurring in the rest of the house could be left behind at the kitchen door. It was filled with their memories. I felt a peace settle over me and I fell into a deeper state of being, the buzzing and the sudden movements of the living fading from my world.

That was when I saw it. There, beside the refrigerator, I saw the figure of a man.

He was like me. He was there, but not quite there. I could see his figure clearly, though it was faded along the edges. I did not think that any of the others could see him. I did not recognize him. He was black, very black, as dark as the coffee now brewing in the urn. He was a stocky man, who must have been as strong as a bull when he was alive. He had broad shoulders and hands like catcher's mitts. His head was shaved and his features oddly friendly given his intimidating frame. He was staring at me as if he wanted something from me. I did not know what he was trying to say. His mouth moved, but I could not hear him. I stepped closer, wanting to understand. His eyes were filled with such pain that I knew at once that he was the spirit that would not leave this house, that he was the source of the cold air and sudden pains that had plagued me on my earlier visit.

I could not understand what he wanted. A veil blocked communication between us. The air around me cooled as I grew closer to the man. He stood stock still, staring at me, trying to send me a message. When I grew near enough, he mouthed a single phrase: 'Help me.'

With that, he faded. Calvano walked right through him, heading for the kitchen sink to wash his hands, and gave no indication he knew he was there.

The spirit was gone. The air solidified again and I was drawn back to the world of the living, where the old man butler started to loosen up. He told them that the maid was gone. Frightened by the disappearance of a second woman in town, Lupe had fled the mansion and no one knew where she had gone.

'Are you sure she's OK?' Calvano asked.

The butler nodded. 'She came to see me first to say that she was leaving and would not be back.' He hesitated and then decided to say more. 'She said the house was just too sad to stay here. She had a new job waiting in another town and she was going to take it.'

Maggie and Calvano looked discouraged. They would never find her now. 'Who will take care of Ms Wylie?' Maggie asked.

The old man shook his head. 'I do not know. She interviewed seven different women before she agreed to hire Lupe.' He turned his back on Maggie and Calvano, as if to shield the resentment in his voice as he added, 'Perhaps her manager can take care of her. He ought to do something to earn his money.'

'Yeah, what's with that guy?' Calvano asked casually as he brought coffee cups to the table and set them out. 'He seems a little below her pay grade, if you know what I mean.'

The butler was fussing with the sugar bowl. 'If you mean he

seems a little sleazy, then yes, I would have to agree. Ms Wylie is better than that.'

'Then what's the deal? Does he have her locked up with contracts? What's the power he has over her?'

The butler shrugged. 'The power he has is that he is the only one in her life who truly seems to care about her.' It was clear the old man would say no more about it.

'So you heard about the second woman who went missing?' Maggie asked him. 'Did you know she was married to Aldo, Rodrigo's brother? We know that Aldo worked here, helping his brother with the gardens.'

The butler sighed. 'I knew you would figure out that we had more people on staff than what you saw yesterday. Yes, we all heard late last night that Aldo's wife was missing. It concerns me. She was a lovely young woman, perhaps a bit overwhelmed by the thought of being a mother, but devoted to her husband. She visited often to bring out his lunch, though my wife was always happy to make lunch for the staff.' He smiled fondly at the old lady who was blissfully snapping beans, her mind incapable of taking in more than that simple task. He, of course, made the lunches but could not admit it, not even to himself.

'Then I suppose you have also heard that Aldo was arrested?' Calvano asked.

'Rodrigo told me,' the butler said, his voice taking on his customary clipped, guarded tone. 'I suggested counsel and offered to help pay the fees.'

Calvano felt compelled to defend his honor. 'It was not our call.'

'Rodrigo will certainly have his hands full now,' the butler replied, making it plain he was not going to discuss Aldo anymore.

Calvano folded his long frame into a chair and sipped at his coffee. 'Holy crap, this is delicious.'

The butler smiled despite himself. 'That's what forty years of practice will do for you.'

'I guess you know the history of this house pretty well,' Calvano said casually, ignoring Maggie's warning glance.

'You want to know about the murders in the orchard, don't you,' the butler said. He sat at the table next to Calvano and poured himself a cup of coffee. It was the first glimpse I'd had of the old man off duty. He didn't look any more relaxed to me.

'That and the rest of the house's history,' Calvano said. 'You've got to admit, it seems a little . . .'

'A little haunted?' the butler suggested. 'I told you it was. When you are as old as I am, you start to like the existence of ghosts. It means your time may not be over after all.'

'You think this house is haunted because of the orchard murder?' Maggie asked, trying to hide her skepticism.

'No,' the butler said. 'Not from the murders in the orchard. That was a killing that could have happened anywhere. It was two homeless men fighting over a bottle of cheap wine and one of them had a knife. It could have happened in the park in the middle of town. It could have happened in the parking lot outside the liquor store. It just happened to occur here, in our orchard, where they had been sleeping for a week or more because of the warm weather. I'd noticed them but thought they were harmless. The grounds here take up over twenty acres. I did not see any harm in letting them stay.'

I had a sudden vision of a steady stream of bums appearing at the back door of the mansion, where his wife dispensed what was left over of the meals she cooked while the butler looked the other way. He was not such a bad guy after all.

'How can you be so sure it's not one of them haunting you?' Calvano asked. 'I heard the one who did the killing died in prison not long after he was sent away.'

'Being sent away was probably the only food and shelter that poor man received his entire life,' the butler said. 'My guess is that he was grateful for it. No, our guest is not either one of those gentlemen. Our guest is older than that. Our guest has been here a long, long time. He has, in fact, been here longer than me.' He glanced at Calvano. 'You seem to be accepting everything I say at face value. That's unusual.'

'I had two Italian grandmothers,' Calvano explained. 'What can I say? I grew up being threatened with the evil eye.'

The old man laughed. It was a rusty sound, like a car trying to start, but it made his wife look up from her green beans with a smile.

'You have no idea who the ghost is?' Calvano asked. 'You never actually see it?'

The butler shook his head. 'I don't even know if it's a he.'

I did. It was a very big and very black and very unhappy he.

The old man glanced up at the clock. 'It is nearly eleven o'clock. Ms Wylie will be awake and wanting her fresh fruit salad.'

'I'll take it up to her,' Calvano volunteered. 'Don't worry, I won't question her. But it will save you the stairs.'

The butler looked embarrassed at the need for this courtesy but he nodded. 'If you see her manager, he will not be pleased.'

'I think I can take that chance,' Calvano said.

'In that case, the tray is ready.' The butler took a perfectly assembled tray holding a bowl of fruit salad from the refrigerator and arranged linen napkins around it. It was clear that he had been doing his job and his wife's job for years, perhaps, masking her condition for who knows how long.

'Adrian . . .' Maggie said in a voice that held a warning.

'Don't worry, boss,' Calvano said cheerfully. 'I just want to bring the lady her fruit.'

The butler handed Calvano the tray, but at the last moment, could not bring himself to let go of it without a final warning. 'You have to knock first and then wait, sometimes for quite a while, while she gets ready to receive visitors. There are no exceptions to this rule. Otherwise, you will upset her and it could take all day to calm her down.'

'Don't worry,' Calvano said. 'I understand. I'm not going to barge in on her.'

The butler released the tray and Calvano accepted it with a solemn nod. I followed him out the kitchen door and down the hall toward the curving grand staircase that led upstairs. I knew that he was intentionally leaving Maggie alone in the kitchen so that she could pump the butler for more information. I also know that while Calvano was intent on questioning Dakota Wylie some more, despite his promise to the butler, he also could not fight his urge to take care of her. She was a pregnant young woman abandoned by an indifferent husband and Calvano thought that she deserved better.

EIGHTEEN

Calvano knocked on Dakota Wylie's bedroom door and waited, as he had been instructed to do. I felt no such sense of gallantry. I preceded Calvano into the room and watched as, still lounging in her bed, the star arranged herself to receive visitors as if she were a queen.

Up close, her face did not seem as grotesque and misshapen as it had when viewed from afar earlier that morning. Yes, her features were swollen. She had clearly had plastic surgery, and something had gone wrong. The fundamental structure of her face had been altered and there was no way the damage could be undone. A once perfectly symmetrical face was now marred by lopsided, unnaturally broad cheeks, frozen eyes and a mouth stretched ever so slightly into a permanent grimace. How could she not see the damage?

Dakota Wylie hurriedly wrapped a scarf over her head and around her chin, pulling it over to cover as much of her face as possible. She slid the oversized sunglasses on and called out in her breathy voice, 'Come in, Mr Jarvis.'

'It's not Mr Jarvis. It's Detective Calvano. We met yesterday.' Calvano waited a moment longer, giving her time to get used to the fact that he was someone unfamiliar to her.

'Oh. It's you. Come in,' she said in a much smaller voice. She crossed her hands over her body as if to protect herself from a blow. I realized she shrank from anything that was not completely familiar to her, that she always seemed to be expecting a blow, if not from someone, then from the world. I thought immediately of her rich and famous husband. Could he? Would he? I remembered the domestic cases I had been called out to in my early days as a cop. Money and fame was no antidote for that kind of violence.

Calvano entered the room casually, as if he always brought Hollywood stars breakfast in bed. 'I'm sorry to barge in on you like this,' he said, taking care never to look directly at her. 'But your butler seems a little bit old to be running up and down the steps. I thought I could save him the trouble.'

'Yes,' she agreed in a voice that was suddenly very sad. Was it real or was it acting? 'Now that Lupe has quit, I don't know what I'm going to do. I feel terrible imposing on Mr Jarvis like that.'

So get your ass out of bed, lady, I thought to myself.

'I don't think he sees it as an imposition.' Calvano placed the tray on the bedside table next to her. 'Would you like me to put this on the pillow in front of you?'

'Please,' she said softly.

Calvano carefully placed the tray in front of her and she looked down at it with no enthusiasm.

'Can I get you something else?' Calvano asked. 'It's normal to have specific cravings when you're pregnant. Did you know that? I had a sister who only ate canned salmon and olives for weeks.'

She looked up at him with some surprise. 'Is it? I didn't realize. No, this is fine. I need to eat it. It will be good for the baby.'

Judging from how she looked, I doubt she had eaten a real meal in over a decade. She was thin in that emaciated way people who make their living on camera get, with bony arms and a head that seems too big for their bodies. I did not see how it could be healthy either for her or for her baby. Perhaps she had no other choice if she wanted to stay employed.

Calvano pulled a chair up to her bedside and sat down without asking. He still did not look directly at her. 'I bet it can get pretty lonely in here,' he offered. 'It's a big house you have here.'

She nodded as she picked up a piece of cantaloupe with her fingers and nibbled daintily at it. Her lips were so swollen she had trouble finding her mouth. It was clear she'd had injections of something in them. Instead of driving me wild, the sight of the cantaloupe bumping against those swollen lips seemed almost grotesque. Why would she think men wanted her to look that way? I was repelled.

'It does get lonely, but Enrique has a lot of business to attend to,' she told Calvano. 'Ever since he married me, his career has taken off again. I guess it was good for his reputation that someone as young as me fell in love with him.'

Calvano studied her carefully, perhaps for the first time. She returned his gaze with wide eyes and a flirtatious tilt of her head and I realized, as I looked around the room, that all the mirrors had been removed from it. Maybe she didn't know what she looked like? I wasn't sure she would have seen herself as others saw her

even if she had studied herself in the bathroom mirrors nearby. I
was beginning to suspect that she had lost touch with reality.

'You really love your husband, don't you?' Calvano asked her.
'I can tell by the way you talk about him.'

'I've loved him since I was a little girl,' she replied in a dreamy
voice. 'I used to stare at his picture in magazines and imagine that
one day he would come and sweep me off my feet and buy me a
huge, beautiful mansion and all the jewels I could ever want. And
cake. I was very young then, you see. I was very interested in cake.'
She smiled again, but this time it was a practiced smile, the one
she reserved for the cameras when she was pretending. 'Not many
girls can say that they grew up and married the man of their childhood dreams.'

'And what about him? Does he love you back?'

It was an unexpected question and she looked startled that
Calvano would ask it.

'What do you mean?' she stammered.

'Here you are, pregnant and clearly recovering from . . .' He
stumbled for the right words, 'Recovering from some sort of minor
automobile accident, perhaps?'

She nodded eagerly at his assumption, completely unaware that
he could see through the excuse he had offered.

'If you were my wife, I would not leave your side,' Calvano
said simply.

She smiled at him, hungry for the compliment. Her shoulders
straightened a little. She was one of those women that doesn't
really exist in her own mind unless she is basking in the attention
of others. When I realized this, what she had done to herself
suddenly seemed so very sad. She was a beautiful woman, not yet
in her prime, and yet she had felt driven to risk her trademark
beauty and endanger the life of her baby – all to look a few years
younger.

'Enrique means well,' she told Calvano. She had not been able
to bring herself to eat any more fruit and it sat, forgotten, in her
bowl. 'I am sure he would stay with me if he could. I think sometimes his agent encourages him to leave without me.'

'Oh yeah?' Calvano asked. 'And why is that? Isn't he your
agent, too?'

She nodded. 'Phil took me on soon after Enrique and I were
married. Lamont, that's my manager, is very protective of me and

he and my old agent just couldn't seem to get along. So it seemed like a good time to make a change.'

I thought of the cocky little man that was her manager and I could totally see that happening. He probably ran everyone off in her life.

'But I don't think Phil really believes in me,' she added suddenly, looking up at Calvano. She needed a compliment from him. 'I think he sees me as just another pretty face. He doesn't believe I can act. But once I have my baby, just you wait and see. I'll be on the cover of every tabloid and in the pages of every magazine, and just as soon as I lose the baby weight, I'll be back and I'll be bigger and more famous than ever. I'll make my husband and everyone else proud of me.'

Calvano smiled as if he believed what she was saying, but even he could see that she had ruined her face – and her chances – forever.

'I'm sorry your maid left you,' Calvano said. 'Did she tell you why she left?'

Dakota Wylie nodded. 'She said that now there were two women missing from town, and she was afraid she would be next. She said she was going to take another job somewhere else and that she was sorry to leave me but she was too afraid to stay in this town.'

'It does seem curious, doesn't it? Two women – both of them Mexican, both of them with ties to this house – missing?' Calvano said.

'What do you mean?' Dakota Wylie asked. 'How are they connected to this house?'

'One visited here and the other is married to one of the gardeners. She often came here to bring him lunch.'

Dakota Wylie looked down at her silk coverlet. 'I didn't know that. But I don't see how that can mean anything. There is no one here who would do something like that.'

'May I ask you about your husband?' Calvano said.

She looked frightened. 'He would never do anything like that.'

'He was married before you, wasn't he? Several times in fact. Do you know what his other wives looked like?'

She nodded slowly. 'They looked like me. He likes blondes. Young blondes, preferably. That is why I am determined to stay looking good for him. But you see, that means that those missing women, well – they just aren't his type, are they? Besides, he's not here enough to have done anything like that.' There was a trace of bitterness in her words.

Calvano felt that he'd pushed it as far as he could. 'When is the baby due?' he asked. 'You must be very excited.'

She patted her belly and smiled. 'In about a month, I think. The doctors aren't quite sure.' She looked up at Calvano. 'Do you know that in all the times that Enrique has been married, I am the first to give him a child? He wants children more than anything in the world and I am going to be the one to give them to him.'

Calvano looked surprised. 'Really? You're telling me that in four prior marriages, not one of those women had his kid?' He did not say what I was thinking: Enrique Romero was like Henry VIII, going through wife after wife in search of an heir, when the problem, in fact, surely lay with him.

'Really,' she assured Calvano. 'I think it's a miracle, don't you? It's a sign that we belong together.'

Calvano looked at her for a moment, unsure of what to say, and I don't think she saw the sadness that I could sense in him. 'Perhaps,' he finally said as he rose to go. 'I hope that you will both be very happy. All three of you, I mean. Your baby will be a very lucky baby.'

'You're a nice man, do you know that?' she told Calvano. 'I didn't know that nice men could be detectives.'

Calvano looked sad. 'Trust me, sometimes I can be not so nice.'

'Oh, I don't believe that for a moment,' she said, touching his hand and letting her fingers linger. 'I think you just might be about the nicest man I've ever met.'

But as if to test Calvano's words, her manager, Lamont Carter, burst into the room at that moment, angry at finding Calvano alone with his client. I should've heard him coming down the hall, but I was too intent on trying to figure out what was going on between Calvano and Dakota Wylie. Was she messing with him, manipulating him or being genuine? It was impossible to tell.

'What the hell do you think you're doing in here?' Carter demanded. 'I'm going to fire that old man for letting you up here.'

'No you aren't,' Dakota Wylie said firmly. 'I like Mr Jarvis and you're not going to fire him.' She never raised her voice in the slightest, but I had the feeling that her manager would do anything she said, anything at all. Certainly, he did not press the point.

'I just brought up her breakfast,' Calvano said. 'That's all.'

'Well, she has her breakfast, so you can go now,' Carter said rudely. His eyes darted back and forth between his client and Calvano, as if he were convinced that they had been plotting against him and he was trying to find a way to counteract their plans.

'Whatever,' Calvano said with a shrug. Then he smiled at Dakota Wylie so genuinely that I honestly believed that he did not see the bruises, the swelling and the tiny bandages at the corners of her hairline. I think he saw a woman so beautiful it made your heart stop; a fairy princess come to life. It's amazing what the heart can do to the eyes.

'You can go now,' the manager said more loudly. Calvano stared at Lamont Carter. His gaze lingered as he scrutinized the other man's shorter frame, letting Carter know that he could posture and threaten and bully as much as he wanted, but Calvano would always outrank him in every way. Carter got the message. His nostrils flared and he clamped his lips tight as he held back the insults he wanted to say.

'Goodbye,' Calvano said to Dakota Wylie. 'It was so nice talking to you.'

Her face brightened with the automatic graciousness of a woman who was used to being adored and wanted to keep it coming. 'It was so nice talking to you,' she chirped back.

To hear that beautiful, breathy voice coming out of that ravaged face was like a sucker punch to the gut.

As for Calvano, he glanced back at the manager over his shoulder and his look held a warning – Calvano would be watching him.

I, of course, could do that quite literally. I stayed behind to see what Lamont Carter would do once he was alone with Dakota Wylie. I was not entirely convinced that the bruises she was hiding were caused by plastic surgery. But the moment they were alone, he hurried over to her, sat on the edge of her bed and gathered her in his arms. She leaned back against him, surrendering herself to his embrace. I had to admit that I had never seen her look so content as she did in that moment, being rocked back and forth in her manager's arms as he whispered soothing words to her. She looked beautiful today, he was telling her, more beautiful than ever, and soon the whole world would know it, too.

I figured there was a better than even chance that Dakota Wylie's baby was going to come out with corn yellow hair and look a hell of a lot more like that short little man than it would look like the great Latin lover Enrique Romero.

Inside the kitchen, Maggie was helping the old man wash the coffee dishes. They were chatting like old friends while the butler's wife beamed at them from her place at the table. She smiled when she saw Calvano, assuming she must know him, not wanting to give away the confusion she felt.

'Ready to rock 'n roll?' Calvano asked Maggie.

She read this tone instantly and dried her hands on a towel. 'Sure. Let me just thank Mr Jarvis for his help.' She shook hands with the elderly butler before they left through the back door but I stayed behind long enough to see Mr Jarvis shuffle over to the kitchen table, a little slower than usual. The effort of appearing happy and in control had taken a lot out of him. He sat next to his wife with a sigh and closed his eyes. He was too old to be coping with so much.

Back in the car, Calvano told Maggie what he had learned upstairs and of how her manager had made it plain he felt a need to protect Dakota Wylie.

'Do you think Gonzales is right, that it's possible her husband is involved with the missing women in some way?' Maggie asked him.

Calvano shook his head. 'I don't think so. She's flaky and she's out of it, but she's right – he's not here enough to pull off something like kidnapping or killing two women.'

'What about the manager? Could he be behind it?'

Calvano shrugged. 'I don't see why he would. There's no motive. He just seems like a really short jerk to me. No surprise there.'

Maggie stared out the windshield. 'Mr Jarvis told me that Aldo was a reliable worker, steady and even-tempered. He was very thoughtful. He even brought in flowers for Mr Jarvis's wife every day, because he knew it made her happy to look at them. He says that there is no way Aldo could be involved in the disappearance of his wife or Arcelia Gallagher. I don't think Flores is involved, either. He's sitting there in a jail cell, Adrian, and he doesn't have anything to do with this.'

'I know,' Calvano said. 'It sucks. But I think the only way we're going to get him out of there is to find out who is responsible. Gonzales is on the war path.'

Maggie's phone vibrated and she checked the number. 'Crap,' she muttered. 'Gonzales wants to see us.'

'That can't be good. You think your ex-husband complained about me rearranging his face for him?' Calvano sounded worried. He'd gone off once or twice before and it was on the record. He was trying to rehabilitate his image and he didn't need it noted that he had punched a member of the media in the nose pretty much just for standing there. Not that the guy didn't deserve it.

Maggie shook her head. 'No, Skip won't tell anyone what happened. He likes to be the big, strong guy and if he tells people that you cold-cocked him with a single punch, well – he'll just look like a dumb ass. This has to be something else.'

'I'm not sure that's much better,' Calvano mumbled. He was afraid of Gonzales and I didn't blame him.

NINETEEN

The media had the station house under siege once again.

'Don't these people ever stop?' Calvano asked. 'Isn't this Sunday?'

Maggie sighed and she sounded tired. 'I don't know what day it is, so I can't tell you.'

They climbed from the car. The crowd of reporters gauged whether they were worth their attention. Skip Bostwick stood among them, a bandage covering his nose. Purple bruises bloomed around each eye. He glared at Maggie and Calvano but looked away without saying anything. He was going to keep it to himself.

'Nice work,' Maggie told Calvano. They pushed their way through the crowd, refusing to answer any questions. Lindsey Stanford had been expecting the brush-off and she was ready. Giving her cameraman a signal, she snapped into on-camera mode and began her monologue. 'Meanwhile, authorities are refusing to cooperate with the media and are stonewalling reporters on their progress. This has led more than one observer to remark that it is unlikely they have any leads in the case. Arcelia Gallagher has been missing for over forty-eight hours and chances are growing that the outcome of this story will not be a happy one. None of

these developments appear to trouble her husband, Daniel
Gallagher, who remains free – despite a growing consensus that
he, and only he, knows what happened to his wife.'

If Lindsey Stanford thought it would rattle Maggie, she was
wrong. Maggie just shook her head slightly and pushed through
the double doors into the station house, past a line of uniformed
men assigned to keep the media hordes outside.

Freddy, the desk sergeant who had ruled the front counter for
decades, called out to Maggie as soon as he saw her. 'There's
some Mexican guy hanging around the lobby who says he'll only
talk to the two of you. He went out for some coffee, but he'll be
back. He says it's important. The guy seemed terrified.'

'What do you mean some Mexican guy?' Maggie asked. 'Can
you be more specific?'

Freddy shrugged. 'He looked like a Mexican guy.'

Maggie gave him a look of disgust and headed for the elevator
as Calvano scurried after her. 'What's your problem?' he asked
as they stepped into in the car.

Maggie jabbed the floor button angrily. 'Did you ever think we
wouldn't be in this mess if this whole town didn't assume that all
Mexicans looked alike?'

But Calvano's conscience was clear. 'No, I don't think that. But
I do think we wouldn't be in this mess if some massive scumbag
hadn't taken Arcelia Gallagher.'

'Point well taken,' Maggie conceded. She seemed reluctant to
leave the elevator when they reached the fourth floor. The closer
they got to Gonzales's office, the slower she walked. She was
directing the investigation and she knew that his priorities did not
coincide with hers. She wanted to find Arcelia Gallagher and the
other missing woman. He wanted to make sure that he came off
looking good in the press, that the case fueled his rise to the top,
and that the local fat cats were pleased with how the town came
off in the national press. None of them gave a crap about Arcelia
Gallagher.

'Have a seat,' Gonzales told them. He was reading an e-mail
on his BlackBerry and barely gave them a glance. Abruptly, he
shoved the device in a drawer and placed both hands on his desk,
staring back and forth between Maggie and Calvano. The silence
in the room lengthened.

'Well?' he finally said.

'Well,' Maggie answered, her voice holding more than a trace of impatience. 'We've spent the morning out at the Delmonte House and I can tell you right now that Aldo Flores has nothing to do with the disappearance of Arcelia Gallagher or his wife. You have a man sitting in a jail cell who has done absolutely nothing, who is clearly a victim as well, and once the press gets wind he is there, he will be crucified.' I had never heard Maggie challenge Gonzales so directly. The case was getting to her.

'It's been forty-eight hours,' Gonzales reminded her. 'We're looking for a body at this point. It will be found and when it does, someone is going to have to pay.'

Calvano was in over his head and remained silent. He understood that Maggie and Gonzales had a complicated relationship, one that stretched back to her childhood when she had grown up wanting to be a cop, just like her father, and Gonzales had promised to hire her one day after she got some experience under her belt. He had done just that right before I died, hiring her away from the Wilmington force and bumping her up a rank.

'Wouldn't it be better if the person who actually did it paid for it?' Maggie suggested.

Gonzales lost his temper. I had never seen that happen before, either. It rose in him and flared before he willed it back under control with monumental effort. I think that scared me more than anything. To know he had that kind of anger in him, and the control to use it for his own purposes was terrifying, even though he held no power over me.

'Aldo Flores has a record in Mexico,' Gonzales informed them. 'He spent two years in jail there for drug running. He is, in fact, a wanted man down there. It took me one phone call to uncover that fact.'

Calvano decided to take one for Maggie. 'Sir, with all respect, we have no way of knowing if that is true or not. I would no more believe what an official of the Mexican police told me than if . . .' He failed at finding a metaphor and plowed onward. 'People down there don't have much choice. It's either do what the drug gangs tell you or die. It's not like up here. You can't possibly know what it is like. He may simply have been trying to stay alive.'

'And you do know what it's like?' Gonzales asked sarcastically.

The old Calvano would have taken the bait. He would have

insulted the commander and been busted back down to his usual ignoble status. But he had learned a lot from Maggie and, this time, he kept his temper under control.

'We would like permission to keep looking into the Delmonte House connection and to pursue Danny Gallagher as a suspect again,' he told Gonzales instead. 'I also think Aldo Flores is a dead end. I think we should follow Danny around, it's been a few days now and he may tip his hand if he's involved.'

'You really think that's worth our time?' Maggie asked Calvano.

'Well, I'd rather talk to Enrique Romero again,' Calvano said. 'But since he's in California, that's a little out of our range.'

'He's not out of my range,' Gonzales said smugly.

'What's that mean?' Maggie looked alarmed.

'It means, leave Romero to me,' the commander told her. 'Go on.'

'For now, the Delmonte House is a dead end,' Calvano explained. 'I don't think it's that poor bastard locked up downstairs, either. So if you take a look at everyone else, the only one who might have known both missing women is Danny Gallagher. He might have known her through his wife.'

'Or Father Sojak,' Maggie pointed out.

A silence fell over the room.

'Follow Danny Gallagher if it makes you happy,' Gonzales finally decided. 'Keep an eye on the priest, too. Tread lightly there. I don't need a diocese on my ass. And remember, I'll take care of Enrique Romero.'

'What's that mean?' Maggie asked again.

'It means I'll take care of Enrique Romero.'

Maggie and Calvano rose to go. They were almost out the door when Maggie turned back to the commander and said, 'Sir, it's pretty insane out there with the media.'

Gonzales would not meet her eyes. He knew that she knew he had been one of the people to bring the media to their town, no matter how much he tried to lay the blame off on others. But he wasn't about to take the heat for it, nor would he pretend he could control them. 'The genie is out of the bottle, Gunn. You'll just have to deal with it.'

Downstairs in the lobby, waiting alone in a corner of the area where victims came to wait their turn to report a robbery or assault, Rodrigo Flores sat with his head in his hands as he contemplated the fate of his brother-in-law imprisoned a floor above him. The desk sergeant nodded toward Rodrigo when he saw Maggie and Calvano, and the two detectives joined him in the waiting room. They sat on either side of Rodrigo and, though they did not say it exactly, made it clear that their sympathies were with him.

'My brother did not do anything,' Rodrigo said miserably. 'He just wanted help finding his wife.'

'We know,' Maggie said. 'We talked to the butler this morning and he said that Aldo was a really great worker and that he would never have hurt his wife. But it turns out that your brother has a record.'

Rodrigo's eyes were dark and angry. 'You don't know what it's like in my village. You don't have a choice. Either you help them or they slit your mother's throat or, worse, they kill your children and drop them on your doorstep.'

Maggie looked shocked. 'We're doing everything we can,' she promised Rodrigo. 'We'll get your brother out of here.'

'But can you help us out with it?' Calvano asked the gardener. 'That place where you work is one weird house. Do you think anyone out there had anything to do with the disappearance of the women? I don't mean the staff, but Mr Romero or his friends?'

Rodrigo considered the question. 'I don't know. They all walk around and act like they're too important to bother with us. What would they want with a Mexican woman? But you never know. Mr Romero has a temper and he doesn't like it when he doesn't get his way. But that one man, the one who is Mr Romero's agent, he would do anything to keep his job and his status. And then you have the man who tells Ms Wylie what to do all the time.'

'Her manager?' Maggie asked.

Rodrigo nodded. 'He is an angry man who wants power but does not really have it. He is always coming outside and telling me and Aldo what to do, even though he has no power over us. Who knows what he would do? And there is bad blood between the short man and Mr Romero and his agent. They hate the little man and tell him to go away all the time. I have heard them make fun of him when he is not around. But I would expect them to hurt one another, not those women.' He looked up at Maggie and Calvano, disgusted. 'They have all the money in the world and still they are unhappy people. Mr Jarvis, the old butler, he says it is the house. He says the house gives you unhappiness.'

'Mr Jarvis needs help with the house,' Maggie told Rodrigo. 'You know that he is trying to take care of his wife and is hiding her condition?'

Rodrigo nodded. 'I know. She has been very bad for more than a year now.'

'Can you find someone to help him out?' Maggie asked. 'Someone to replace the maid?'

Calvano made a strange sound, something that was halfway between a grunt and a victory cry. 'I know someone,' he said, his voice rising in excitement. 'Rodrigo, I am going to send a woman out to you who will help Mr Jarvis until you can find someone permanent. Will you see that she gets hired?'

Rodrigo shrugged. 'I will try. No one wants to work out there. All my people say the house is cursed. If you send me someone, and they can speak English and take care of Ms Wylie, I am sure she will be hired. At least for a little while.'

Calvano nodded, looking satisfied. He patted the gardener on the back. 'Tell your brother to hang in there, man. We won't forget about him.'

Rodrigo nodded miserably and stared after them as Maggie and Calvano left the station, taking a side door to avoid the crush of reporters.

'What was that all about?' Maggie asked as they circled around to their car.

'Alice Hernandez,' Calvano said. 'The hot Hispanic chick in vice.'

'What about Alice Hernandez?' Maggie asked, irritated at his comment in too many ways to count.

'We can put her in the house undercover,' Calvano explained. 'They'll see her as just another Mexican maid, and she's fluent in both Spanish and English, so she can keep an eye on everyone there while we look into the husband and the priest.'

'How do you know so much about Alice Hernandez?' Maggie asked. 'Which is not to say that this isn't a good idea.'

Calvano smiled. 'A gentleman never tells.'

'I know that, but you are not a gentleman.' Maggie studied him for a moment. 'Wait a minute. You really like her, don't you?'

Calvano acted like he had not heard her.

'Seriously, Adrian?' Maggie said. 'You do know that Alice Hernandez could kick your ass in the dark, right? And that she really has it together? You would not be able to just go out with her and then move on, like you do with everyone else.'

Calvano looked miserable. 'It doesn't matter. She won't go out with me.'

Maggie laughed. 'Of course she won't go out with you. Who wants to be just like the four thousand other women you've gone out with?'

'It's not that many,' Calvano protested.

'But it's enough for Alice to steer clear,' Maggie pointed out. When she saw her partner's expression, she softened. 'Really, Adrian – I'll back you in whatever you want to do. But I'm just saying, Alice Hernandez is not someone you mess around with lightly. Don't start something with her that you are not prepared to finish.'

'Maybe I finally want to finish something?' Calvano said. He sounded more than a little defensive.

Maggie patted him on the back. 'Good for you, my friend. Good for you.'

TWENTY

I had never given much thought to the families of victims I'd had to deal with when I was alive. God help me, I think I looked at them as an annoyance, secretly irritated at their panic and steeling myself for the inevitable criticisms that would come when I failed to find out who had killed their loved one. It is painful now to think what it must have been like for them to look at the disheveled, reeking cop that I had been and know that I was their only hope. Staring at Danny Gallagher now, huddled on the edge of a rocking chair in the nursery he and his missing wife had decorated for their child, I could not help but wonder how many people like him I had let down in the past. How had I overlooked their misery? How had I been able to ignore it? Most of all, I wondered what I could do to atone for it.

Fortunately, Maggie and Calvano were better at handling the grieving than I had ever been. One of the beat cops guarding Danny's house had led them into the nursery with the explanation that Danny had been huddled there all morning, which was pretty much what he had done the entire day before. When he left them alone with Danny, he was shaking his head in disapproval. In his world, men did not lock themselves up in a room sobbing. They manned up and tried to solve their problems.

Maybe Danny Gallagher needed to do just that. But his fear and his sorrow were real. He looked destroyed. Deep circles rimmed his eyes, which were swollen from tears, and the wound from where he had been punched was spectacular. He had not yet changed his clothes from the day before. His head was band-aged, apparently from where a bottle has been bounced off it by some indignant citizen, who was convinced he had killed his wife and so took aim at Danny when he was trying to put gas in his truck early the day before. I wondered if Danny had fallen asleep in the rocking chair, clutching the teddy bear he now held tightly for comfort. I wondered if this nursery was the only place he felt safe.

Calvano and Maggie both knelt in front of him so that they would be at his eye level. Maggie placed a hand on one of his knees and her voice was soft. 'Danny, you need to get some sleep. You need to be strong. When we find her, she's going to need you.'

Danny stared at them hollow-eyed. I'm not even sure he'd heard her.

Calvano had less patience. 'Snap out of it, man,' he told Danny, prying the teddy bear from his hands and placing it in the crib against one wall. 'We need your help. Huddling up here isn't going to help your wife or convince anyone you're innocent. Can you hear me?' He waved his hands in front of Danny's face until he had his attention. 'Snap out of it, man.' His voice rose. 'We need your help. We need to ask you some questions.'

Danny Gallagher shook his head as if he were trying to fling his worst fears from his mind. He sat up straighter, running his hands through his hair. 'I want to help,' he said in a rusty voice. 'I'll answer any questions you have.'

'Let's get you some coffee first,' Maggie suggested.

They led the guy into the kitchen, where the beat cops guarding his house had a pot of coffee ready at all times. Maggie made Danny sit at the kitchen table and brought him a cup, while Calvano found bread and made the poor guy some toast. I'm pretty sure it was the first thing he had eaten in over a day. He didn't look like he was enjoying it.

'We painted the nursery yellow because we weren't sure if it was going to be a boy or a girl. We wanted to be surprised.'

'Quit talking in the past tense,' Calvano told him. 'Your wife's not dead and we're going to find her.'

Danny nodded miserably.

'Did she ever talk to you about going out to the Delmonte House?' Maggie asked.

Danny stared at her, trying to remember. 'I think she said something about one of the workers out there thought the house was haunted, or something. It had bad spirits. The nuns wouldn't let Father Sojak get involved, so Arcelia brought him out holy water and a bunch of other superstitious remedies her grandmother taught her about when she was little. She came back and said the staff had calmed down about it and that was good enough for her.' He looked up. 'Why did you ask me that? What does it have to do with her disappearance?'

'We don't know,' Maggie said. 'Did she have any other connection to the Delmonte House?'

Danny Gallagher looked confused. 'No. I don't see what that house has to do with Arcelia. What are you getting at?'

'We're just trying to figure out where your wife may have been right before she disappeared, especially if it was out of her normal routine,' Calvano explained.

'Arcelia didn't really go anywhere that wasn't part of her routine,' Danny said. 'Work kept her really busy. She was always volunteering to help with the school fund-raisers and things like that. After that, just about every other moment she had free, if she wasn't helping me, she was at St Raphael's with Father Sojak and the nuns. She helped new immigrants assimilate into the community.'

From the way he said it, I knew he had no idea that his wife had been involved with helping illegal immigrants. He had no clue that underneath the marble floors of St Raphael's, there was a whole world of hidden refugees who slipped out at daybreak to work in the fields or houses of our town and then slipped back in to stay the night.

'How close was her relationship to Father Sojak?' Maggie asked. Her voice was neutral.

Danny Gallagher was not offended. 'They weren't having an affair, if that's what you're getting at.' He looked up at Maggie, confident in his belief. 'Father Sojak is one hundred percent married to his faith. I am certain of that. He is the real deal. And my wife would never, ever have cheated on me. I never had any suspicions about them and I never would.'

Maggie took him at his word and moved on. 'Did she ever talk about a man named Aldo Flores?' she asked.

'I don't think so. Was he the man who wanted her help out at the Delmonte House with the evil spirits? I think his name was Flores.'

'He's that man's brother,' Calvano explained. 'They both worked as gardeners at the Delmonte House.'

Danny shook his head. 'I don't think she ever mentioned him. We didn't have a lot of time to sit and talk in the days right before she . . .' His voice faltered. 'She was starting to get really tired because of the pregnancy and needed to nap a lot. And I was tired from working the fields. This time of year is critical. The fields need a lot of irrigation. I'd come in from the fields to find her asleep and, more often than not, fall asleep next to her. We'd end up having a midnight supper and then go right back to bed.' His voice trailed off as he thought of those simple evenings with his wife and I knew he was wondering if they were gone forever.

'Can you think of anyone who didn't like your wife?' Maggie asked him. 'Did she have an argument with anyone? Did anyone complain about her at the school?'

Danny shook his head. 'Everyone loved her,' he insisted. 'Everyone. The only time I've ever seen anyone get angry at her was my father.' He hesitated. 'He wanted Arcelia to campaign for him when he ran for re-election, but she wouldn't to it. She thought he was just using her because he wanted the Hispanic vote. She was afraid of the publicity, that her picture might end up in the paper and some of the men who had held her down in Mexico might see it somehow. My father was really angry, but that was over a year ago. And he would never do anything to hurt her.'

'You sure about that?' Calvano asked. He knew, as we all did, with the apparent exception of Danny, that his father had not been repeatedly re-elected mayor because he was a nice guy. He had probably hurt many people on his way up the ladder.

Maggie shot a warning glance at Calvano, but it was too late.

The comment had rocked Danny's confidence. He stood up abruptly. 'I've got to take a shower,' he said. 'I've got some things I need to do.' He walked from the room, leaving them in the kitchen.

Maggie looked at Calvano for his reaction.

'Ten to one, he's going to go talk to his father,' Calvano predicted.

'Let's make sure we're there when he does,' she said.

TWENTY-ONE

I never gave a crap about politics when I was alive. Maybe if they had started talking about taxing my beer I might have, but all I really remembered about local politics was a blur of images on the television set above the bar, offering what seemed like the same old parade each year of beefy men surrounded by other beefy men, all looking exactly the same. Sometimes the mayor was Irish, sometimes the mayor was Italian. One day, if Gonzales got his way, the mayor would be Hispanic – and on his way to being a US Senator.

Danny Gallagher's father, Terrence Gallagher, was just the latest in a series of mayors chosen by the handful of men who really control our town. I didn't know if he was a good guy. I didn't know if he was a bad guy. I did know he lived in a house big enough for four families, even though it was just him and his obscenely young wife. She must've been his third try. She was a tiny little brunette with a college coed hairdo, wearing skin tight black pants and a tight sweater. No wonder he was sitting at his kitchen table watching her bend and stretch as she prepared him dinner.

What Terrence Gallagher didn't know, was that I was sitting at the table with him, waiting for his son to arrive. Maybe Maggie and Calvano could not get close to their discussion, but I could and I intended to.

'It's just terrible,' his wife was telling him. 'Can't you do something about it? We can't have people running around snatching women off the street.'

'For Chrissakes, can you give it a rest?' Terrence Gallagher asked. He shut his newspaper in annoyance. 'I told him not to marry her in the first place. I said she'd take off once she got his money. You can't assume these people have been kidnapped when they go missing. They got this whole route going to and from Tijuana, you know. If you ask me, for all we know, she's running drugs.'

'How can you say that?' his wife demanded. His comment had made her angry. 'You know Arcelia would never do something like that. And she's having your grandchild any minute. Honey, you can't just sit there and ignore this. It's your own son's wife. What is the matter with you?'

I gave her credit. She was young, but already she knew how to control the old man. She was also smart enough to know that when the doorbell rang, it was probably not good news. 'I'll get it,' she told her husband. 'You stay here and take a deep breath.'

Terrence Gallagher needed a deep breath or two. Like all the other man down at town hall, he looked like he had eaten too many steaks, washed down by too much whiskey, and smoked way too many cigarettes in his lifetime. His gut spilled out over his pants and his face was flushed deep red. I could practically watch his cholesterol levels rising as he dined on the meat loaf his wife had set before him. And I know his blood pressure rose even higher when his wife brought Danny into the kitchen and left them alone so they could talk.

'Any word?' the mayor asked his son, pushing his newspaper to one side.

'You tell me, Dad.' Danny Gallagher slid the chair out from the table and its legs scraped against the floor, causing a screeching sound. His father looked up, startled. Danny was agitated and I'm not sure the old man had seen his son that way in years.

'How would I know?' the mayor asked. 'I'm the last person anyone keeps informed about it. I know as much as you do. Probably less. You want to know more, watch television like the rest of the world.'

'The reporters on television say I'm the one who did it,' Danny reminded his father. 'And they're going to keep saying it until we find out who did take her.' Danny had finally found his strength. He did not sound panicked or in shock. He sounded angry and determined. 'Dad, if you had anything to do with this . . . If this is some sort of campaign stunt or payback because Arcelia wouldn't campaign for you, so help me God – I will come after you. How could you do this to us?'

His father was genuinely shocked. 'How can you think I would have anything to do with this?' His voice rose. 'Danny, she's your wife. I would never lay a hand on her. I would never let anyone hurt her.'

'Don't give me that, Dad,' Danny said. 'I know what kind of friends you have. And I know who their friends are. I know how you got this big house and about the money you launder for them. I know that they would harm Arcelia without blinking an eye. So help me God, I'm telling you, if you had anything to do with this . . .'

Terrence Gallagher looked horrified. He pushed the newspaper away and leaned toward his son. 'Danny, you listen to me – I know how much you love her. I would never, ever let anyone harm her. Besides, why would we hurt her? She's done nothing wrong. She didn't have to help my campaign. Sure, it would have given me a boost. But I was going to win anyway, and I did. Let it go.'

'And, yet, here you sit, doing nothing while my wife is gone and my child is missing.' Danny's voice wavered. 'You talk family, but look at you. You left me and Mom without ever looking back and you've had how many wives since then? What do you care about my wife? You don't even care about your own.'

His father stood abruptly. 'I'm going to have to ask you to leave, Danny. I'm going to let this one go. I know how upset you are and how frustrated you must be. But I can't help you.'

It was difficult to tell whether Danny Gallagher really thought his father had something to do with his wife's disappearance, or if I was just feeling thirty years of resentment coming to a boil. But I did know, without a doubt, that Danny Gallagher blamed his father for everything that was wrong with this world and that he probably had for decades.

I felt sorry for him then. Even if they found his wife, even if his life went back to normal with his farm to tend and a child filling his house with laughter, the anger he felt for his father would still simmer inside him, clouding everything he did.

I knew because I had been there. I did not like the reminder of how resolutely I had clung to old betrayals or how I had embraced my suffering so willingly.

When Danny stomped out of the kitchen, I followed him, brushing past the stepmother, who was far closer to Danny's age than to her husband's. She was standing in the hall, eyes wide and lower lip quivering. She had heard it all and his words had rocked her.

I knew then that this crime, like all crimes, was going to ripple through the people in Arcelia Gallagher's life. When it was over, whether she was found alive or found dead, no one would ever be the same.

Danny burst out of his father's house, slamming the door behind him, and headed for his truck. He was too angry to notice Maggie and Calvano parked on a side street, tracking his movements. I could not bear being near Danny, the pain that spilled from him was contagious, so I joined Maggie and Calvano in their car. I was just in time to hear the tail end of a conversation.

'I say we go talk to your old man,' Calvano was saying to Maggie. 'He can give us more background in less time than it would take for us to pull out files or look up headlines.'

'Someone needs to follow him,' Maggie said, nodding at Danny Gallagher. He was sitting in his truck, head bowed, strength gone. His fear and panic had returned.

'So call it in,' Calvano suggested. 'Danny's been stuck in a funk for two days now, barely able to move. So if he found the energy to come see his father, then I say there is at least a chance his father was involved. If anyone knows whether that's a possibility, Colin will know.'

'You're right,' Maggie said, nodding. She reached for the radio. 'Besides, I need to check and make sure Skip hasn't tried to get to him.'

Calvano was appalled. 'You're telling me your ex-husband would actually try to milk your father for information?'

'Not if he remembered the last time he saw my father,' Maggie said. 'I wasn't there, but I heard it involved a shotgun.'

'Remind me to stay on your old man's good side.'

'You just have to stay on my good side,' she told him. 'My father follows my lead.'

TWENTY-TWO

C olin Gunn had spent a lifetime on the force, working his way up to detective and, eventually, becoming the epicenter of the department in that way only someone who cares more about solving cases and less about being promoted can become. He knew everything there was to know about our town at one point, and he knew everything there was to know about the people who were supposed to protect it, too.

I am sure Colin Gunn had been many things to many people, and that his life had consisted of many remarkable moments. He was a man who had lived each day head on. But in the end, he had chosen to define his life in three ways, and most people knew him for one of these reasons: he had been a policeman for over forty years; he had loved his wife deeply and taken care of her when she grew ill; and he was Maggie's father.

There may have been some people who thought Maggie rose in the ranks because of Colin Gunn, but no one who knew Maggie thought that. She was an even better detective than he had been, perhaps because she had so few other distractions in her life. She showed no self-consciousness about adoring her father or about turning to him for help. Whenever she had a big case, it was tradition that she consult him on it at least once. Both of them were the better for it.

The thing about Colin Gunn, though, was that he was one of the few people who could tell that I was still around. Which made perfect sense. He had also been one of the few to notice that I was still around back when I was alive.

It wasn't that he could see me in my present state. It was more like he could feel me and, he claimed, smell the combination of sweat and whiskey I'd exuded when alive. But he never let on that he knew that I was there, at least not when others were around. He didn't want anyone to think that he was getting senile. He was still fiercely independent, though confined to a wheelchair because of his strokes. It had seemed impossible that such a vibrant man could show signs of poor health – I remember hearing about his last stroke when I was still alive. The news had raced through the department grapevine and penetrated even my fog of self-centered pity, placing an icy finger on my heart with the message that it could have been me standing face-to-face with Death. And, of course, in my case, it had turned out to be true.

When Maggie and Calvano visited him to ask about Danny Gallagher and his father, Colin was sitting on his front porch, as he often did, keeping an eye out on his neighborhood. This time, however, I noticed that he had a shotgun leaning up against the low stone walls of his porch within easy reach. I gave it a wide berth and perched on the wall in a corner, eliciting a quick glance.

'Make yourself at home,' Colin growled at me.

It was good to have a friend.

'Seriously? You're openly packing now?' Maggie asked him. She looked at the shotgun and then back at her father. 'Really, Dad, we're going to start getting calls about you from the neighbors.'

'Don't give me that,' her father said gruffly. He waved each of them toward the chairs he kept ready for any and all visitors. 'Pregnant women are disappearing off the streets of my town and you better believe I am going to be ready.'

'Two women have disappeared,' Maggie said wearily. 'And we're really not sure whether one of them just decided to leave on her own or not.'

'Gonzales tell you that?' her father guessed astutely. 'He wishes. He hates it when the case involves someone Hispanic. He doesn't like the reminder he's one of them. I wouldn't listen to him on anything about this case. He can't be objective.'

Calvano's eyes widened and he said nothing. He was like that around Colin Gunn. It was as if he feared being the object of the old man's ire and so he stayed silent most of the time, soaking up the departmental tidbits that Colin dispensed with childlike wonder.

'That's why you're here, right?' Colin asked Maggie. He had caught Calvano's expression. 'You want me to help with the Arcelia Gallagher case?'

She nodded. 'Most of our leads take us into places where we're either not wanted or we can't go. I'm sure there are fifty illegal immigrants in this town who could tell us something, but they're not talking. Danny Gallagher seems to think his father might have had something to do with it. And then the trail keeps leaning back out to that creepy Delmonte House on the edge of town, but it's guarded by money and power way above this town's pay grade and I don't know if we're going to be able to crack it, or even if it's worth it. We need your help figuring it all out. I've never had a case this frustrating before, with every door getting slammed in our face, sometimes literally.'

Colin nodded thoughtfully. He knew that Maggie had a lot of pride. She would not ask for his help unless she was stumped. 'That house has a history all right,' Colin said. 'But I don't see how it could be related to your girl. Whoever took Terrence Gallagher's daughter-in-law was either stupid or has a lot of nerve, that's for sure. Terrence is very well connected, as they say.' He touched the side of his nose and nodded.

Calvano risked weighing in. 'You're saying that being the mayor's daughter-in-law should have protected her. That you think whoever took her didn't know who she was.'

It was a perceptive theory and it could well be true.

'You don't think the mayor is involved?' Colin asked them. 'I'd put my money on an outsider.'

'We don't think he's involved, but there is a chance his son does,' Maggie said. 'We followed him out to his father's house today. He seemed pretty upset.'

'Those two have a history.' Colin shook his head. 'The mayor has a pretty poor track record of treating his family well. But I don't see why he'd harm his daughter-in-law.'

'What do you know about the Delmonte House?' Calvano asked him. 'I remember there being a murder out there when I was a kid.'

'And back in the twenties,' Colin said. 'That house has a way of getting to people. I've talked to more than a few people who worked out there and left. They say the house holds an unhappiness that's contagious. That's why it's had a lot of owners over the years. Larry "The Wag" Pisano lived there until he and his wife moved to Boca about fifteen years ago. I think it's been through a couple of owners since. The next-to-last one sold it to that big deal movie star a couple years ago.'

'Do you think any of its history could be relevant to the Arcelia Gallagher case?' Maggie asked.

Colin shrugged. 'I've got no idea, but I can tell you this – that house needs to be burnt to the ground. It's caused people nothing but unhappiness since it was built. Your great-grandmother worked there as a maid, you know.' Maggie looked surprised and he added, 'You think it's such a big leap to go from being a maid to being a policeman's daughter?'

'Or being a detective yourself?' Calvano pointed out with a grin.

'It's true,' Colin said. 'My grandmother worked out there her whole life, back when the current house was first built. She said it was the unhappiest place on earth. I didn't hear her say that, of course, but it's always been passed down in our family. Don't you remember the stories from when you were young?' He looked at Maggie disapprovingly. Sometimes she was a little too modern for his tastes. 'The original owner, Delmonte, made his fortune by inventing some tiny little piece of sewing equipment, something that mattered way back then. He married a young and beautiful wife then built the house for her and gave her everything she wanted. But it was never enough. She always wanted more. He died still trying to make her happy and she sold it off. Then there was a murder there, back in the twenties, when some old woman, the lady of the house, shot her gardener dead because she found out he had a girlfriend and she had been under the impression he was interested only in her.' Colin shook his head. 'Then you had that murder in the orchards, those two bums fighting over a quarter bottle of wine. People say the house makes you covet things you cannot have. If I were you, I'd look into the house.'

Maggie laughed. 'Come on Dad, listen to yourself. You sound like a crazy old man. You seriously believe that stuff?'

Colin shrugged. 'I don't know. I grew up hearing all sorts of rumors about that house. Some people say it was once a stop on the Underground Railroad, this was before the present house was built. Others say the man who built it buried gold on the grounds to keep it from his wife, who liked to spend every penny he had, and that it's still hidden on the grounds somewhere, maybe buried or in one of the orchards. Even if you don't find the missing girl, maybe you'll get lucky and find the gold.' He smiled, knowing that he sounded a little over the top and enjoying the effect it had on his daughter.

Calvano took him seriously. 'We're putting someone out there, undercover, to work in the house,' he said. 'It was the one of the last places where Arcelia Gallagher was seen and I do think they're hiding something.'

Colin Gunn nodded his approval.

'You have any ideas about how we can get the illegal immigrant community to talk to us?' Maggie asked. She was not as convinced as her partner that the Delmonte House was their best lead.

Colin shook his head. 'You can bet most of them attend St Raphael's. They give them the fish-eye at St Michael's because that's where all the money goes to mass. Maybe they could help at St Raphael's.'

'They're not being very helpful,' Maggie said. 'I'm not sure what's going on, but I think Father Sojak is hiding something.'

'He could just be protecting his flock,' Colin said. 'Maybe he doesn't want to give up their names if they're illegals? And he'd get in trouble with the bishop if they found out his church was welcoming illegals. There was a time they would have tolerated it, but they're worried about the political repercussions these days. Father Sojak may be hiding it from his superiors as much as he's hiding it from you. If you can find a way around that, he may talk.'

Maggie and Calvano nodded, thinking it over. They had already tried that and it hadn't worked yet.

'Maybe you should talk to that worthless peacock you married once upon a time?' Colin told Maggie. 'I heard he's in town. Looks like someone beat him up pretty good, too. He was on the news saying he'd been pursuing some illegal who knew something about the case and the guy beat him up in an alley. Wish you guys could find out who it was. I'd like to shake his hand.'

Calvano rose abruptly. He walked over to Colin and stuck out his hand, startling the old man. 'We've got to get going,' Calvano said. 'But it's always good to see you, sir.'

'Come back soon,' Colin said. He was no stranger to abrupt departures. 'I'll break out the whiskey next time.'

Maggie gave her father a kiss and skipped down the front steps the same way she had probably skipped down them thousands of times as a child. She was laughing at Calvano's inside joke as she left. Colin watched his daughter with pride as she sped away with Calvano riding shotgun.

'What was that all about?' the old man said, half to himself and half to me. I couldn't answer him, of course, but I wished I could have clued him in on what was so funny. Something tells me Colin Gunn would have appreciated how Maggie's ex-husband really got his black eye.

'You know, Fahey,' Colin suddenly said. I was startled to hear my name. 'You ought to come around here more often. You and I have a lot in common.'

I couldn't answer him, of course, but he waited a moment, as if I had, and said, 'We're both just sort of hanging around, waiting for the big finish to happen.'

He smiled in my direction. 'The difference between us, my friend, is that I found a lot of meaning in my life. You, son? Well, you looked like you were drifting. If you're still hanging around, then maybe it's not too late. Take it from me – if your life has no meaning, for Godsakes, find some.'

TWENTY-THREE

If, as Calvano seemed to think, all roads led to the mansion on the edge of town, then I would take one of them. I knew that the vice cop, Alice Hernandez, would be showing up in the morning and applying for the job of maid, but I considered myself the *ultimate* undercover operative and I wanted to get there first. Yes, it was a small badge of honor to wear, but it satisfied my pride. Besides, it was my chance to see how the presence of a newcomer would change the household. To do that, I first needed to see what it was like before Alice Hernandez arrived.

Like all big houses, the Delmonte House felt lonely. I wandered the empty halls and sterile rooms without even another spirit to keep me company. My unhappy friend was elsewhere, perhaps off searching for whatever it was he so desperately needed. He had left wisps of his unhappiness, though, and I felt his desperation as I passed through them. I knew I should help him. He was a fellow traveler, after all. But I just could not understand what it was he wanted or how it might connect to Arcelia Gallagher.

The house was in that period of calm that comes when its inhabitants are winding down for the night. Dakota Wylie was lying in bed, a cool washcloth over her bruised eyes as she dozed the groggy sleep of the medicated. The television in one corner of her bedroom played what seemed to be an endless loop of her old television show. I wondered if she ever left her bed, or ever left her old life, and I went in search of others.

Her manager, Lamont Carter, was sitting in the dark of a small movie theater that had been installed on the first floor. He, too, was watching an episode of the television series that had made Dakota Wylie famous. He felt coiled and angry, even alone, as if the fight he wanted to pick was with the entire world. Up on the screen, his client was bouncing around Hollywood's idea of a dorm room with the unconscious, coltish grace of girl who has just crossed over into womanhood. Her heart-shaped face was perfect, with features that seemed carved out of ivory. I watched her until I could no longer bear to acknowledge the terrible truth of what she had done to her face in an effort to retain that beauty. I left Carter to his solitary worship, wondering if he realized that his client would no longer bring him so much as a dime. Her beauty was gone. Surely he realized that by now.

The old butler was sitting at the kitchen table doing a crossword puzzle and enjoying a cup of hot tea. His wife was sleeping in a bed in a room off the kitchen, her face smooth and unworried. I wondered if her husband ever stood and watched her sleep, remembering what his long life with her had once been like. It was probably the only time when he felt he had her back again.

Outside in the gathering evening, Rodrigo the gardener was collecting his tools and stashing them in the shed. He had worked long hours that day without anyone to help him. I would have felt sorry for him, but I felt that he knew more than he was saying about Arcelia Gallagher's disappearance. Maybe he was remaining silent to protect his family, but it was robbing another man of his.

Or maybe he really didn't know where Arcelia Gallagher was after all. He definitely moved with the easy air of a man whose conscience is clear. I followed him for a while, enjoying the summer air and the sounds of the birds as they settled down for the night. First, Rodrigo checked all the doors and windows of the house to make sure they were locked – a task he performed, I felt certain, to spare the old butler the chore. Each time he reached a new entrance into the house, he stopped and made the sign of the cross, then sprinkled droplets of holy water on the ground at his feet, marking a perimeter around the mansion.

When he was done securing the house for the night, both literally and spiritually, he took off across the lawn and I followed
him, enjoying the smooth expanse of green that had once been
tilled diligently by farmers, long before the crops had been bull-
dozed and the trees razed to make room for the huge house that
towered behind us. Birds flew from the ground shadows as Rodrigo
approached, while, overhead, the evening gathered. I could see no
purpose to his walk, except perhaps to enjoy the night. There were
worse ways to pass the time. The air was cooling and smelled of
loam. It was a heavenly place to be.

But as Rodrigo reached the edge of the far lawn and turned
back toward the house, I stepped through a pocket of despair
so profound it nearly brought me to a halt. It was *her*. I could
feel it.

I looked around, but saw nothing but open lawn for acres in
either direction and, yet, I could clearly feel Arcelia Gallagher and
her fear. She had been here and part of her lingered.

The gardener continued toward the house, whistling to himself
as if his nightly ritual had cleared his mind and heart of troubles.
I hurried after him. As he reached the shed, instead of heading
toward his bedroom at the back of the house, he pulled a bicycle
out of the small building, donned a bright orange safety jacket
and began peddling toward town.

I had never been the best cop in the world, but even I realized
that a man who traveled the world by bicycle would have a tough
time kidnapping and concealing a pregnant woman. I doubted
Rodrigo had been the one to bring Arcelia Gallagher here.

As I watched the orange of his jacket bob off into the dusk, I
caught a glimpse of headlights behind a thick stand of oaks across
the road. It was an odd place for a car to park. I moved closer. A
beat-up old Chevy was idling in the trees between two fields still
worked each day by the farmer who lived across the highway. The
car had cut across the pasture to reach its hiding place, where it
had a view of the Delmonte House.

I was curious to know who was in the car, and why, thinking
perhaps Maggie and Calvano had sent someone to watch the house.
But before I could check for myself, the car pulled out of the
grove and made its way slowly across the field and on to the road.
The Chevy slowed as it passed the Delmonte House, then pulled
into a driveway a quarter-mile down the road and doubled back,

passing by the house once again. I waited behind the split-level fence that lined the road in front of the mansion until it came so close to me that I could see a man and woman sitting in the front seat.

When the car pulled to a stop a few yards beyond me, I went over for a better look. The man was big and beefy with a buzz haircut and the jowls of a heavy drinker. He wore a plaid shirt unbuttoned at the top to reveal a grimy white tee shirt underneath. The woman next to him was in her fifties and wore a pink flowered blouse that strained against her ample chest. Her hair was dyed an unflattering shade of blonde and her heavy make-up accentuated her age. They stared back at the house, mesmerized, as best I could tell, by its size and splendor. Finally, the man started the car again and, continuing on another quarter-mile, once again turned around. This time, he stopped a few yards short of the front gate.

What in the world would the pair of them have to do with anyone in the Delmonte House? They were clearly from a different world. Their car had once been green but the paint had flaked off to reveal much of the metal base beneath and there were rust spots corroding the body's edges. The license plate on the back of the car had been issued by Alabama and was splattered with mud. They had traveled far to see the house. The back seat was heaped high with cardboard boxes and paper bags filled with household possessions. It looked like they were living out of their car.

As the engine ticked in the silence of the night, cooling, the couple remained in the Chevy, staring through the gate at the mansion. At last, as the darkness settled around them, the man opened the car door and unfolded himself, stretching in the night air. He was tall and broad shouldered with a drinker's belly that tapered down to spindly hillbilly legs. He wore jeans and a pair of cowboy boots with pointy toes that looked like they had kicked more than one man in his time.

The man tucked his shirt into his jeans, hitched up his waistband and started swaggering toward the low fence to the left of the gate. He hopped it easily and went tromping up the driveway toward the house. So much for security. The old butler would be no match for him.

But before he could even ring the doorbell, a figure came racing out a side door toward him. It was Lamont Carter, Dakota Wylie's manager. He held a handgun and looked like he was prepared to use it.

The man from the Chevy immediately held up his hands and backed up, smiling. Carter did not return the smile. 'Get in the car, turn around and drive away,' he told the newcomer. His voice was confident. With a gun in hand, he had no fear of the larger man. And his tone told me that he knew him well.

'Is that any way to treat—'

'Get in the car and drive away,' Carter interrupted. He poked the gun into the bigger man's chest, forcing him back a step. 'I mean it.' He stared at the other man, who inched down the driveway until he was pressed against the gate. Still aiming the gun at him, Carter unlocked a side gate and kicked it open. 'Go on, get out of here.'

'If you want us to leave,' the other man said, 'you're going to have to give us some cash.'

'Oh, it's like that, is it?' Lamont Carter asked.

'You're damn right it's like that,' the big man retorted.

The two men stared at one another for what felt like minutes but was probably no more than a few seconds. They were gauging each other's resolve. Lamont Carter was the first to give. 'Get back in your car and wait. If you so much as get out of the car again, I swear to God I will shoot you both dead on the spot.'

'Better make it a lot,' the bigger man called after Carter as he headed for his car.

The woman with the garish make-up was waiting for him, her mouth a scarlet 'O'. She had obviously overheard their exchange and looked a little frightened.

'How much is he getting us?' the woman asked her companion as he climbed back into the front seat with her. She had a thick Southern drawl.

'Enough,' he said sullenly. 'At least for now.'

'Let's get us a motel room and a couple bottles for later, then maybe find us a steak dinner and a bar where we can score a bump or two. Hell, maybe three. We're rich now.' The woman smiled, revealing bad teeth, and her eyes lit up. I guess it was her idea of a perfect evening.

The man looked disgusted and didn't bother to hide his contempt for her. 'You seriously can't think of anything better to spend our money on than that?' He shook his head. 'You deserve to be poor. You know that? You deserve to be poor.'

The woman knew enough not to argue. She turned on the radio, selecting a country music channel, and smiled secretly to herself as if she were already imagining how she would spend the money. The man was less complacent. He seethed with anger. However much money Carter returned with, something told me it would not be enough.

I waited with the couple, wondering if they would say something to reveal who they might be. But they were done talking to one another.

Lamont Carter returned with a thick envelope of bills and knocked on the car window. He handed it to the larger man without comment. The man thumbed through the money greedily and smiled. He cast a gleeful look at Carter. 'This ought to last us for a while.'

'That better last you for the rest of your life,' Carter told him. 'And if it doesn't, I can take care of that problem, too.' He held up the gun and stared the older man down.

'Come on, Barton,' the woman said. 'He always was an ungrateful little bastard. I need a hotel room and a drink.'

The older man turned the key in the ignition and gunned the engine, fishtailing down the shoulder of the road, spewing rocks and gravel behind him. When he reached the asphalt, he turned abruptly and went squealing off down the highway, the car engine roaring to life with surprising strength.

Lamont Carter stared after them as he gently caressed his gun. He hated them, that much was clear, though his hate felt more like a habit than a burning emotion. He was not seeing the last of them and he knew it. But whatever lay ahead, something told me that Lamont Carter was ready for it.

TWENTY-FOUR

I went in search of Maggie and Calvano. I had learned plenty that night, though I wasn't sure how much it mattered, and I had no way of letting anyone know. I knew now that Lamont Carter was being blackmailed, though I didn't know why, and I knew that Arcelia Gallagher had been at the Delmonte House while in an extreme state of despair and might very well still be there. I didn't know how long ago she had been there, but only a life-threatening situation could have produced the emotion I had felt lingering in the field.

It was completely dark and though my town should have felt peaceful in the summer night, the streets were empty. People were afraid. Curtains and shades had been drawn against prying eyes and an air of suspicion filled the air.

Earlier that day, I knew that patrol cars had been sent to rescue Danny Gallagher from a group of young men who had surrounded his truck at a convenience store, intending to take justice into their own hands. The patrolman had reported back to Maggie that Danny just sat there as the teenagers climbed over his truck and began to rock it back and forth.

'It was like he was made out of stone,' one of the cops explained. 'It was like he thought he deserved it.'

It seemed the whole town now thought Danny Gallagher deserved it. Though he had been rescued, he had finally been forced to leave his farm and was staying at an undisclosed location set up by his father. At least his old man was stepping up to help.

Meanwhile, Gonzales had apparently grown so desperate for positive press that he had actually agreed to go on Lindsey Stanford's talk show. I had watched incredulously, in some stranger's living room, as Gonzales turned on the charm, said little, yet appeared to be perfectly forthright. He had managed, without quite coming out and saying so, to make it sound as if Aldo Flores was under suspicion and Enrique Romero was refusing to cooperate with the police. He had also flattered Lindsey Stanford so shamelessly that she had refrained from her usual hardball style.

In this world, when you're as shallow and willing as Gonzales to kiss ass, things always break your way.

Maggie and Calvano, of course, were stuck doing the actual work. I caught them just as they were leaving the station house, cups of coffee and late-night sandwiches in hand. I was pretty sure they'd been meeting with the rest of the case team and, judging from their faces, nothing of value had been uncovered.

I knew the moment I took my place in their back seat that they were headed to the church to see Father Sojak again – Calvano looked as if it were his rights being violated and Maggie looked determined.

'If what we had wasn't good enough for a judge, why are we
going there again?' Calvano complained.

Maggie sounded impatient. 'Because we have nothing else to
go on. It's as if she vanished from the face of the earth and the
only people who know where she might have gone are too afraid
of us to say anything. We have to get through to someone. We
can't keep bumbling around in the dark. We have to find a
direction.'

'What are you going to do if Father Sojak says no?' Calvano
asked. 'We can't force him to cooperate.'

'I really don't know.'

But Father Sojak didn't say no. In fact, he met them at the door
of the rectory with so much friendliness that I suspected he had
somehow known that they were coming. The trio of nuns who
served the church were clustered behind him, the old nun shielding
the younger ones with her body.

'We have to speak to some of the illegal immigrants who knew
Arcelia Gallagher,' Maggie said simply. 'We have had no other
leads and we're desperate.'

'Come in,' Father Sojak said, opening the door. 'We've been
expecting you.'

Maggie and Calvano followed him in, baffled at his generosity.
Not me. He was slick. He would raise less suspicion if he treated
them with courtesy. I knew what he was hiding: an entire basement
full of illegal immigrants beneath our very feet. The last thing he
wanted to risk was having that room discovered.

Everyone headed toward the small sitting room where the old
priest had been snoozing a few days before. He was there once
again, fast asleep in his old armchair, and apparently the others
who lived at the rectory were used to treating him as just another
piece of furniture. They all took seats without commenting on his
presence. After a brief glance at the priest, Maggie and Calvano
followed their lead.

'Since your last visit, I have asked the sisters to speak with
some of our parishioners who may have come in contact with
Arcelia,' Father Sojak said. He nodded at the older nun.

The nun faced them with determination. 'We have, in fact,
spoken to as many of them as we can on your behalf.' She sounded
defiant when she said this, as if she had not appreciated being
treated as a suspect and wanted it known that she was on their

side. 'Most of them knew nothing, only the same wild rumors that you yourself have probably heard.'

'What rumors?' Calvano interrupted. He looked interested.

'Oh, you know. Things like she went out to the Delmonte House and the spirits got her. We can't always keep these people from interjecting their own superstitions into our religion, you know.'

Maggie went for the low blow. 'I seem to recall your religion is pretty superstitious to begin with,' she said.

The nun looked at Maggie sharply. 'Didn't I have you in one of my classes when you were a girl?' she asked. Her voice held a hint of steel.

Maggie actually looked alarmed. It was a reflex, I think, from a childhood spent in Catholic schools. 'No, you did not. Please continue.'

'As I said, we talked to as many of . . .' the nun's voice faltered and she began again. 'We talked to as many of the people who will not speak to the authorities as we could. I would say we interviewed over one hundred of them. Wouldn't you say so, Heather? Felicia?'

The two younger nuns cooed their agreement like a pair of turtle doves and then subsided into an embarrassed silence.

Calvano was such a dog. He was blatantly giving the young nuns the once-over, appraising what his gender had lost when they joined the convent. He stopped ogling long enough to ask, 'Did you find out anything of interest? Will any of them talk to us?'

'Yes and yes,' the old nun said primly. 'We have a meeting room where we hold receptions for church functions and there are two people waiting there to speak with you.'

Maggie looked back and forth between Father Sojak and the old nun. 'That's efficient. Have they been waiting there for us all day?' She seldom resorted to sarcasm, and for good reason. It made her sound mean.

'I had Heather fetch them when we saw you pull up,' the older nun said quickly. 'They have been here all day, yes, but only because we have encouraged them to stay until we could reach you. We did not want them disappearing again.'

It was a lousy cover story. I knew that whoever had volunteered to speak to the police had been whisked from the room downstairs at the same time one of the younger nuns had dashed below to warn everyone to remain quiet until after Maggie and Calvano left. But the cover story was accepted without question.

'Well, take us to them,' Maggie said, sounding more than a little suspicious that they were cooperating so willingly.

'I could summarize what they told us,' the nun named Heather said in a nervous voice. 'If you don't speak Spanish, I would have to be there anyway to translate.'

'Why don't you tell us what they told you?' Maggie said to her. 'And then we will go question them ourselves. Between the two of us –' she nodded toward Calvano – 'we know a little bit of Spanish.'

I had no idea if this was true, although I suspected it was an exaggeration.

'There is a man in our congregation who says that someone approached his wife asking if they could buy her baby,' the youngest of the nuns said. She looked appalled at her own words. 'He was quite upset about it.'

'I'm not following,' Maggie admitted.

'Don't you see?' The other young nun said. 'Arcelia Gallagher is pregnant and now she's missing.'

'Are you saying you think Arcelia Gallagher sold her baby?' Calvano asked skeptically. 'According to her husband, this was their dream come true.'

'That's what we thought,' the nun named Heather said timidly. 'But a woman waiting to see you will tell you that the same thing happened to her. An American man approached her and offered her money for her baby. She told no one but Arcelia Gallagher about it, she says, and Arcelia was quite upset. She told the woman that it was time to stop rich Americans from preying on her people.'

'Did she say where she was when she was approached?' Maggie asked.

The nun looked apologetic. 'I didn't think to ask. But you can ask her for yourself.'

'Let's go then,' Maggie decided, rising. 'I want to talk to these people myself.'

As everyone followed Maggie's lead and rose to go, the old priest stirred in his chair, opened his eyes briefly, looked straight at Calvano and muttered, 'You better have wiped your shoes this time, Adrian. I'll not have mud in the rectory.' He fell back asleep again.

We all stared at Calvano. He shrugged and smiled, looking –
just for an instant – like the reluctant altar boy he had once been.

'Figures,' Maggie mumbled at Calvano as they followed the
nuns and priest out of the sitting room door. But no one else
noticed what I had seen – while everyone's attention was on the old
priest, one of the younger nuns had hurried ahead, down the hall.
No doubt to warn the others.

But Father Sojak and the nuns had made one mistake when
they devised whatever plan they had in mind to assuage their
consciences while still protecting the people below. They had
forgotten that Calvano had attended the church as a child and
would know every nook and cranny of it. Just as they were
attempting to hustle him out a back door, Calvano paused at the
entrance to the basement.

'Hey, I remember that door.' He laughed. 'We used to steal
cookies from the pantry in the rectory and then run down to the
basement to eat them. There was some freaky stuff down there,
if I recall.'

He put his hand out and grabbed the knob. A wave of fear rose
in the priest and the nuns. They froze, waiting for his next move.

'What's the basement used for now?' Calvano asked. He opened
the door and stuck his head into the darkness, peering down the
steep steps. 'If I recall, there's a room big enough to park the Queen
Mary in down there.'

'Oh, we just use it to store furniture we collect to give to the
poor,' Father Sojak said hastily. He was good. He opened the door
to the basement wider. 'Would you like to take a look?'

'No,' Maggie said impatiently, even as Calvano answered 'yes'.
They stared at one another, both annoyed.

'The people waiting to talk to you have waited for hours. They
can wait a few minutes more,' Father Sojak said calmly. 'Follow
me.'

That crafty old fox. He had faith indeed. He let them calmly
down the stairs into the basement hallway, flicking on lights as he
did so. Their footsteps echoed behind me in the hallway as I
hurried ahead, wondering what had happened to the room of illegal
immigrants. As I approached the door to the great room, I felt a
wave of fear so thick I could not believe that Maggie and Calvano
could not sense it as well.

From the outside, the room looked like just another basement

storage area. It was dark from the outside and, on the inside, beds
and other furniture had been piled against the entrance so that it
was nearly impossible to open the door even a crack. The stacked
mattresses made it completely impossible to see inside the door
windows as well. It was a good cover. If Maggie and Calvano
really wanted to enter the room, it would take a long time to clear
a path. They'd likely give up before long.

The fear of the people inside that room was remarkable. So was
the silence. Entire families huddled together in the darkness,
seeking out beds and blankets to provide themselves with cover.
Parents held their hands firmly over their children's mouths so that
they could not make a sound. Young mothers held their nursing
babies to their breasts, pre-empting their cries. The men smelled
of sweat and fear. The women held their breath. It was as if the
entire room breathed in and out as one as they waited, knowing
from the light leaking in under the door jamb from the hallway
that they were on the verge of discovery.

I realized, then, in that instant how little these people had and
how very much they were willing to risk in order to start a new
life for their families. They were willing to huddle in the darkness
like animals just to have a second chance. And in that moment, I
found myself rooting for them. I prayed that Maggie and Calvano
would walk by.

But the sounds outside the door made it clear that they had
stopped at the entrance to the room. All around me, fear and
memories too terrible to share rose up. The people huddled in the
darkness of the room trembled and their children clung to them,
seeking comfort, frightened by their parent's fear.

'This is it,' Calvano announced. He laughed. The doorknob
rattled and the door inched inward, but immediately knocked up
against a barrier of furniture. Calvano gave up and shut it. 'You
are not kidding. If you need any more furniture, and I can't say
it looks like it, my mother's trying to get rid of a bunch of ugly
crap from her sister's house.'

Father Sojak laughed. 'Oh, we'll take it. You'd be surprised how
many people need help these days.'

'Come on,' Maggie interrupted them. She was getting impatient.
'Let's go back upstairs. I need to talk to those people.'

'Of course,' Father Sojak said. 'Did you want to look around
anywhere else?'

'No,' Calvano said. 'My partner's the impatient type.' He laughed and Father Sojak joined in, just two men laughing at the foibles of women.

Boy, that Father Sojak was good. I only hoped he would stay on the side of the angels.

Their footsteps echoed in the hall, growing fainter as they left the basement room behind. I could feel the fear receding with the sound of their footsteps. People begin to breathe once again. Still, no one dared say a word.

Their relief, though silent, was immense. They were safe, at least for now.

TWENTY-FIVE

Upstairs, in a room filled with plastic tables and chairs, a nervous-looking Hispanic man sat at the center table, while a younger Latino woman with curly hair and eyebrows plucked to thin arches waited nearby to be questioned by the police. I wondered if they had simply been nominated to throw Maggie and Calvano off the track of those who hid in the darkness below them or if they really did have knowledge of Arcelia Gallagher.

Maggie and Calvano decided to speak to the older man first. Although he had volunteered to speak to them, at least according to the nuns, he looked angry and uncooperative when they joined him at his table. The younger nuns took a seat on either side of him, stereo translators. The one named Heather spoke for the Hispanic man first.

'He is quite upset that you are holding Aldo Flores in jail,' she explained after his reply. 'He keeps asking when you are going to take him to jail and keep him there, too.'

To her credit, Maggie looked embarrassed. 'Please tell him that we apologize for these actions. We did not agree with imprisoning Mr Flores. We have no intention of bringing him downtown. If he will speak honestly to us, and give us a way to get back in touch with him in the future, he has our word that, for now, our conversation will stay between us.'

The young nun translated Maggie's words but the older Mexican man did not relax. I didn't blame him. But, gradually, with coaxing from the two young nuns, the story that emerged was this: two months before, as his wife had been shopping at a small grocer's in their neighborhood, an American man wearing a dark jacket and a Philadelphia Eagles baseball cap had gestured to her and asked if she spoke English. When she nodded yes, he had held out a fistful of thousand dollar bills and waved them at her. 'These could be yours,' he'd said. He nodded toward her swollen belly. 'I have a client who is interested in adopting a child. He is willing to pay thousands of dollars for yours. You could start over and live in a big house with servants and be just like an American,' he had told her.

The man telling the story looked even angrier as he repeated the American's words. He did not like that the American had taken his wife for a fool who was willing to sell not only her baby, but her heritage, for a fistful of dollars.

'What did this man look like?' Maggie asked, and waited as one of the nuns translated.

The man shook his head. His wife could not remember much more and he would not permit the police to question her. He had sent her somewhere else with their baby so that they would be safe and he was not telling them where. He did not want the same thing happening to her as had happened to two other women in their community. She had told him before she left all she knew about the man who had offered her money for her baby. 'He was American and angry, as American men often are,' she had told her husband. He added that the American man had not argued with his wife when she refused his offer, but had spat the Spanish word for whore at her and stomped away.

'The man knew a little Spanish?' Calvano asked. The Hispanic man looked at Calvano with contempt. When translated, his answer became, 'I would not call the ability to dishonor women as speaking my beautiful language. Many Americans have picked up the worst of our colloquialisms. That does not mean they speak our language.' The nun had imitated his dignity with perfection and Calvano looked properly ashamed at the rebuke.

'Did your wife see where the American went after he walked away?' Maggie asked him.

The man said, no, his wife had been quite upset by the encounter and had fled home, calling him on the way to report what had happened. They had discussed telling someone, but were afraid to approach the police. They told themselves that the man was just passing through, looking for someone desperate for money, and would keep going. Who were they to try to stop him? But now, the man continued with an abashed expression, he wished that they had done more. Perhaps they could have spared others pain? Perhaps the American had taken the two missing women?

After several more questions about the time of day the man had approached his wife, and if she had noticed him before that day, and other attempts at extracting even the smallest detail about the encounter, Maggie and Calvano let the man go. He had promised to stay in touch with the nuns and would be available if they needed him further. Neither Maggie nor Calvano looked convinced that he would follow through. They were certain, as I was, that he would join his wife wherever she had gone for safety as soon as he could, now that he had told them what he knew and his conscience was clear. But they were unwilling to take him into custody officially. They did not want Gonzales throwing him in jail, too. One Aldo Flores on their consciences was enough.

The young woman with curly hair waiting to see them held something in her arms that she jiggled with an automatic efficiency as they approached her table. It was the baby that, according to the nuns, a man had tried to buy from her. Apparently, having had someone try to take it from her once, she now intended to keep it as close as possible to her in the future. The baby was wrapped in pink and white blankets and though it was no more than a few months old, tiny gold studs had been affixed to its ears.

Most women attempting to establish rapport with a new mother would coo over her baby or ask questions about it. Maggie did not even try. She gave it a cursory glance to establish that it was there, and confirmed that it was the baby the man had tried to buy. The young mother was shy and it took much coaxing to get her story out of her. In the end, she was able to tell them that when she was approached, she had been pushing a cart filled with fresh produce as she gathered food for her family's evening meal. It was just two weeks before her eventual delivery date, and the man had come out of nowhere, frightening her as she stood on the sidewalk between two specialty shops.

'I thought he was going to rob me,' she said. 'But then he

showed me a big stack of money and said that he would make me
rich if I would give him my baby. I told him that I would never
sell my baby. That he was sick and must go away. He got angry.
He said I would have many more babies. That I should be smart
and make money from them.' Her voice cracked as she described
the man's behavior. One of the nuns patted her on the back until
she regained her composure and continued with her story. The
man had spat on the ground beside her feet and stomped off, angry
that she had refused his offer.

'I would never give my baby to someone like that,' the woman
protested, as if Maggie and Calvano thought she had intended to
sell her child. 'I would never sell my baby to anyone, but especially
not to a man like that.'

Under the questioning, she revealed that the man had been only
a little taller than she was. He had been wearing a brown leather
jacket and a baseball hat. She did not remember what the hat had
looked like. She could not remember much about his face, except
that he had angry eyes and his mouth was cruel. A sketch artist
would not be able to do much with that, and neither Maggie nor
Calvano looked hopeful. But at least she had watched the man
leave and had seen him get into his car and drive away.

'Do you remember the make and model?' Calvano asked eagerly.

The woman looked confused when the nun translated. 'It was
a big car,' was all she could offer. 'It was silver and would take
much money to buy. It is the kind of car that rich people drive.'

It wasn't much, but it was something. There weren't that many
wealthy people in my town. It was either the politicians, the mob
bosses – or the pair of movie stars who lived on the edge of town.

'When did you tell Arcelia about what had happened?' Maggie
asked the girl.

She had told Arcelia about the man and his offer about two
weeks ago, and Arcelia had asked her questions just as they were
doing. She had told them the same things she had told Maggie
and Calvano. The man had been driving a silver car, like rich
people drove, and he had been angry at her for refusing his offer.

'Did you get the feeling that Arcelia knew who you were talking
about?' Maggie asked. She looked at the nuns and said, 'It is very
important that you translate the question exactly.'

The young mother took Maggie's question seriously, mulling it
over before she answered. 'Yes,' she said. 'I believe that Mrs

Gallagher knew who I was talking about. I think this because she grew very angry and started talking about how people with money thought they owned the world, thought they owned us, and that they must be stopped.'

'What did she say she was going to do to stop them?' Maggie asked.

The woman shrugged when she heard the translation of the question. 'She did not tell me what she was going to do,' she explained. 'But I thought she was going to talk to the man. I got the feeling that she was going to tell him he must stop trying to buy babies in our town.'

Maggie and Calvano looked at each other. While they had learned more than they had expected, the information could lead them nowhere. The man had approached the women several weeks apart, which meant he was a local or at least staying in town. On the other hand, all they really had to go on was that he wasn't very tall and he drove a silver car.

Still, it was better than nothing and nothing was all they'd had to go on until now.

'If you hear of anyone else with a similar experience, we need to talk to them,' Maggie told the nuns. They nodded solemnly.

'What she really means to say,' Calvano explained, 'is that we need you to question each and every one of all the other women illegals who are pregnant or have young babies to see if they were approached by the same man. If so, we need to speak to them ourselves. This could be our most important lead.'

Maggie looked startled but said nothing. She knew Calvano was right. If the illegal immigrants in town would not speak to the police, they had no choice but to use the nuns as their go-betweens.

TWENTY-SIX

Maggie and Calvano were exhausted but they would have no rest that night. They had just finished a late-night dinner when the call came through – Gonzales wanted to see them and he wanted to see them now.

By this time of night, Gonzales was usually finishing up an

evening of wining and dining all the right people to further his career. I had never known him to be at the office this late. I rode along, curious to know what might have happened to inspire this meeting.

The station house was deserted and blessedly calm. Not even a drunk awaited booking. The news hounds were finally gone and I knew the bars nearby were probably jumping with visiting journalists. Maggie and Calvano hurried through the lobby to the upstairs offices while I tagged along, energized by their urgency and wondering if this was what my life would have been like had I cared more about my job when I was alive.

Gonzales was waiting for them in his office. He was watching the re-run of his appearance on Lindsey Stanford's show, perhaps seeing for the first time that her follow-up guests and rants had turned away from who might have taken Arcelia Gallagher to focus on illegal immigration. Gonzales looked irritated, but then Lindsey Stanford had that effect on nearly everyone. I couldn't tell if he was angry because he had been a part of the show, she had anointed herself judge and jury, and the whole country was letting her get away with it, or because he was embarrassed that his people were the focus of such intense scrutiny.

He gestured for Maggie and Calvano to sit. In another rare break in his routine, he poured himself a glass of whiskey in front of them. The smell of it drifted across the room. It was irresistible. Even in death, I was still an alcoholic. Gonzales took a long sip then drummed his fingers against the glass. He did not bother to offer either Maggie or Calvano a drink.

'You had something for us?' Maggie asked. She was tired and in no mood for his usual maneuverings.

'I do indeed,' Gonzales said. He handed them a manila folder thick with photographs. 'I just printed these out. I called in a favor and some locals have been tailing Enrique Romero since he arrived in Los Angeles.'

'Why?' Calvano asked, unable to stop himself. Like me, he was wondering why the hell Gonzales had bothered to have Romero followed. Yes, the television star had left town as soon as the investigation opened. Yes, he was condescending and annoying. And, yes, as owner of the Delmonte House, he at least deserved scrutiny. But calling in a favor like that from another police department was using up a pretty big chit.

'I don't like people who blatantly ignore our jurisdiction,' Gonzales said abruptly. He banged his glass on his desktop a little too hard. For a moment, I thought the glass had cracked.

Maggie had opened the folder and was staring at the first photograph with a look of astonishment.

'Is it her?' Gonzales asked. 'Romero went straight from the plane to her hotel room. They spent about an hour and a half inside before they were picked up by a car and driven north to some restaurant where they had dinner and, as you can see if you look at the rest of the photographs, several hour's worth of drinks. He also saw her last night.'

Calvano was staring over Maggie's shoulder. Why should I be left out? I joined them.

Maggie looked around the office and shivered. 'Can you turn the air conditioning down?' she asked Gonzales. He ignored her.

Calvano was too engrossed in examining the photos to care and I didn't blame him. We were staring at what looked like a photo of Arcelia Gallagher and Enrique Romero in an embrace.

'This woman is not pregnant,' Calvano said. 'It's not her.'

He was right. Enrique Romero, movie star and heart-throb to many, including his own ignored wife, was shown in a series of photographs kissing, groping, laughing with and clearly wowing a beautiful young Hispanic woman who looked remarkably like Arcelia Gallagher. But she was not pregnant and, from the looks of her body in her clingy red cocktail dress, she had not been pregnant in this century, not unless she knew something about regaining her figure that no woman I had ever known knew.

'She could have had the baby already,' Gonzales said. 'She was due in less than a month, right?'

'I don't think it's her,' Maggie said. 'Although the resemblance is startling.'

'Are you sure?' Gonzales asked. 'It explains everything – she goes out to the Delmonte House, meets the man of the house and boom. Chemistry kicks in. You know how it goes. If someone like Enrique Romero wants something, he gets it. He probably moved her out there so that they could be together without interference.'

Calvano was staring at Gonzales, trying to hide his disgust. 'I don't think that Arcelia Gallagher would do that to her husband,' he said. 'It seems completely out of character.'

Gonzalez waved a hand dismissively. 'People will do almost anything when they're offered a limitless bank account, a big house in Malibu and fame. Arcelia Gallagher was raised in poverty in Mexico. You'd better believe she jumped at the chance for a better life.'

There was something in his voice we'd all heard before. I knew that Maggie and Calvano were wondering, as I was, why Gonzales had it in for people who looked like him.

'I still don't think it's her,' Maggie said quietly. 'It would help if there were better photographs of her *face*.' Gonzales missed her sarcasm.

'Call in the husband to look at the photos,' Gonzales told them. 'He'll know if it's his wife.' He looked disappointed. He had deigned to dabble in their investigation and had hoped to pull off a coup, probably to show them that he still had all the right moves.

'Now?' Maggie asked. She glanced at the clock on the wall. 'This seems like a pretty big thing to spring on him this late.'

'If he wants to find his wife, he'll cooperate,' Gonzales told her.

Maggie rose, willing to obey him for now. But I noticed that she kept the news of what she had found out from the two witnesses at the church to herself. She did not want Gonzales interfering with her investigation any more than he already had.

'Does this mean that Aldo Flores can be released?' Calvano dared to ask. It really bugged him that the poor guy was still in jail, a convenient suspect on hold until someone else came along.

'No, it does not mean that Aldo Flores can be released,' Gonzales said irritably. 'Call me if it turns out to be her.' He sat back down at his desk and stared at his empty drink moodily. He hated the case and wanted it to be over.

The woman in the photograph was not Arcelia. Danny Gallagher raced to the station house as soon as he got the call, frantic to find out if his wife was safe. He had grabbed the photographs out of Maggie's hand and, when the first one proved disappointing, spread them out across the conference table, looking from each to each with a hopefulness that broke my heart to witness. He wanted it to be his wife. He wanted her to be safe. He was willing to accept anything – even the possibility that she had run away with another man – so long as she was safe. But he had been forced to acknowledge that while the woman in the photograph resembled Arcelia, it was not his wife.

'I'm sorry, man,' Calvano said gently, patting him on the back. Danny Gallagher had begun to cry again, the combination of hope, followed by hope lost once again, proving too much for him. 'I'm sorry.'

'Let's all get some sleep,' Maggie said. 'We'll start again in the morning.'

'No,' Danny said. He wiped away his tears. 'Not yet. I want to visit Aldo Flores.'

'Why?' Calvano asked, unable to help himself.

'Because he's the only one who knows what I'm going through,' Danny said. 'He's the only one who can really understand.'

I could feel the possibilities flitting through Maggie's head, but she did not really think that Danny Gallagher and Aldo Flores had somehow conspired with one another to kill their pregnant wives. 'You can see him,' she decided. 'But everything you say to him has to be in English and I'm going to be right there beside you listening in.'

Danny nodded and they rode down in the elevator to the second floor in silence. The guard outside the holding cells looked a little confused when he recognized Danny Gallagher, but Calvano gave him the nod and he backed away.

Aldo Flores was sitting up on his bunk, unable to sleep, staring out a square window in the wall of his cell. He recognized Danny Gallagher at once and went over to the bars, his voice cracking as he asked, 'What is it? Have they found your wife? Was she alive?'

'No, man,' Danny said. 'They haven't found her.' He grasped the other man's hand and held it tight. 'I didn't mean to get your hopes up. I just wanted to come by and tell you how sorry I was that your wife is missing. That your wife and baby are missing.'

Aldo Flores did not hesitate. 'Me too, my brother, me too,' he said. He reached through the bars with his free hand and patted Danny Gallagher on the arm. 'I know what you're going through, what your head is telling you right now, and I'm sorry it happened.'

'Yeah, but you're in there and I'm out here,' Danny said. 'It doesn't seem fair, does it?'

Aldo Flores was unconcerned with how differently he had been treated. He just wanted his wife and baby back. And he wanted to make the man who was suffering as much as he was feel a little bit better. He stared at Danny's injuries. 'Maybe I am safer in here,' he said.

'Maybe,' Danny admitted.

'Can you do something for me?' Aldo asked Danny. He sounded almost apologetic.

'Anything,' Danny told him.

'Make them understand that someone else did this. They won't believe me. They are never going to find who took our wives if they don't look beyond you or me.'

'I will,' Danny told him. 'I promise that I'll make them understand.'

'Thank you, my brother,' Aldo Flores said. 'Do you want to pray together?'

Danny nodded. Both men bowed their heads and began to pray. I didn't think there was any doubt by anyone in the room about what they were praying for – which is why I bowed my head and joined in.

TWENTY-SEVEN

The dead of night can wreak havoc with your soul. There is something about the darkness, and the way the rest of the world is silent, that causes your regrets to rise and run through your mind, reminding you of your failures again and again. I often think that the biggest reason why I drank was to escape those bleak hours in which I was forced to confront the choices I had made, the decisions I had waited to make until it was too late, and the actions I had failed to take.

It is also during the dead of night that I have often discovered the truth about human nature. Or at least about those truths we hide from others.

I returned to the Delmonte House in the wee hours of that night, determined to make contact with my fellow traveler again or, perhaps, hoping to catch a glimpse of the true nature of those who lived within its walls. I could feel Arcelia Gallagher near. I had walked through the unmistakable essence of her despair earlier on the lawn and I now knew how to recognize it. I could feel it even more keenly in the dead of the night without interference from others. I could feel her everywhere. I could also feel the unhappy presence who had struggled to make me understand its needs. Wherever it had gone earlier, it was back.

As I passed through the empty foyer of the house, the moon came out from behind the clouds and threw its light off the marbled floor. I followed the moonlight through room after room, feeling the other presence near me but never quite seeming to make contact with it. I stopped in the drawing room and turned slowly in a circle, hoping to catch a glimpse of the other presence. There, over in one corner, I thought I saw the outline of something manlike, about the size of what I had seen in the kitchen. It could have been a trick of the light, but it felt tangible and sad, so sad, as if all the sorrows of the world had converged in that one spot. As the night shadows settled around me, the shape took form. It was a rough outline of a man, filled with a thousand tiny stars that sparkled like diamonds as they danced within the confines of the amorphous shape.

I shut my eyes for a moment and with a rush of insight, there it was – I was somewhere else, somewhere hot with a blinding sun overhead, and I was looking at a mother being ripped away from her children. I could hear their screaming and the mother sobbing, and I could feel the anger that rose in me like a beast. White men were dragging my wife away. She was flailing and struggling against them, crying out the names of our children. I was struggling, too, straining against the chains that bound me. I could feel the bite of the metal in my skin. And then, just as suddenly, I was back in the library and I was myself again.

That was the connection. The being that wandered this house had once had his wife and children taken away from him. He knew where Arcelia Gallagher was. He knew she was a mother and that someone, somewhere, was grieving for her. He was trying to tell me where she was. 'I am ready,' I thought, trying to will my acceptance to my fellow traveler. 'I am ready for you to show me.'

I felt a heaviness growing within me, as if I was once again carrying the burden of flesh and blood. I grew drowsy, an equally unexpected sensation, and began slipping into an inky void. I felt the sensation of falling, as if I were spiraling backward through time and space. It was that shape, I thought to myself as I lost control and fell into the void, it was that shape with the stars dancing inside its borders. It was the unhappy spirit, inviting me into its world. I felt myself free-falling through what felt like miles of space until I found I had stopped, without any sense of slowing. I was staring at a crying woman huddled in the corner of a dank, dark room. The walls were made of heavy clay reinforced with wooden timbers. The floor was dirt as hard as concrete. A tray of half-eaten food had been kicked into one corner and the woman was sobbing quietly to herself in another. Her thick hair fell over her face and her hands were clutched across her swollen belly, though one arm was affixed to a hook in the wall by a handcuff and chain.

I had found Arcelia Gallagher.

The amazing core of strength I had sensed within her was fading. She sobbed in the darkness of her prison, fearful for her life and the life of her unborn child. The air was cold and smelled of earth. I knew we were underground. No light broke the darkness and, yet, I could see her enough to know she was huddled beneath a sweater for warmth, one she had spread over herself like a blanket.

The room was little bigger than a large bathroom. No more than four men could have stood in it at one time. I counted the days that she had been down here, breathing in the dank air, and I marveled that she seemed as healthy as she did.

A great weariness enveloped her. She was no stranger to suffering nor to sorrow, or even physical cruelty. But she had already endured the unmanageable once upon a time, and lived through it, and perhaps keeping those memories at bay had taken away all her strength. She was not equipped to endure more suffering, not in her condition. I could feel her hope leaking from her, draining as surely as water down into the earth.

There was nothing I could do. There she was – the woman we were all searching for, still alive, still pregnant, yet barely holding on. The baby inside her was strong. But its strength meant that it was drawing energy from its mother, sapping her own strength, taking from its host what it needed to survive.

I felt helpless and ashamed and inadequate. Why had the other spirit sent me here? What did it want me to do?

As I thought of the other being, I could feel it near me. It was both near and not near. Part of it *was* me, I thought irrationally. Or maybe he had lived here, in this place, and lingered still. Then

I had it – the thought flashed through me with certainty: he had died in here.

My realization scared me. Death lived in this strange room. It hovered in its corners. It filled the air. It was embracing Arcelia Gallagher in its arms.

I wondered if she could sense my presence. I wondered if it comforted her or frightened her. I wondered what the other spirit wanted me to do. I tried to think of how I could help her. There was so little that I could do.

Arcelia's sobbing subsided. She no longer had the strength to cry about her confinement. She needed to sleep, she wanted to sleep, but her fear was keeping her awake. I could feel the bad memories pressing in on her, memories of times past when her freedom had been taken away from her and angry men with quick fists and cruel imaginations had visited her again and again. I knew that the longer she stayed in this strange dungeon-like room, the more those bad memories would return. I had to do something to help her.

I willed myself to enter her mind. It was a meager ability but all I had to offer. I fought through the bad memories and called on newer ones, conjuring up sunny days spent on the farm helping her husband till the soil and happy evenings arranging the nursery for the baby to come. I entered those memories, and I felt their warmth. I felt the sun on my skin and heard the buzz of the bees and I smelled the sweetness of strawberry jam. I could feel the rough wood of the kitchen table and a lightness in my heart as I looked up and saw my beloved crossing the room toward me. I concentrated on it all. I felt every ounce of its beauty, and the warmth of being loved and the gloriousness of feeling safe. I clung to her happy memories.

It was difficult. Her darker memories called to me. Always the remembrance of cruel men with cruel appetites threatened to over-shadow the joy. But I turned my back on the darkness again and again. I followed the light and the goodness she held in her heart. I found her hope and I fanned it back to life, I meandered through her memories to an even simpler time when she was a child beneath the hot Mexican sun, the earth parched around her but the steps to her simple home swept clean of the desert sand. I could hear her mother singing in the kitchen and smell a rich aroma from something spicy bubbling on the stove. There were pigs rooting in the brush nearby and the air was filled with the laughter of her brothers and sisters as they chased one another, shrieking, through the front yard. Yes, I thought, this was the place where I needed to keep her. This was where she had been loved and cherished. This was where she had been free beneath an endless desert sky with acres of sunlight and unbound vistas beckoning everywhere she turned. Yes, I would keep her in that place as long as I could. I would keep her there so that she could breathe. I would lead her there so that she could sleep.

TWENTY-EIGHT

I do not know how long I stayed in that strange hypnotic state. It could have been hours or it could have been minutes. But slowly I felt myself rising back to the surface of my world and found myself in the drawing room of the mansion with the morning light just starting to leak through its windows. The old butler's wife was sitting in a chair by the empty fireplace, staring intently at me. Her expression was blank but her eyes unwavering in their focus on me. I smiled at her but she did not respond this time. She was lost in a world even more inaccessible than the one I inhabited.

I knew now for certain that Arcelia Gallagher was being held somewhere nearby. But where to begin to find her? Perhaps by determining who in the house had taken her. It could not have been the old butler. He was far too frail. Perhaps the gardener after all? Perhaps Rodrigo's carefree attitude was not a sign of a clean conscience but, rather, the sign of a psychopath? I thought of what I had seen the evening before – Dakota Wylie's manager paying off that odd couple in the beat-up Chevy with the Alabama plates. They looked like just the types to have done Lamont Carter's dirty work for him. But why? And did Carter even have it in him? Yes, he was angry, but he was also passive. I had seen him give in to Dakota often, unable to keep from indulging her whims.

I drifted upstairs, hoping to find his room. That would tell me more about him.

The master bedroom where Enrique Romero lived, apparently

without his wife, was lavish beyond good taste and devoid of any personal objects. It could have been an opulent suite in a Vegas hotel. I wondered how many nights he had spent there, if any. His whole life here seemed a sham.

The next bedroom over was empty and waiting for guests that never came. Two more bedrooms appeared to be the same. But a fourth bedroom in the middle of the long hallway had to belong to Lamont Carter. He wasn't there, but it definitely looked and felt like him. It was strangely lowbrow, given the rest of the house. A huge widescreen TV covered most of one wall and he had arranged leather couches in front of it like a living room. There was a bar built along another wall. Empty glasses and dishes littered its countertops. His bed was round and unmade, its black silk sheets draping to the floor. It was like an adolescent boy's dream of the perfect bedroom, a fantasy of what life in the Playboy Mansion might be like. And yet, it was also an unhappy room, filled with resentment. Lamont Carter felt out of place in this room, I thought. He felt out of place in this house.

I left his room and continued down the hall to the far end, where Dakota Wylie passed her days in the shadows. She was still asleep, curled up beneath her white comforter, her loose blond hair hiding her battered face. Lamont Carter slept next to her, pressed against her so closely they would have appeared as one if Lamont had not been on top of the covers, fully dressed, his gray slacks and black silk shirt a startling contrast to the snowy white of her coverlet. He was cradling Dakota Wylie in his arms and his chin fit perfectly into the curve of her neck. They were nestled like spoons in a kitchen drawer, breathing in and out as one.

I did not know what to think. They felt so peaceful. Her anxiety had been banished; his anger and rough edges were gone. It was as if this was the place they both belonged.

I drifted through her room, counting the endless bottles of perfume and jars of cream guaranteed to keep her young forever. I admired the length of the marble bathroom that led off her bedroom and thought of how my wife Connie would have loved to have had all that counter space instead of the cramped life I had given her. Rows of cosmetics lined the counters of Dakota Wylie's bathroom, but I knew they were useless to her right now. Nothing could touch her skin in its present condition. It was still raw from surgery. Would her face ever heal to a semblance of normalcy? I wondered. Had she destroyed herself forever?

I heard the murmur of voices and returned to the bedroom. Dakota Wylie had woken. She touched the back of Lamont Carter's hand, reassuring herself that he was there.

'I'm right here,' Carter murmured, still half asleep and yet seeking to reassure her.

'Did he call?' Dakota asked. She closed her eyes again, perhaps knowing the answer but not yet understanding what her life had become.

'He's not going to call, Dixie,' Carter told her, using a nickname for her I had never heard before. 'He was just using you. You have to accept that. He's not worth it. You're going to be more famous than he ever was. I think it's time we move on.'

Dakota Wylie opened her eyes. They were the clearest I had ever seen them and she sounded lucid. The drugs had not had time to cloud her system. 'I signed a pre-nup, Lonnie,' she whispered. 'I'm not going to get much if I walk away. Besides, I don't believe you. I think he loves me. He would never have tried so hard to win me if he hadn't.'

Carter groaned and rolled over on his back. 'He came after you because that agent of his told him to. He needed the boost for his career. You have to accept it. He used you. The only thing we can do now is use him back. The pre-nup doesn't matter. Once you have the kid, he'll have to pay you millions. He can't walk away from his kid. His managers won't let him do that. It would be terrible publicity.'

'How much longer do you think it will be?' Dakota Wylie asked. Her voice grew dreamy. 'Maybe when I have the baby, it won't matter about Enrique. I could love the baby and the baby would love me back.'

'Soon, soon,' Carter promised her. He wrapped his arms around her again. 'Soon it will all be over.'

Dakota was staring at the walls of her bedroom, her mind far, far away. 'A man comes to me at night, you know,' she said. 'He talks to me. He tells me things.'

Carter raised his head from the pillow to look down at her. 'What are you talking about, Dixie? What man? What does he say to you?'

She was self-absorbed to pick up on his anxiousness. 'I can't see him. I can only hear him. He whispers to me. He keeps telling me the baby is coming, the baby is coming. Help the baby, he tells me.' She smiled. 'Isn't that beautiful, Lonnie? I am going to help the baby. I'm going to take care of the baby. And the baby will love no one but me.'

'That's crazy talk, Dixie,' Carter said more sharply. 'You can't talk like that. People will think you're crazy.'

She took his rebuke without rancor. All she cared about was what she wanted. 'But I'm going to get to take care of the baby, right? I'm still gonna have my baby?'

'Of course you are. Now go back to sleep. Sleep is good for you.'

They fell back into a half-sleep, still intertwined. There was something strong and unalterable that bound them together, but it was clouded in too many emotions to separate the memories out from the here and now. Between them, there seemed to be years of sadness, with moments of joy but, more often, remnants of cruelty. There was love there, but resentment, too, and always an undercurrent of fear they could not seem to escape. Most of all, I could feel that they needed one another, that neither one of them would be able to flourish without the other.

How had they reached that point? I wondered. What had they gone through together to get there?

I wanted to learn more. I wanted to watch them longer, but a knock at the door startled them both. Carter leapt to his feet and, with a deftness that made it clear he had done it before, ran to the bathroom and slipped inside it. Dakota sat up in bed, arranged the bedclothes around her and anchored herself with pillows as if she did not have the strength to sit up on her own. 'Who is it?' she called out.

'The new maid is here,' the old butler said through the door. 'I would like you to meet her before I give her the final go-ahead.'

'Come on in, then,' Dakota Wylie said. She arranged the scarf around her face so that it covered much of it and slipped the oversized sunglasses on to conceal her eyes.

The old butler shuffled into the bedroom. Alice Hernandez, the undercover cop Calvano had nominated for the task, and who he apparently carried a torch for, trailed in behind him, looking as innocent and bewildered as she possibly could. I was not fooled. Her tiny frame and huge brown eyes hid a scary competence and a legendary thirst for justice. I had heard about her even before my death and she was even more talked about now. She was smart and driven, and had turned down promotions to stay on the vice squad, where she had an astonishing arrest record. She had a reputation for going straight for the pimps and johns instead of the girls. She was particularly brutal on johns who preferred under-age prostitutes and had once broken a man's arm after she caught him with a twelve-year-old runaway in his car. The man was now serving fourteen years and his lawsuit against the department had gone nowhere. That case was just one reason why other cops called her 'The Terminator' and said she was invincible.

You could tell none of that now. She looked like nothing except a young Hispanic woman in her late twenties, who looked bewil-dered at the English words being used around her, even though she spoke English better than most of the schmucks on the force.

'Does she speak any English?' Dakota Wylie asked as she automatically evaluated Alice to see if she was prettier than her or in better shape. In my opinion, she was both, but apparently Dakota did not feel threatened and nodded in unconscious approval.

'A little,' the old butler said. I felt bad that he was being hood-winked. 'Well enough, and I speak enough Spanish to manage her and I think she will learn more very quickly. She is obviously intelligent and can help out in the kitchen as well.'

'That's fine. Why don't we try her then?' Dakota said with a touch of loneliness in her voice. She needed a friend. 'I know some Spanish, too, not that it did me any good when it came to keeping Lupe from leaving me. I hope this one stays.'

'I hope so, too, Mrs Romero,' the butler agreed. 'I will send her back up once she has filled out the necessary paperwork.'

Alice Hernandez remained docile and agreeable during this exchange, looking about the room with appropriate wide-eyed wonder. I had a feeling that same wide-eyed wonder had made her very effective when it came to prostitution stings. When she didn't have you in a chokehold, she seemed no older than a teenager.

'She'll be right back up,' the butler promised. He gestured for Alice to follow him and she obeyed, still acting as if she did not understand much English.

'Mr Jarvis?' Dakota called out just they reached the door.

The butler stopped, startled to hear his name. 'Yes ma'am?' he asked cautiously.

'I just wanted to thank you for everything you do. You take such good care of me.'

'Yes, ma'am,' the butler said automatically as he shuffled out into the hall, Alice trailing after.

TWENTY-NINE

I had been a famously incompetent detective when I was alive, known for my ability to tolerate an equally infamous partner. No one had ever requested that I be assigned to their case and many a colleague had begged off from being assigned to one of mine, knowing it was headed for failure. My ineptitude had isolated me over the years and I had seldom felt part of a team. But that morning, as I searched the halls of the mansion, wondering what it had been like in its glory days, I felt the comfort of knowing that Maggie and Calvano were searching for the man who had tried to buy a baby and that Alice Hernandez was keeping watch on the house. Their efforts left me free to search for Arcelia Gallagher.

I knew she had to be in the mansion somewhere. The unhappy being who roamed the halls with me knew where she was. If I could find him again, I might find her. But how do you find something you cannot see?

I could feel the house around me, as sad and forlorn as a person who has spent too much time alone. The sights this house must have seen through the years, the drama, the dreams realized and denied, the love and the hate that it had held. Irrationally, I wondered if the house itself had played a part in what happened to Arcelia Gallagher. Maybe the house changed those who lived within its walls? Maybe the unhappiness of its former occupants really did linger and infect those who followed?

I thought of the clay walls I had seen Arcelia chained to in my vision and checked the basement first. The house had been built on top of the remnants of another house. The old basement from the first house was boarded off and extended westward. But the wall was no barrier to me and I checked every corner of the old basement carved into the earth. I found nothing but spiders and a long forgotten silver baby rattle with bells attached to it, dropped into a corner. Curious, I thought. What an artifact to find in the darkness of such a room. There were a few tunnels leading off from the old basement and I followed them as well, but they led to nowhere and ended within a few yards in small rooms barely big enough to stand up in. I wondered what their purpose had been. Perhaps Maggie's father was right about the house that had stood on this property before the Delmonte House? If it had been part of the Underground Railroad, the tunnels could have been used to conceal hidden slaves. It would be easy enough to disguise the entrance to the openings with shelves filled with canned food and other provisions. Could Arcelia Gallagher be in one of them? If so, I could not find her.

I returned to the newer basement. It consisted of a tidy series of storage rooms to hold the many possessions the house's owners could not give up. I found several rooms of opulent white and gold furniture, the fantasy of a young girl who had made it big. The furniture had probably been banished to the basement as tasteless by whatever decorator Enrique Romero had hired to create his tabloid-worthy home.

There were plenty of places where Arcelia Gallagher could be, but all of the rooms felt lonely. The whole basement had a deserted, musty air to it. I thought of how few people were trying to maintain the house and was not surprised. Indeed, a layer of dust coated each step that led back upward to the house. I don't think anyone had been in the basement for months except for me. Certainly, Arcelia Gallagher had not been there. I could not feel a trace of her anywhere.

Upstairs, the house was coming to life, its stillness replaced by the clatter of silverware, pipes running with water, and doors being opened and shut. I left the house to its inhabitants and walked the grounds next, checking every outbuilding, but did not feel so much as a twinge that Arcelia Gallagher was near. I roamed the amazing gardens and the stands of trees that rimmed the vast lawn, searching for signs that she had been there. Nothing.

I returned to the house and checked every room, every closet, every recess I could find but felt nothing to indicate that her presence. I finally returned to the open field where I had felt her presence so strongly and there it was again – the essence of her despair as palpable as it had been when I was inches from her. Arcelia Gallagher had to be near. But where? I was in the middle of an empty lawn. It made no sense.

A wave of cold washed over me, followed by a sensation that felt as if someone had grabbed my heart and tugged it, turning me inside out on myself. It only lasted a few seconds and, yet, it left me stunned. I stood, alone beneath a summer sun, and looked around, knowing that the other spirit was near.

All I saw was the mansion's gardener, Rodrigo Flores, tilling a patch of ground along the edge of the field. A neat row of bushes, roots bound in burlap, had been lined up by his side, ready to be planted. He had stopped to wipe the sweat from his brow when his cellphone rang. He glanced at the number and answered it. He stood abruptly and froze as he listened to what his caller had to say. To my astonishment, after hanging up, he lifted his arms toward the sky, his face wreathed in a smile, then dropped to his knees, praying with his head bowed solemnly. When he was done, he rose and began to run toward the house.

Had they found her? I wondered. Had Arcelia Gallagher been found?

I followed Rodrigo to the back door of the mansion. He washed up in a bathroom near the kitchen, where the butler's wife sat at the table, staring blankly into space. Rodrigo stuck his head in, toweling dry after his wash, started to tell the old woman something and then shrugged and left as quickly as he arrived.

I was about to follow, when the old woman turned right to me and said in a surprisingly deep voice, 'There is only one in trouble, but you must find her now.'

When she lapsed instantly back into a reverie, I had no choice but to continue to follow Rodrigo. He walked so briskly toward the front road that even I had trouble keeping pace. When he reached the split-level fence that rimmed the mansion's grounds, he hopped up on the top rail, hooked his heels over the lower rail and lifted his face to the skies again. He stayed that way, immobile and reverent, until a car pulled up to a stop in front of him. Father Sojak sat at the wheel. The two exchanged words in Spanish – interesting, as I had not known that Father Sojak was fluent – and Rodrigo hopped in the front seat beside him, grasping his hand and shaking it vigorously.

I was no fool. I hitched a ride.

Father Sojak drove quickly toward downtown. I could feel relief flowing through him. Sometimes, the two men would speak and then Rodrigo would return to his happy contemplation of the world rushing by.

I was surprised when Father Sojak pulled up outside the station house instead of the church. Rodrigo leapt from the car before it came to a complete stop. I followed him as he pushed through the media crowd and was let into the station house by the guards, who recognized him from his many prior visits. As he approached the front desk. Freddy, the desk sergeant, waved him upstairs toward the holding cells where a few were always set aside for high-profile prisoners in demand by the brass, lawyers or the media. I knew that Rodrigo's brother, Aldo, was still being held there, pondering what had happened to his wife and why no one cared about her as much as they cared about Arcelia Gallagher.

As Rodrigo rushed up the stairs towards his brother's cell, I saw Freddy reaching for his desk phone. Someone in the department had asked him to keep an eye on the brothers and they would likely be there soon.

The holding cells were hardly Alcatraz and, at this time of the day, deserted except for the high-profile prisoners. The guard on duty recognized Rodrigo and waved him toward his brother before returning to reading his newspaper with a bored expression. The two men met at the bars and linked fingers as Rodrigo whispered furiously in Spanish to Aldo. Aldo gave out a yelp in response and leaned his head against the bars as Rodrigo reached through the bars and cradled his brother as best he could, given the barrier between them. Aldo was sobbing. Rodrigo kissed the top of his head and it was impossible to tell whether the two men were laughing or crying. The guard looked up, his curiosity finally aroused. Rodrigo grasped both of his brother's hands and whispered to him in Spanish. I thought I saw something pass between them, an object of some sort, but it happened so quickly I could not be sure. Aldo was still at the bars, head down, when Rodrigo left the room as quickly as he had entered.

Aldo fell to his knees in his cell and began to pray. He muttered furiously in Spanish. He was still in this position when Maggie and Calvano entered the holding area a few minutes later.

Calvano looked at the guard with a quizzical look on his face. The guard shrugged. 'I'm no expert,' he said. 'And I don't speak a word of Spanish. But I am pretty sure the guy is praying because he's happy. His brother was just here and whatever he had to say looked like good news to me.'

I could see the realization hit Maggie and Calvano: there was only one reason why Aldo Flores would be so happy. There was only one thing that could have triggered this outpouring of emotion – his wife and baby had been found.

'Get a translator up here quick,' Maggie ordered the guard.

The guard heard the urgency in her voice and reached for the phone. A young woman with black glasses and spiked hair arrived soon after. She listened solemnly as Maggie explained the situation. She nodded, then gestured to Aldo Flores and asked him a series of questions in rapid fire Spanish. Aldo did not hesitate to answer. He spoke eloquently and joyously, his words a waterfall as they tumbled from his lips. The young translator's eyes widened and she smiled along with him before she turned to Maggie.

Yes, she explained, Aldo's wife had surfaced. She had called St Raphael's to say that she was safe and staying with relatives at an undisclosed location. Apparently, she left of her own accord. She had not realized that her husband was being held by the police until someone told her they had seen Aldo's photo on the news.

'Where is she?' Maggie asked her. 'Why did she leave?'

'He does not know exactly why she left,' the translator explained. 'He says she was frightened by something. Or, more accurately, by someone. She says a man tried to steal her baby. She panicked and left to stay with distant relatives. She is safe and the baby is safe. She told someone to let her husband know where she had gone, but apparently that person was picked up by Immigration before he could get word to Mr Flores.'

'She just took off?' Calvano asked skeptically. 'Without telling her husband?'

'She says that the man who wanted her baby was very powerful and rich. She was afraid to tell her husband for fear he might accidentally tell him where she had gone.'

'Who in the world would have that kind of power?' Maggie wondered out loud.

It was Calvano who made the connection. 'Aldo's employer would have that kind of power,' he said. 'I bet this goes straight back to the Delmonte House.'

'We need to talk to Aldo's wife,' Maggie said. 'She could tell us who it is. If she knows he was rich and powerful, then she

knows who he is.' Maggie looked at the translator. 'We need Mr
Flores to get in touch with his wife. It's urgent. Can you get him
to cooperate without frightening him?'

The translator looked startled by this but she came back strong.
'I will try,' she told them. 'But you are not likely to get his cooperation if he's being held as a suspect.'

That meant dealing with Gonzales. I knew Maggie did not like
the idea. 'Tell Mr Flores that if he will help us get in touch with
his wife, we will get him out of here as soon as we can. I give
him my personal word that it will happen.'

The translator nodded and began speaking rapidly to Aldo. They
went back and forth for a while, but I could sense the translator's
heart was not in it. She knew Maggie had asked for Aldo's cooperation before he was released because, once out, it was likely he
would disappear and join his wife, wherever she was. They would
never find him again. The trouble was, I'm not sure the translator
blamed him.

'My money's on Enrique Romero,' Maggie said to Calvano as
they waited. 'He's trying to buy a baby for the publicity.'

'Why would he do that?' Calvano asked. 'His wife's about to
have one.'

'Twins,' Maggie said, not entirely seriously. 'Everyone in
Hollywood is offloading a kid. If he can come up with twins, it
gets him the headlines.'

'Seriously?' Calvano laughed. It was the first break they'd had
in the case and it had made them both a little punchy. 'If you ask
me, I still think the butler did it.'

'I'm going to call Alice,' Maggie decided, reaching for her
phone. 'She's on the inside. She'll be able to help us figure out
who it is.'

'Only if it's someone at that house,' Calvano pointed out. 'This
could still have something to do with Danny Gallagher. His father
is the mayor. I call that rich and powerful. It could still be a lot
closer to home.'

'I'm calling Alice anyway,' Maggie said. 'I'm going to tell her
to meet us somewhere.'

'You know what?' Calvano said abruptly. He was watching
the translator talk to Aldo, trying to figure out what direction the
conversation was heading in.

'What?' Maggie asked.

'If Aldo's wife was found alive, maybe there's hope for Arcelia Gallagher. Maybe it's not too late.' He sounded as if he were afraid to even say it out loud, as if somehow that might jinx the possibility.

'Maybe,' Maggie said cautiously.

'You're one of those people afraid to hope, aren't you?' Calvano asked.

'Maybe,' Maggie said again.

The translator had tried to convince Aldo for as long as she could, but she looked apologetic as she approached them. 'I'm sorry. Mr Flores will not cooperate. He is angry at being in jail. He says you must first let him out and then he will get in contact with his wife.'

'Can't say I blame him,' Calvano admitted, surprising the translator. He looked at Maggie. 'You're the one who gets to tell Gonzales.'

THIRTY

Alice Hernandez had promised to meet Maggie and Calvano on a corner of the property shielded from the house by a curve of woods. Maggie pulled the car over and waited. Gonzales had blown her off, saying he was deep in a crisis and would have to deal with Aldo Flores later. What could be more important than tracking Arcelia Gallagher's kidnapper? Maggie had complained about it to Calvano all the way to the Delmonte House.

Venting had not helped. She remained frustrated at not being able to talk to Aldo's wife. Worse, Calvano kept taking Aldo's side, saying he didn't blame the guy for not cooperating until he got out, which irritated Maggie. It made me glad I was invisible.

'Where is Alice?' Calvano wondered out loud for the third time.

'Relax, hotshot,' Maggie said. 'She's not due for another five minutes.'

'What if all of this has to do with drug smuggling after all?' Calvano said. 'What if this house is nothing but a big fat two-story red herring?' He remembered something and asked Maggie about it. 'Hey, did you ever hear back from your friend at the FBI about whether or not Arcelia Gallagher's name was in their system?'

'Yeah, I got it back today. But there's nothing in it. She's not involved in drug smuggling.'

I knew Maggie had just lied to Calvano. I didn't know why, or exactly what she had lied about, and Calvano hadn't notice, but I sure had – and I wondered why.

Alice showed up exactly as promised, darting from the woods and into the car before anyone driving by could see her. She sat inches from me, unaware I was there. I enjoyed her clean, powdery smell. If I had still been inclined to human impulses, I would surely have appreciated the maid outfit she wore. It included the short black dress and little white apron of male fantasies.

Calvano definitely noticed. 'Hot, Hernandez,' he commented, leering at her from the front seat with exaggerated enthusiasm.

'Put a cork in it, Calvano,' she shot back. Her ability to squelch romantic offers from her fellow officers was as legendary as her arrest rate. I didn't know why Calvano would want to risk her scorn, but he seemed helpless not to try. She leaned forward, although there was no one but me to overhear. 'I have to hurry. That poor old butler is completely overwhelmed. He's trying to take care of his wife and do his job and she's being a little erratic today. She's really agitated about something, but no one can figure out what it is. He needs some help. I have to get back.'

'Aren't you the old softie?' Calvano said.

'Put a cork in it, Calvano,' Alice repeated. 'You are not half as cute as you think you are.' She had his number. 'That is one weird household to go with one weird house,' she said. 'The lady of the house is a mess. Her face looks like hamburger and, from what I can tell, she only gets out of bed to pee. Even then, I'm surprised her manager doesn't offer to wipe her ass for her. He never leaves her side.'

Maggie laughed. I guess it was OK when women made jokes like that. She sure wouldn't have laughed if it had been Calvano.

'Have they said anything about Arcelia Gallagher?' Maggie asked.

Alice shook her head. 'No. And I've been listening. I can hear the old butler coming from about a mile away. He shuffles and breathes like he's on the verge of a heart attack, so it's easy for me to keep track of him. I've been listening to the girl and her manager all morning, and I've still done more work than the old maid ever did, by the way. But mostly it's the manager telling her majesty how beautiful she is, and how she's going to be famous again one day, and about how the husband will have to pay attention to her once she appears in the tabloids with their baby. It's pretty sad. He's like this creepy cheerleader urging her to indulge in her worst psychological dysfunctions. He'd be a great manager in Hell. He's definitely earning his ten percent the hard way, too, and he's probably doing other stuff for his cut of the take, if you know what I mean. It's like one can't function without the other.'

Calvano did not like what she was implying, but he said nothing. Brooding was not a good look for him, but I admired his loyalty to Dakota Wylie anyway.

'I'm surprised you haven't run screaming from the house with the ghost hot on your tail yet,' Calvano said instead, in a very misguided attempt at teasing her.

'Don't make jokes about the ghost,' Alice told him as she cuffed his ears. 'It's real. And it's real creepy. I can't wait to get out of there.'

'Did the gardener come back to work after he visited his brother?' Maggie asked. She was in no mood to talk about ghosts. I decided not to take it personally.

Alice nodded. 'He came right back here from the station house, judging by the time he arrived, and he was really happy, even gave the old lady a peck on the cheek. Then he went out back and started working again. I've got to tell you – I'm not taking him for a kidnapper. I saw him feeding apple slices to some chipmunks about half an hour ago. He's not exactly a criminal mastermind.'

'Anyone come to the house for a visit?' Maggie asked. 'Did you see anything unusual at all or find a silver car in the garage?'

'Well, you were right about the cars – there's a whole collection of collectibles in the garage. The place is huge and it's climate-controlled. Two of the cars are silver, but they are also very distinctive. A Rolls-Royce and a DeLorean. I think if your guy had been driving one of those, someone would have mentioned the make. Other than that, the best I can offer is that I think it's kind of weird that the lady of the house never leaves her bed. I have to dust the rest of the bedroom every ten minutes, mostly so she can have someone to talk to.'

Now she was starting to irritate Calvano. He didn't like her making fun of Dakota Wylie. Unfortunately for Calvano, Alice Hernandez apparently liked irritating him and she stepped it up when she noticed his expression.

'Go ahead, ask me anything about how she got her big break into show business,' she urged him, punching his shoulder. 'I did everything but the windows while she talked to me this morning.'

Calvano ignored her.

'Did you see anything that might conceal a hiding place?' Maggie asked. 'Any place where someone might be keeping Arcelia Gallagher?'

Alice shook her head. 'I checked all the rooms, the closets, the hallways, even the bathroom closets. I checked dimensions and looked for discrepancies. Definitely no hidden rooms. Haven't been able to check her majesty's room closely yet, though. No chance.'

'Maybe you should try harder,' Calvano suggested testily.

'Maybe I should,' Alice agreed. 'But I have to do it when her majesty is not in the room, and since she spends every moment of her waking life wallowing in her bed, it's going to be tough.'

Calvano glared at her but Alice just smiled back agreeably, revealing perfectly lovely white teeth and an enchanting smile that was completely lost on Calvano, at least at that particular moment.

'Did her husband call her today?' Maggie asked. 'Gonzales is itching to nail Enrique Romero for everything.'

'I bet he is,' Alice said. 'I heard Romero complained about him to the governor for something Gonzales said about him on Lindsey Stanford's show. The commander got ripped a new one.'

'What?' Maggie turned to look at her. 'Where did you hear that? *How* did you hear that before I did?'

Alice smiled enigmatically. 'You have your sources and I have mine.'

Calvano groaned. 'Now Gonzales is going to be even hotter to get Romero for this, whether he did it or not. Or Flores. Basically, the commander is not going to rest until he can pin it on someone who is Hispanic.' He looked over his shoulder and leered at Alice. 'Play your cards right, Hernandez, and it could be you.'

Maggie gave him a withering look. 'Did Romero call his wife today?' she asked Alice.

Alice shrugged. 'I think so. Her majesty was on the phone crying and begging someone to come back, talking about how he couldn't leave her because they were having a child together. It was pretty pathetic. You would never catch me talking to a guy like that.'

When she gave Calvano a look like he was to blame for the entire male species, I started to wonder if maybe there wasn't something already up and running about those two. They disliked each other a little too much for there to be only casual feelings between them.

'But whoever she was talking to wasn't buying her act,' Alice added. 'She hung up just as unhappy as when she had started.'

'That guy is a jerk,' Calvano said suddenly. 'If my wife was on bed rest and having a baby, I would not fly to the other side of the country and cheat on her before the plane engine had cooled.'

'Cheat on her?' Alice asked. 'What do you do know that I don't know?'

Maggie filled her in. 'Gonzales called in some favors from the LAPD and they came up with some photos of him cheating on his wife with a hot-looking woman who looks exactly like Arcelia Gallagher. Except it isn't her.'

'No kidding? You mean this whole business of him marrying an endless parade of anorexic blondes is just for the publicity? I can't decide if that's pathetic or hilarious. You know he gets condemned in the Latino press for turning his back on 'his people', whatever the hell that means, and now you're telling me he actually prefers hot Latinas?'

'Apparently so,' Maggie said with a shrug.

Calvano could not resist the opening. 'Play your cards right, Hernandez, and maybe he'll hit on you. I bet that would be your dream come true.'

'Nightmare, maybe,' she snapped back. 'He's not my type. I like Italian food better.'

I'm quite sure she had not meant to say that out loud, at least not in front of Calvano. She flushed and the silence in the car, while brief, was electric.

Calvano was the first to break the silence. His voice sounded a little high when he said, 'Whatever. The guy is still a world class jerk for cheating on his wife.'

'That may be, Adrian,' Maggie said. 'But we can't arrest him for being a jerk.' She turned to Alice. 'Nothing else at all you think is out of the ordinary?'

She hesitated, but she had something, all right. 'Sometimes I think that old butler is not as old and slow as he lets on,' she said. 'I may have caught him eavesdropping earlier today. I came around the corner and saw him down the hall, standing near Carter's bedroom. I turned around and went the other way before he saw me. But I am pretty sure he was standing outside of the door, listening in on Carter.'

'I told you, the butler did it,' Calvano said triumphantly. Both Maggie and Alice ignored him. Boy, it was a tough crowd.

'I don't know if Carter was in his bedroom at the time, though. He is always in *her* bedroom, from what I can tell,' Alice continued. 'I think it's creepy. I'm thinking Enrique Romero also thinks it's a little creepy. Maybe he's paying the butler to keep an eye on Carter for him?'

'That could be something,' Maggie mumbled, but she did not sound convinced.

'We're sure this chick is pregnant, right?' Alice asked.

'Why do you say that?' Maggie said.

Alice shrugged. 'I don't know. She never gets out of bed, so I can't tell you for sure, but she seems pretty damn skinny to me. If there's a kid in there, it's starving to death. And she doesn't act pregnant to me.'

'Romero hasn't had a kid in four or five prior marriages,' Maggie admitted. 'We checked on it. That tells me he's shooting blanks. Maybe they're planning to adopt and her pregnancy is a ruse?'

'She could be faking it,' Calvano agreed reluctantly. 'Or just sort of misrepresenting it, and as soon as the adoption goes through, they'll announce it to the papers as their own. They wouldn't be the first couple in Hollywood to do that.'

'As soon as the adoption goes through?' Maggie asked. 'Or as soon as the kidnapping goes through?'

This time Alice took Calvano's side. 'I don't think she's involved with any kidnapping,' Alice said reluctantly. 'She's not organized enough. I'm not sure she's pregnant, but I am sure she is not involved with Arcelia Gallagher's disappearance. She doesn't have it together enough to kidnap someone. She couldn't kidnap her own lunch. Not that she eats lunch.'

'Lamont Carter might have it together enough,' Maggie pointed out.

'Now, him I would believe,' Alice admitted. 'He gives me the willies.'

This was, of course, the perfect opening for Calvano to make a dirty remark. It was proof that he really did like Alice Fernandez that he held back and instead said, 'Keep an eye on Carter, will you, Hernandez? And watch your back. The guy could be dangerous.'

'Will do. Call me on my cell if you get anything I need to follow-up on. I've got to jump. The old guy needs help in the kitchen.'

'Sheesh, you really like the old guy,' Calvano said. Was he jealous of the butler? I doubted irrational jealousy was what Alice Fernandez liked about Italian men.

'There's nothing wrong with caring about other people,' Alice told him and her tone was scathing. 'You ought to try it sometime.' She hopped from the car and disappeared into the grove of trees, the white bow on her uniform bobbing up and down like a rabbit's tail until she disappeared.

'You are so out of your league,' Maggie told Calvano when she noticed him watching Alice leave. 'That woman is way too smart to go out with you.'

'So says the woman who not only went out with the number one douche bag in America, but actually married him, too.'

'Touché,' Maggie said. 'Speaking of which, wonder who Skip is blaming for his black eye today?'

They would not get a chance to find out. Alice came running back to the car and this time she was all business. 'Did you say that Arcelia Gallagher was driving an old black Volvo when she disappeared?'

'Yes,' Maggie confirmed. 'It was a 1986 Volvo sedan with gray interior and it has a bumper sticker on it that says something like "Eat Organic" on it.'

'I just found it,' Alice said. Her voice rose with excitement. 'I was cutting through the woods, when I saw a corner of its trim catch the sunlight. It's right off the road, barely in the woods, and someone has piled a whole bunch of branches around it. I'm sure it's hers.'

Maggie and Calvano were on it instantly. 'OK,' Maggie said. 'We'll call it in. But don't say anything to anyone back at the house. I'm going to have them process the car quietly, understand? I don't want anyone in that house alerted that we found it. Our best hope for finding Arcelia is for someone to lead us to her – and they're only going to do that if they think no one is watching them.'

'Understood,' Alice said. And with that she was off again.

THIRTY-ONE

I did not stay to watch the forensic team process Arcelia Gallagher's car. I knew it would take them a long time to get to it without being seen on the main road. I also knew that their evidence gathering would be even more painstaking than usual. Maggie was after a search warrant for the Delmonte House and she needed irrefutable evidence that someone who lived in the mansion had been in Arcelia's car to get one. She would not want any mistakes made. I wondered if they would even find anything to justify a warrant. As it was, the car was just over the line on to the neighbor's property. She had a tough fight ahead. This might be her only shot and she didn't want to blow it.

Instead of watching them work, I returned to the mansion to see if I could find out on my own who had taken Arcelia Gallagher and where she was being hidden.

Alice was in the kitchen preparing a sandwich for the butler's wife. She put it down in front of the old woman, then sat and encouraged her to lift it to her mouth and take a bite. But as I watched the two women, I felt a current of animosity wind its way into the cheerful kitchen and discovered Lamont Carter standing in the hallway, looking in at them. His eyes narrowed as he watched Alice.

This was not good. How long had he been standing there and why was he watching Alice? Carter said nothing, however, and stayed hidden from their view. After a moment, he turned and left. I followed him – and just like that, there it was. I could feel traces of Arcelia Gallagher's hopelessness clinging to him. He had been near her. I was certain of it. Lamont Carter had taken her and I knew why.

Carter headed for Dakota Wylie's bedroom. She was propped up against her pillows, groggy from pills, watching herself on television. Carter sat in the chair next to her bed and crossed his legs. His foot jumped up and down as his knee jiggled nervously.

'I don't like the new maid,' he told her.

Dakota blinked her famously blue eyes at him, trying to focus on what he was saying. It took a moment for his words to filter through. When she answered, her voice was slower than usual. 'Oh, Lonnie, you don't trust anybody. My room is cleaner than it has been in six months. You've got to learn to trust people. You're so hard.'

'And if I weren't a hard man, where would you be?' he asked, his eyes flickering away from her as he unconsciously surveyed the room, taking in its size and height, toting up the value of the insanely expensive furnishings. Yes, possessions meant a lot to him.

'I can't do this much longer,' Dakota Wylie said to him. 'I want Enrique to come home. I miss him.'

Carter shook his head. 'You've got the worst taste in men, Dixie. The worst.'

'Better to have bad taste than no taste at all. I worry about you, Lonnie. Why are you always alone? Don't you want someone in your life?'

'I don't need anyone in my life,' Carter said. 'I have you.' He took her hand and they turned as one to stare at the television screen where a younger Dakota Wylie walked across a fake campus, capturing the hearts of all with her effortless beauty. The two of them together suddenly seemed too much for me to take, but I made myself stay and watch them, lost in their own private world and happily oblivious to anyone's needs but their own, until Carter stood and announced he had business to attend to. Dakota waved him away, too enraptured with her younger self to pay much attention to his leaving.

I had felt traces of Arcelia Gallagher's despair clinging to Lamont Carter, so I knew he must have been near her recently. I had learned that emotions that strong did not simply disappear, they clung to the people who had been there when the emotions were first created. And I was not going to let Carter out of my sight until I found her. He spent the rest of the day in his room, making fruitless phone calls to people on the West Coast, hoping to land a meeting to discuss a new television series for Dakota. It sounded like word had leaked out about her plastic surgery, probably through her husband, I thought to myself, and Carter did not have any luck all afternoon. No one would even take his calls.

Between each call, he left to check on his client. She spent the entire day in bed, as she had spent so many other days, clutching a pillow to her belly and staring at the television in a dreamy, drug-induced haze while her sitcom played endlessly in the corner of the bedroom. How long had she been like this? I wondered. Weeks? Months? How long could she stay like that without affecting her baby? If she was even pregnant.

Lamont Carter would sit with Dakota for a few minutes each time he checked in, lying to her about what he had arranged during his phone calls. One day he would have to come clean and explain to his client that she had ruined both her face and her livelihood. It was not going to be anytime soon, though, if his lies were any indication.

Each time Carter left, I followed him back to his room where he would make more unproductive phone calls and occasionally pour himself a drink from the bar in his man cave. He was a strange man. Small and coiled, stronger than he looked at first glance, and completely withdrawn from the world. In his closet, he had rows of nearly identical black shirts and gray slacks lined up, with leather oxfords beneath him. He had a look that clearly meant affluence to him, and one look only. There was little else in his wardrobe.

As the afternoon wore on, I realized that Alice Hernandez was right: the butler was indeed keeping an eye on Lamont Carter. Several times, when Carter was getting to leave his room, I arrived in the hallway first and spotted the butler disappearing around the corner. I could also feel him outside the door, listening in, and I wondered how much he knew.

Finally, just as dusk was starting to gather, Carter visited the kitchen and asked the old man for Dakota Wylie's dinner. 'She's extra hungry tonight,' he told the old man. 'She's eating for two, you know?'

The old man looked skeptical, his eyesight wasn't so bad that he didn't know that Dakota Wylie was wasting away to nothing. But he still prepared a tray piled high with sandwiches and fruit.

It seemed to be all anyone in the house ever ate. He added a huge glass of milk and returned Carter's stare by saying, 'She needs the extra calcium, sir. Especially if she plans to breast feed.' If he was being sarcastic, he hid it well.

Carter took the tray from the old man without bothering to thank him and started down the long hall toward the main stairs. Just before he reached the foyer, he darted down a side hallway, pushing his way out of a small door that opened on to a flower garden arranged beneath the library windows. He looked around to see if he was being observed, then pulled a small electric lantern out of a hiding place in a boxwood hedge. Spotting Rodrigo cleaning his gardening tools in the shed, Carter quickly walked across a patch of lawn and darted behind a hedge of tall bushes. He walked faster, lantern and tray in hand.

Carter had planned well. By the time he turned the corner and started across the main lawn, it was dusk. He was almost invisible in the strange yellowish light that comes when neither the day nor the night prevails. By then, he was moving so fast that the milk had sloshed over on to the tray, leaving little in the glass, but he did not slow his step.

Halfway across the field, he glanced up at some cherry trees growing to his left. When he was about ten feet from the edge of the lawn next to the trees, he placed the tray on the grass and knelt. He started searching the grass with his hands, seeking something only he knew was there. Even though he had to have been there many times before, it took him nearly a minute to find what he was looking for. Glancing around to see if anyone was observing him, he reached deep into the lush turf and pulled. A square of lawn opened upward to reveal an opening in the earth and the top of a ladder leading beneath the lawn.

The rumors were true: the house *had* been a stop on the Underground Railroad. I wondered how Carter had discovered it. Probably by searching for buried gold, I thought. He was the type who would have heard those rumors and believed them.

But his real pot of gold lay beneath the earth – his only ticket to magazine covers and fat contracts now that Dakota Wylie had ruined her face. Arcelia Gallagher was slumped against the earthen walls of an underground room, the same prison I had seen during my strange vision the night before. She was either half asleep or losing strength. She barely opened her eyes as Lamont Carter climbed down the ladder, the tray of food still balanced on one hand and the lantern looped over the other. He had the arm strength of a chimp and would be a formidable opponent to anyone who tried to take him on.

There was a plate of food already at her feet, mostly untouched, stiffening and turning brown in the stale air.

Carter stared at the food before he looked up at her and said, with confident authority, 'If you don't eat more, you will kill your baby. Is that what you want? To kill your baby?'

Arcelia Gallagher glared at him with contempt. 'I have been tortured by real men,' she spat at him. 'I have stood up to men who make you look like the little boy you are.'

I thought for a moment he might hit her. Instead, Carter placed the tray of food on the dirt floor by her feet and laughed. 'How does it feel to disappear?' he asked. 'How does it feel to know that you will never see the sun again? Look around you, this is your tomb. As soon as the baby is born, you will watch me climb that ladder for the final time and, after that, you will never see me – or the sun – again.'

She lunged for him, but one wrist was handcuffed to a bolt embedded in a plank shoring up the wall and she could not reach him. 'They will find you,' she predicted. 'They will find you and they will kill you.'

Carter laughed again. 'No, "they" won't find me. "They" won't find you either. Wake up. The world is convinced your husband is your killer. No one will ever take a look at me.'

Arcelia Gallagher gasped suddenly and pulled her legs toward her. Carter smiled. 'Those are labor pains, aren't they?' His voice shifted, taking on a heavy southern drawl. 'I knew the baby was near. It won't be long now.'

He leaned in closer to see her better and her legs lashed out with surprising strength. She caught him right in the groin. He tumbled backward, cursing and grabbing at his crotch.

'You will never get my baby. I will kill you if you try,' she screamed at him.

He lay in the dirt for a moment, fighting to regain control. Amazingly, he stood calmly and began to brush off his clothes. 'You shouldn't have done that. I could have made it easy on you. I could have given you something to dull the pain.'

He stared at her swollen belly from a safe distance. 'Now I

don't really care. You can scream as loud as you want, no one can hear you here. And the screaming sure as hell won't bother me. If you haven't had the baby by morning, I'll cut it out of you. Come to think of it, it would be my pleasure.'

The love I had seen him show Dakota Wylie had disappeared. The hardness that lurked behind his eyes had taken over his whole being. He radiated hatred toward Arcelia Gallagher, toward himself, toward the entire world.

'You can't expect me to deliver the baby down here,' Arcelia said. 'You're putting its life in danger.' Even faced with death, all she wanted was to protect her baby's life.

'Babies are born in squalor every day,' Carter told her. 'Don't you know that babies are born into dirt and filth to parents who don't give a shit every single minute of every single day? You think that having a baby is special? You think just because you're going to have one, it makes me want to protect you? Think again. I don't give a shit if you're its mother. I don't even give a shit about the baby. But I need it, so I intend to keep it alive. All it has to do is make it to the house. All you have to do is stay alive until I take it.'

I felt a sort of buzzing rush across the room, a stinging as if a swarm of bees had flown by. Carter flinched. He had felt it, too. I knew then that the second spirit was here in the underground room with us. Once I realized that, I could feel so much more coming from my fellow traveler: terror, violence, extraordinary pain and a thousand memories of a life left behind all washed over me. I could see his memories as vividly as if they were happening now and I was a part of them.

I saw a man, tall and broad-shouldered with dark-colored skin helping a young boy fill a sack with fallen apples. I saw the same man looking up at the top of a cabin made of rough-hewn wood and felt his pride that he had built it. I looked through his eyes across the floor of the cabin at a stout woman bent over a pot of bubbling food mounted over a roaring fire burning deep in a stone hearth. In a handful of seconds, I lived his life with him, feeling joy and pain and sorrow. I saw, once again, his wife and children being taken from him, the pain as fresh as the first time I had felt it. And then I felt his death. I felt the blows raining down on me, the carving of my flesh, the seemingly endless ripping and hacking away at my body. I felt the life drain from me as the world darkened. At last, I felt his stillness and I knew why he had stayed in this place, why he was here keeping Arcelia Gallagher company.

He had been killed here, in this terrible cavern. This was where his bones lay.

Carter looked uneasy. He had felt the spirit's presence, too, as a predator might sense an even bigger predator in the jungle. He backed away from Arcelia Gallagher and nodded toward the food he had just brought. 'Drink the milk. The baby needs it for the calcium.'

As he started up the ladder, I followed with a glance back toward Arcelia Gallagher. She slumped back against the wall, eyes closed, her hands resting on her belly. God help her if the contractions truly had begun. Once the baby was born, Carter had no use for her.

Darkness had fallen in the upper world. The air was cool and filled with the sounds of spring frogs peeping and the hoots of owls setting out for their evening meals. I smelled fresh grass and new life and marveled that it could exist mere feet above such hell.

Carter replaced the hatch to the cavern and made his way quickly across the lawn. As he reached the edge of the courtyard in the back of the house, he saw the same thing that I saw: the butler standing in one of the kitchen's French windows, watching Carter hurry back toward the house.

Carter did not break stride. He walked through the back door, turned the corner into the kitchen and headed straight for the butler. He wrapped one hand around the old man's neck and pushed him up against the wall, lifting him up off the ground. 'Mind your own business, old man,' Carter told him.

The butler instantly turned red. His toes were barely reaching the ground and his arms flailed for something he could grab on to. Carter was relentless – and so absorbed that he did not notice what was happening behind him.

The butler's wife had lost her vacant stare. Seeing what was happening to her husband, she stood and reached a knife on the counter within a few steps. She grabbed it and walked calmly over to Lamont Carter, the knife held high above her head. The butler saw what she was doing and began to flail. Carter looked over his shoulder and let go of the old man, darting to one side just as she slashed down with the knife, missing his body by inches.

Carter stood with his back against the sink, staring at the old lady, as the butler slumped against the wall and gasped for breath.

'Leave him alone or I will kill you,' she said in the same, strangely deep voice I had from her earlier.

Carter did not move.

The old woman looked back at him with a blank stare then shuffled to her table. She placed the knife on it and sat down as if she had done nothing more important than shut the door. The silence in the room was profound.

I tried to understand what was happening, to read her memories in hopes of knowing what had motivated her. But her mind was blank. She had lapsed back into the void. Or, I thought, never left it in the first place.

Carter stared at her as if she was possessed. I was starting to wonder the same thing myself. 'That's it,' Carter said. 'The two of you will be gone by morning.'

'You have no power over me,' the butler said, rubbing his throat. 'You can't fire me.'

'I can tell them about your wife,' Carter said. His voice was devoid of any emotion. He was a robot fueled by hate. 'If I tell them about your wife, how she does nothing and sits there staring into space all day, how she's violent and threatens people with knives, you can bet she'll lose her job. She'll lose her health insurance, too. Who will take care of her then? You'd have to quit your job, wouldn't you?'

The butler stared at Carter. It was impossible to read his expression but I could feel what he was thinking. He was old and he had seen angry men before, he had seen selfish men before, too. Perhaps he had even been there when hatred had overwhelmed others. He knew enough not to fight back.

'I thought you'd figure it out,' Carter said to him calmly. 'Stop following me or you're a dead man. Killing someone old like you would be as easy as pushing you down the basement steps. Your bones would break like peanut brittle.'

Lamont Carter had two men inside him. One was guarded and angry; the other violent and angrier still. Yet I had never seen him anything less than tender when it came to Dakota Wylie. I thought of the power she had to tame his hate and I knew that, without her, he would be lost. But what a terrible force they were when they were together.

The old butler watched Carter leave the kitchen before he rushed to his wife's side. She was still sitting at one end of the kitchen table, staring into space. It was impossible to know whether she understood what had just taken place. He kissed the top of her head and held her close, as if she had been the one threatened and not him.

'Something bad is going to happen, Muriel,' he whispered to her. 'I can tell. I felt it before and you know what happened then. I can feel death gathering around this house. It's hungry. All we can do is make sure it's not one of us.'

THIRTY-TWO

Three times before midnight, Carter descended the steps into his hell on earth and checked on Arcelia as she lay, gasping, trying to endure the spasms that overtook her body at increasingly frequent intervals.

I knew the baby was coming. I could tell because, despite the fear and hatred that filled the room whenever Carter came to check on her labor, I felt an undercurrent there, barely a ribbon, perhaps, of something pure and light growing inside Arcelia Gallagher. It was as warm as an ember inching toward flame. The life inside of her was gathering its strength, determined to make a great journey.

Arcelia herself was astonishingly strong. There she was, trapped beneath the world, all on her own and about to give birth for the first time. She had only her captor to keep her company and he was anything but supportive. He did not hold her hand, nor did he hand her badly needed water. He simply clambered down the steps, waited as long as he needed to in order to time her contractions and left again without ever saying a word. She could have been a cow giving birth to a calf for all he cared.

Just before midnight, as I was despairing that Maggie was getting nowhere with her attempts to find enough evidence in the abandoned car to bring a search team to the house, I felt a change come over Arcelia. The terror and the anger left her, to be replaced by something I had never experienced before. I could not tell if this was of her own will or a reaction she could not control, but all of her being seemed to turn inward as the hours passed. It was as if every scrap of strength she had, every hope for happiness, had been distilled and was now being directed toward that tiny life in her belly, toward her child, the child that, once born, would be taken from her while she was left to die.

The circumstances no longer mattered to her. She had astonishing strength. I stayed with her for long hours at a time, trying to bring her comfort, trying to will her all of the love I had not shown my own family when I was alive. Surely it was still there somewhere. Surely, knowing I was there and praying for her to survive, would do some good, wouldn't it?

I think the other spirit was there as well. However unhappy he was, whatever it was that caused him to linger in this world, he seemed to have put his own needs on hold, as I had. I could feel little more than a presence, a comforting sort of solidity in the air, but I hoped it gave Arcelia Gallagher the surety that she was not alone.

There were times when I could not stand it any longer and I returned to the surface, my mind racing as I sought a way to let someone, anyone, know what was happening. It was maddening to see the world going on as usual – to see the forensics team still combing over the vehicle, inch by painful inch; to see Rodrigo lying in bed watching television; to watch as the old butler shuffled across the kitchen with a glass of milk for his wife, his bruised throat swathed in an ascot; to witness Alice Hernandez gently probing the butler for information, never noticing that he was hiding something from her. It filled me with despair to know that beneath their very feet, a woman lay trapped and in pain, faced with the impossible task of giving birth to one life while trying to save her own, yet none of them knew she was there.

I could not bear to leave Arcelia Gallagher alone for long and so had no idea whether Maggie and Calvano had found anything to lead them closer to her. I saw Alice Hernandez on her cellphone once, crouched behind the corner of a bookcase in the sitting room where no one could overhear her. But I came upon her too late to hear what she was saying. Just as I arrived, she stored her cellphone back in her pocket and began to dust the shelves again.

Close to midnight, I found Dakota Wylie in her bedroom, pacing restlessly from window to window, her sheer negligee trailing after her. She was not any more pregnant than I was. But she knew the baby was coming. Her pacing told me that.

I wondered if she knew where the baby she waited for was coming from. Her mind seemed so fragmented, so incapable of holding a single thought and so muddled with bits of fiction and reality that I wondered if, perhaps she was descending into madness. Only a desperate woman would be able to believe that taking another person's baby and passing it off as her own would fool anyone for long. Maybe she thought Carter had arranged to adopt a newborn and knew little else. I could not tell what she knew even when Carter came to visit her, for he was full of information about media interest in her upcoming birth and predictions that she would garner every entertainment headline as soon as they released the photos to publications.

He predicted a bidding war, and when I looked at Dakota Wylie's altered face I had to wonder about his grasp of reality. Yes, they might pay for photos of her with her child, but the headlines that went with those photos would destroy her psyche forever.

Dakota did little but stare dreamily out the window, thinking of how her husband would welcome her and his baby back with open arms. Carter gave her another handful of pills to take and she licked them from her palm dreamily, swallowing them without water. He had her doped to the gills. If he was able to keep a doctor from examining her, it might be easy to see her loopiness as exhaustion. She might be able to pull off playing the part of a new mother after all.

'I have to go check a few things,' Carter told Dakota. He led her gently back to her bed and helped her into it, then arranged the bedclothes around her and turned out the lights. 'Just sleep. When the baby comes, I'll bring it to you.'

'How can you expect me to sleep?' she drawled back in a sleepy voice. 'It's so exciting. I'm going to be a mama.'

A flicker of impatience rippled across Carter's face and I felt a glimpse of what he was feeling. Dakota drifted through the world without any awareness of how complicated and hard it could be, leaving it to him to navigate the rough spots. She had no idea what it took, but that was his job and he would have to do it.

As Carter left the room, he ran to Alice Hernandez just outside the door. Startled, he dismissed her with a wave. 'Ms Wylie is sleeping,' he said. 'You're dismissed for the night. We have it all under control.'

'Have all what under control?' Alice asked back, doing her best to sound as if English was not her strong suit.

'Ms Wylie's care, of course,' Carter said sharply. I felt a flash of impatience flare in him. 'I am sure you are tired. It's been a very long day. You do not have to work until this late at night.'

Coming from anyone else, it might have sounded normal. But Lamont Carter was not the type to be thoughtful of others. It aroused Alice's suspicions even more. She looked at him a moment too long and then nodded, walking down the hall without answering. I could not tell if it would be enough to inspire her to keep a closer eye on him tonight, though.

Was there no one who could help?

As Carter strode through the hallways, coiled and intent on finishing his plan, I despaired anew that anyone would discover Arcelia Gallagher in time. When Carter headed for a side door, I knew he was going to check on her again.

I followed him as he slipped through the rose garden, glancing from side-to-side to make sure he was not being observed. The moon was covered in clouds and the grounds were cloaked in darkness, making Carter nearly invisible. In a moment, no one would be able to see him.

I had not counted on the old butler. As Carter cut across a corner of the backyard, I saw the old man framed in the kitchen window. He still wore an ascot wrapped tightly around his neck to hide the bruises from Carter's earlier attack. He had seen Carter slipping from hiding spot to hiding spot and his suspicions were aroused. Unconsciously clutching the ascot to protect himself, the old butler watched Carter heading toward the great lawn. I was at his side within seconds, frantically trying to reach him, trying to access them through his memories, to do anything I could to get him to follow Carter.

The butler was old and physically weak, but he was not a coward. He knew that Carter had to be up to something – and he was angry at himself for not fighting back earlier when he had been bullied. Shutting the other kitchen door to keep his wife from wandering away, the butler stepped out into the night and began to follow Carter.

He had to hurry to keep Carter in his sight, but the night shadows made it easier for him to stay close without being seen. As for Carter, he was too focused on making sure Rodrigo was still in his room to notice the butler. Not once did he look behind him.

The butler stumbled over the roots of a tree, losing his balance. But he reached for the tree trunk and caught himself in time. I died a thousand more deaths in that interval. He was too old and frail to recover quickly from a fall. I put the thought out of my mind and continued onward with him. He reached the edge of the great lawn in time to spot Carter on his knees, searching the grass for the hidden handle.

I could feel the old butler's heart beating in his chest as surely as if it had been my own. It felt like a jackhammer. The old man knew that something was up. He looked back toward the house, one hundred yards in the distance, looming up in the night, and I could feel his longing to return to the safety of its rooms. Lights glowed in a handful of windows, a cheery reminder that it would be easy to come in from the darkness. But curiosity kept him there, behind a hedge, picking out the figure fumbling in the grass. Something else kept him there, too – I could feel old regrets in the butler, along with shame and a weary recognition that he had failed to act when he should have in the past. I could not sense the circumstances, but I could feel him gathering his courage and resolving to stay where he was. This time, he would take a stand.

Carter found the handle and lifted the hidden hatch upward, then disappeared down the entrance hole into the earth. A few seconds later, the hatch was lifted back into place above him, rendering the opening invisible. But the old butler had seen what Carter had done.

He did not waver in his watch. He stood in the darkness, trying to control his ragged breathing, his old hands trembling with both excitement and a touch of palsy. He hated Carter and this, he knew, might be his chance to get revenge. He knew Carter was up to something, but I do not think he realized it had anything to do with Arcelia Gallagher yet.

The minutes stretched by, each an eternity. High above, stars started to emerge from the darkness, appearing to blink on one by one as the wind swept the cloud cover across the night sky. The air was cool and smelled of fresh growth. For those above the earth, it was a heaven sent summer night. For those below, who could say? I did not dare leave the old butler. I feared he would lose courage if I did. Whether I was helping him or not, I was there by his side, willing with every fiber of my being that he stay strong.

After what seemed like an hour, but could not have been more than five minutes, the hatch opened and Carter re-emerged into the night. His eyes swept the dark lawn to see if anyone was watching, then he clambered up the ladder and replaced the hatch after him, sealing Arcelia Gallagher in her tomb. He had not been down there long and he carried nothing in his hands but his lantern. The baby had not yet been born. But I knew Carter would be back soon.

The butler had grown rigid and his breathing had become more rapid, perhaps dangerously so. But I did not have time to worry about him. Carter was darting back across the lawn, heading for the house to make more of his phone calls to the West Coast. He had photo auctions to conduct and tabloids to call. He had money to make. Arcelia Gallagher was just a means to his ends.

The butler stood immobile until Carter disappeared into the darkness of the distance, then waited a moment longer just to be sure. His heart was pounding in his chest and I could hear a roaring in my ears. The old man was alive, too alive. I feared his frail body could not take it. Finally, he moved cautiously toward the hatch and across the lawn, each step tentative as he sought his way through the night, fearful he might fall. It was all the harder for him because he did not want to take his eyes from the spot where Carter had emerged from the earth. It was slow going, but at last he reached the area and carefully dropped to his knees, wincing at the pain it caused him.

He searched the cool grass with his hands, seeking the handle he knew was nestled in among the grass. He found nothing. I wanted to scream in frustration, what if he was in the wrong place? Even I, who had watched Carter go in and out of the hatch all day, could not be certain of where the opening lay.

The old butler remained calmer than I did. He shifted his position slightly and leaned as far forward as he could, and checked the new perimeter all around him, finding nothing. Adjusting his position yet again, he searched a wider circle being careful not to miss an inch of grass. It was maddening. It was frustrating. It sent me spiraling into even greater depths of despair but, at last – at long glorious last – the old man found what he was looking for.

With a glance to make sure that Carter was not coming, the old man tugged on the handle hidden in the grass. The hatch hinges had been well wheeled and the lid opened easily. The old man peered down into the darkness.

I could hear Arcelia's moans coming from below. I found her lying back against the dirt wall, her legs stretched out and her hands cupping her belly. Despite the coolness of the underground room, her body was drenched with sweat. She was breathing rapidly and fighting to stay in control. Her heart was hammering in her chest and she was too intent on bringing her baby into the world to have noticed the hatch opening above her. What if she did not notice the butler above her at all? There was no way he could clamber down that ladder. What if he simply shut the lid and left?

The metal stairs rattled violently. Arcelia looked upward. Was the butler actually trying to come down? No, there was no one on the steps. It was my fellow traveler, the unhappy spirit who had terrorized the house for so long. He was up to his old tricks, but this time they might save Arcelia.

'I need a doctor,' Arcelia shouted towards the opening. 'Please, if you want my baby, you have to bring me a doctor. I think something is wrong. I can't do this by myself.'

She laid her head back against the wall and panted.

The old man's voice wafted into the room from above. 'Who is that? Who is down there? Are you OK? Who are you?'

Hope flooded through Arcelia Gallagher in a tidal wave of adrenaline. She sat up straight and her voice rang out strong and clear. 'Help me,' she shouted. 'My name is Arcelia Gallagher. My husband is Danny Gallagher. I have been down here for days. Please. Don't go anywhere. You must help me. My baby is coming. I need help.'

There was a silence and I feared irrationally that the old man had given up and left.

'I can't make it down the ladder,' he finally said, sounding apologetic. 'I'm going to go for help. I'm sorry. But I will be back soon, I promise.'

'No,' Arcelia shouted helplessly. 'Don't leave me. Please. He'll come back. Please don't leave me down here alone.'

'I have to. I'm so sorry. I can't make it down the ladder. I just can't.'

She had been strong for a very long time. She had endured

things no person should ever go through. But the news that her
rescuer was simply going to turn around and leave proved too
much for Arcelia Gallagher. The helplessness came and she began
to cry as she slumped weakly against the wall and waited for the
next wave of contractions to hit her.

'I will be back,' the old man promised. 'I promise. No one will
stop me.'

No one? I knew Arcelia was thinking the same thing that I was.
If he was too weak to come down the ladder by himself, it would
be all too easy for Carter to overpower him if he was
discovered.

The old man needed help. I left Arcelia reluctantly, returning
to the surface where the butler was replacing the hatch. But he
was no fool. He left it open until he could crack a small lower
limb off from a nearby fruit tree. Returning to the hatch, he placed
the limb across the opening then shut the top on to it. From afar,
Lamont Carter would not be able to tell that the hatch had been
discovered, but fresh air could still get through to Arcelia Gallagher
and it would mark the opening for others.

The old man wiped his hands on his pants, pausing to collect
his breath. His heart leapt in his chest like an animal struggling
to break free. I wondered if his frail body could contain it. I could
feel his desperation as his mind processed what was happening to
Arcelia below, the danger of Carter being so near and his own
physical weakness. If he tried to help, his life would be in danger.
He was taking many risks.

But I had not given the old butler enough credit. His body was
old, but his courage had been awakened. His shoulders straightened
with resolve and he took off in a rapid walk toward the back of
the house where Rodrigo slept. The first thing he was going to
do, I realized, was find Rodrigo and send him down to help Arcelia.

Rodrigo. If he was helping Carter, the old man was dead and
I did not think I could bear to see him pay such a price for his
courage. I followed close behind, worried for him.

Rodrigo was in bed, watching television, when the butler reached
him. He looked up, alarmed, as the old man pushed through the
door, gasping for breath.

'What is it?' Rodrigo asked. 'Has something happened to my
brother?'

The old butler's words were barely distinguishable and his

breathing had taken on a whooping sound. 'Below. Below.' He
pointed outside. 'I found the woman they are looking for. She's
in a dungeon below our lawn. Near the cherry trees. Carter did it.
I followed him. I saw the woman. She needs help. Her baby is
coming.'

Rodrigo looked stunned, and in that instant my hope died – why
had the butler not considered the fact that Carter might have an
accomplice? Why had he not remembered that Rodrigo had been
one of the last people to see Arcelia Gallagher before she
disappeared?

'Did you hear what I said?' the old man asked. 'We have to
call the police. The missing woman is below the great lawn.'

Rodrigo fumbled for his cellphone. Perhaps he was not helping
Carter after all. But then he froze. 'I gave my phone to Aldo in
jail so he could call his wife. I told him he could keep it until
tomorrow.'

'Then you must go to the woman,' the butler said. 'You must
help her. I cannot get down the ladder. If you help her, than I will
go for the police.'

Rodrigo leapt from the bed and grabbed a long pole with a
wickedly sharp cutting edge from a corner in his room. He had
other tools there, makeshift weapons against the spirit he feared.
He fumbled in his pockets and took out a pocket knife long enough
to be illegal in our state. I froze, fearful of what he might do next,
but all he did was extend both weapons so that the butler could
choose. 'You need a weapon in case Carter comes back,' Rodrigo
said. 'Take one of these.'

The butler waved him away. 'I'm not strong enough. He would
only use it against me.'

'Where is she?' Rodrigo asked. 'The great lawn is very big.'

The butler looked panicked for a moment as the enormity of
what they needed to do overwhelmed him. I could feel him thinking
of the vastness of the lawn, the hopelessness of the dark and the
cleverly hidden hatch buried deep in the grass. Courage, I willed
him. Strength and courage. You must stay calm.

'I tore a limb off a cherry tree to mark the opening,' he finally
remembered. 'Go to the lawn by the cherry orchard, find the tree
with a limb torn off and then head straight into the lawn. I left
the entrance open a few inches, with a branch wedged in it. You
will find her there. You must close the top after you. If Carter

comes, he will try to hurt you. Your only hope will be to surprise him on the way down. Take a lantern. It is dark in there. And a blanket, she will need something to lie on. Take a blanket.'

Rodrigo grabbed the blanket from his bed and ran out the door. I followed him, desperate to know if he could find the opening. He sprinted to the gardener's shed, scooped up a lantern and kept running. As I left the shed, I could hear the old butler wheezing inside the house, struggling for breath. But I had no choice but to follow Rodrigo. He might need my help.

It was Rodrigo's world and he knew it even in the dark. He loped across the lawn toward the spot where the butler had directed him. If he had been in it with Carter, he would have gone straight to the hatch. Instead he was heading for the trees.

He found the cherry tree with the limb stripped from its trunk and paced carefully back across the lawn, staring intently at the ground, searching for the opening the old man had promised. He passed it the first time and my heart sank, but he turned around and began to search again. This time he tripped over the opening. He dropped to his knees and opened the hatch door wide. He called down in Spanish and Arcelia answered him. Rodrigo scrambled down the ladder and I followed, needing to know that Arcelia would now be OK.

Her breathing was coming faster and her contractions were barely a minute apart. The ground below her was wet. Her water had broken. The baby would be here soon.

Rodrigo folded the blanket underneath Arcelia so she had something to lie on. He could do nothing about the handcuff that bound her to the wall. He encouraged her to lie flat on her back. Murmuring to her in reassuring Spanish, he lifted her dress and checked on the baby's progress. His moves were confident and I knew that a baby struggling to join the world was not new to him. A profound sense of relief flooded through me, clearing the way for me to feel a force that had surely been there in the cave all along: a ferociously brilliant spark of energy and love, all centered on one spot within Arcelia – new consciousness taking form.

Rodrigo adjusted the lantern and checked the baby's progress. He shouted something to Arcelia that made her pushed down harder. The air around us vibrated. I could feel a billion atoms dancing and whirling, coalescing at the point where the baby struggled. Arcelia panted, gasping for breath, and Rodrigo murmured more encouragement. The two of them had become one, had somehow agreed silently that they would do this together, that they would bring this new life into the world.

Arcelia relaxed for a moment. The baby was still and she panted in the quiet. Then, as if remembering something, she looked up at Rodrigo and murmured Carter's name.

I'd forgotten about Lamont Carter. If he knew that the old man had discovered him, the butler would not last a minute. I had to go check on him. The baby would be safe. Rodrigo knew what he was doing and Arcelia was strong.

A sudden wind swept through the cave, even though Rodrigo had replaced the hatch cover. It smelled of grass and rain. It was my friend, my fellow traveler, letting me know that there were two of us there, unseen. Letting me know that I could leave. He was there to help.

I fled, my fear for the butler increasing. Carter knew that millions rested on the baby. It would not be long before he left his room to check on Arcelia. I feared what would happen to the old man then.

THIRTY-THREE

The butler had reached the kitchen table and been unable to go further. Trembling, he sat, trying to regain his strength. As I waited with him, trying to lend him my strength, a shadow appeared behind him. The old man sensed a presence and whirled around, prepared for the worst.

His wife stood in the kitchen, looking down at her husband with the same vacant eyes she had greeted the world with for over a year. But then she said, quite distinctly, in a low voice that I knew somehow came from the other spirit, 'You must find the master keys and lock him in his bedroom.' Then she calmly reclaimed her customary seat at the kitchen table and lapsed into silence.

The butler was so startled he stood abruptly and grabbed the table to steady himself. 'Muriel?' he asked his wife. 'Muriel, are you there?' She stared at him with vacant eyes, but a silver fork lying on the table in front of her began to spin slowly in a circle before it flew off the table and clattered to the floor.

The butler rushed to an immense sideboard against a wall. Frantically opening drawer after drawer, he shoved his hands deep into the back of each until, at last, he emerged triumphant holding a large silver key ring. One single key dangled from the hoop, an old-fashioned skeleton key polished to a sheen. It had been the ultimate symbol of power once – the butler's key, used to lock each room in the house from the hallway when the mansion shut down for the season, a precaution that made it harder for thieves to steal the family treasures.

'Muriel?' he asked his wife hopefully once more before he left the kitchen, but she was back to staring at the tabletop, oblivious.

The old man hurried through the halls toward the grand staircase. I was close behind. I felt strange vibrations in the air all around me, perhaps even the vibration of the walls themselves, as if the house was alive in some way and urging the old man on.

When he reached the upstairs hallway, the butler slowed his steps and crept silently down the center of the narrow carpet. Carter's room was in the middle of the corridor and the butler had to stop to get his breathing under control before he approached it. But once he reached the right door, the sounds of Carter's voice against the backdrop of a noisy television show leaked out from underneath it. Carter would not have been able to hear the old butler wheezing if he had tried. He was on the phone, arguing furiously with someone over the size of a fee. He never even paused in his rapid-fire sales pitch when the butler inserted the master key into the lock of the bedroom door and gently turned it to the right. The click, though no more than an echo, seemed as loud as a gunshot.

'What are you doing?' a voice whispered to the old man's right.

The butler gasped and backed up against the hallway wall.

Alice Hernandez stood there, staring at the old man curiously. She glanced at Carter's door and gestured for the butler to follow her down the hall. When they reached the top of the steps, she wasted no time in explaining who she really was. 'Why would you lock him in his room?' she asked, pulling her badge from the pocket of her maid uniform and showing it to the old butler. 'I'm working here undercover. Why were you locking Carter in his room?'

I thought the old man might start sobbing with relief. He grabbed for the railing and steadied himself before explaining, 'I found the woman you are looking for. Carter's been holding her in some sort of cave beneath the great lawn. I think maybe it's an old room from when the house was part of the Underground Railroad. She's about to have her baby. I sent the gardener to help her, but if Carter finds out, he will kill us all.'

The old man unwrapped the ascot and showed his bruises to Alice. 'I'm not strong enough to fight him off, as you can see.'

Alice took him by his elbow and escorted him down the stairs. 'Listen to me very carefully,' she said, keeping her voice calm. 'I need you to show me where Arcelia Gallagher is, and then you must stay above on the lawn until the police get here so that they can find us as quickly as possible. You must wave them over while I go down inside the room to protect her.'

'I don't think I can walk to where it is again,' the butler said, ashamed. 'I don't think I have the strength.'

'I want you to tell me exactly where this place is,' Alice told him. 'Remember that I am not familiar with the grounds and tell me exactly where it is.'

The butler explained about the cherry trees and the great lawn, but warned her that Rodrigo had closed the hatch above him to avoid Carter being tipped off.

'In that case, I am going to need you to come out to the great lawn with me,' Alice said, the urgency rising in her voice. 'I know it will be hard for you, but I may need your help finding it. Can you do that? Can you do that for Arcelia Gallagher and her baby?'

The old man nodded, but he looked frightened and I could feel his heart thumping in his chest, erratic and ragged, pushed to its limit. His frail body could not take much more.

'I'm going to run ahead,' Alice told him. 'I'll call the police on the way. But promise me you will follow me. Promise me you will not give up. If I don't find the hatch, I'll wait by the cherry trees.'

The old man nodded but Alice had already taken off, running through the hallway of the house. I followed, watching as she raced past the old woman in the kitchen and burst out the back door. She bounded down the steps in one leap, hitting the ground below with athletic grace. She was strong and ran like a gazelle, her heart beating confidently in her chest as her lungs took in the night air and the fresh oxygen fueled her legs. She reached the great lawn within a minute and loped to her left. Once she reached the cherry trees, she pulled a cellphone from her pocket and, barely winded, had Maggie on the phone within seconds.

'I found her,' she told Maggie. 'She's being held in some sort of cave underneath the lawn of the mansion. The old butler found her, actually, and I caught him trying to lock Lamont Carter in his room. Carter is the one who took her.' She was silent as Maggie asked her something. 'Yes, he's locked inside. I don't think he's noticed anything yet. But he's dangerous. You need to send an ambulance. The old man says she's having her baby. I'm trying to find the entrance now.' She described the spot on the lawn where the butler had told her the hatch would be and promised Maggie that someone would be waiting above ground to show them the way.

'Hurry,' she told Maggie. 'Please, just hurry. The butler is going to guard the room from above and if Carter gets out and finds him, he won't survive.'

As soon as Alice hung up, she walked straight into the lawn in the direction the butler had directed her to. She found nothing, but that did not slow her. Dropping to her knees, she swept her hands around her in a wide arc and began to call out Rodrigo's name. She pulled the grass, she buried her hands deep in the turf, she raised her voice and called out his name louder. It was maddening. But the moon above was full and a cloud blocking it moved past at that moment, causing pearly light to pour over the tree line and send shadows dancing across the lawn. The top of one of the cherry trees looked like a figure pointing directly to where the hatch handle was hidden.

'Rodrigo!' Alice cried out, frustrated. 'Can you hear me, Rodrigo? Where are you?' She pounded the earth in frustration and her mind registered something different in the grass beneath her fists. She pounded again and felt the bounce, then began frantically digging through the grass seeking the handle to the opening. At last, triumphantly, her fingers closed around it and the lid raised, gloriously, upward.

'Rodrigo,' she called down the steps. 'It's me, Alice. I'm coming down. Are you OK? Is Arcelia OK?'

Alice had asked the question in English and he replied in the same. 'She's OK. She's a strong lady, but the baby is almost here.'

'I'm coming down to help. An ambulance is on its way. Is there room for me?'

'Yes,' Rodrigo called up. 'Come down.' He added something in Spanish and Alice climbed on to the ladder, hesitating when it came time to close the hatch. Should she leave it open or close it to avoid tipping off Carter that his plan had been discovered? In the end, she did the same thing the butler had – she shut the hatch with the branch of the tree wedged in it, so that only a sliver of light from the lantern below leaked out into the night.

I followed, praying the butler could make it back across the lawn so the police would not have to search, as Alice had. But I saw no sense in me staying above, there was nothing I could do, and the breathtaking energy I had felt earlier beckoned to me from below the surface. I wanted to be there when the baby was born.

THIRTY-FOUR

The underground room filled with Arcelia's breathing and the encouraging murmurs of Alice and Rodrigo. After trying unsuccessfully to unshackle Arcelia, Alice ripped part of her apron and wrapped a bandage around Arcelia's wrist to protect it from being cut by the metal as Arcelia struggled to give birth. The hard-edged cop I had heard about disappeared as Alice murmured a never-ending stream of reassuring words in Spanish.

Rodrigo had assumed the role of the midwife. He knelt in front of Arcelia, lantern at his side, his hands ready to catch the baby the moment it emerged. I wondered if any of them could feel what I felt: an epicenter of energy, like the eye of a hurricane, whirling joy and hope in one miniature maelstrom centered on the baby emerging into the world. I felt my lifetime whistling through me and heard a thundering, as if thousands of years of human existence were galloping past me in seconds. I caught glimpses of eons past, shadows of figures huddled on windswept plains, living in tents, racing on horses as part of a vast army. I smelled oceans and mountains and flowers and sweat. I was filled with the most amazing essence so poignant and glorious it was electric. I felt as if I was being reborn.

Rodrigo shouted something in Spanish and Arcelia pushed harder, willing not just her muscles but her whole heart and soul toward her baby.

The air in the room felt as if it were whirling faster, the light from the lantern sparkled and danced, and then – in a moment of hush so abrupt it stunned me – time, space, even the world itself, seemed to stop. A small head emerged into the glow of the lantern, covered in mucus and blood, paused for a moment to turn left and then right. Arcelia gave a groan and pushed harder. In a rush of liquids and cries from everyone there to help the baby along, a new being slid out into the world and into the arms of its unlikely savior: a sweaty, middle-aged bachelor more used to breathing life into roses than human beings.

Rodrigo shouted something in Spanish and I knew enough to understand what it was – it was a healthy baby girl. Rodrigo had taken off his flannel shirt and folded it by his side. Cradling the baby carefully in one arm, he wiped her face with his tee shirt and pulled the mucus from her nose, then smoothed the caul from her eyes and cleared her brow. Thick black hair sprung from her head like a rooster's comb as Rodrigo dried it with his shirt. The baby was still for one heart-stopping moment before she burst out into an indignant, cave-filling cry that sounded more beautiful than any music I had ever heard. Both Arcelia and Alice began to cry as Rodrigo wrapped the baby in his flannel shirt and placed her in Arcelia's arms.

Overcome by what happened, Rodrigo sat back on his heels and watched the two women huddled together over the child, bathed in the glow from his lantern. He was thinking the same thing I was thinking: life remained a miracle.

Arcelia kissed her baby's face over and over and held the squalling child to her. All the strength she had shown for the past week – culminating in the astonishing power she had shown that day – had been worth it. It had led to this. She had done it. Her baby was safe.

It was a uniquely human moment. I felt as if the universe, whose secrets still eluded me, had nonetheless given me a gift. I felt connected to the baby nestled in Arcelia's arms and the three adults clustered around it. I felt connected to my fellow traveler, who lingered in the room with us, and I felt connected to every one of the billions of human beings who walked the earth above me, all oblivious to my being. I had lived my whole life as an outsider, feeling out of step with the world and unworthy of my existence. But in that moment, for the very first time in either my life or my afterlife, I felt as if I was supposed to be there. I was part of the plan.

I was so stunned with gratitude that, like the others, I forgot the danger that lay above. When the hatch lid above us opened, it was Alice who reacted first. She leapt to her feet and started up the ladder, without hesitation, ready to face anything to protect the child.

'Damn girl,' Calvano's voice floated down from above. 'Easy there. It's only me.'

Alice slumped against the ladder in relief, staring down at Arcelia and her baby. 'The baby is here and it's healthy. But we need an ambulance. And something to get the cuffs off of her. He chained her to the wall.'

'Ambulance is here,' another voice promised. It was Maggie. 'Is there room for the EMTs to go down?'

'No,' Alice said. 'I better come up.' She sounded reluctant to leave.

Calvano reached down to give her hand and she grasped it automatically. As their hands touched, I felt something electric pass between them – was it something new or a residual of what had happened below? Maybe what I had felt in the cave when the baby was born lingered to forge connections between people, I thought. Maybe it always happened that way. Maybe it all came down to that.

As Calvano hoisted Alice up into the night air, I heard him say, 'What in God's name are you covered with, Hernandez?'

'Afterbirth,' Alice told him, laughing with relief. She could relax. Arcelia and her baby were safe.

Calvano's reaction made Maggie laugh and that, too, was a glorious sound. It had, against all odds, ended well.

Rodrigo would not leave Arcelia and I don't think she would have let him let him if he had tried. She was gripping his hand with the resolve of someone who intends never to let go. He stayed by her side as the emergency medical technicians climbed down to join them and freed her from her metal restraints, then fashioned a pallet to lift both Arcelia and her baby to the surface. I had no doubt that she could have – and would have – climbed up that ladder one hundred times, if need be, if it meant safety for her child, but the ambulance attendants insisted that she ride up in style instead, emerging from the ground in a giant papoose, receiving a round of applause once she reached the surface.

I joined her and there – spread out against the great lawn of the mansion – stood what looked like an army of people ready to help. Calvano and Maggie were in the forefront and behind them clustered rows of uniformed officers who had answered the call for help. Investigations like this one never ended well and everyone wanted to be a part of the triumph.

Which one of them had found the opening to the hatch? I wondered. Then I saw the old butler slumped against one of the cherry trees at the side of the lawn, his head bowed as he gasped for breath. He had been forgotten in the excitement of bringing Arcelia and her baby to the surface. I saw him suddenly jerk, like a puppet whose strings have been released. He clawed at the tree and crumpled to the ground. He twitched and sprawled, then lay completely still.

Not a person other than me had seen him.

It couldn't end that way. The old man had pushed himself in unimaginable ways, he had helped save Arcelia and her baby more than anyone. How could he die like that, on the very edges of victory, overlooked? It wasn't fair. I couldn't let it happen. But I had nothing to bargain with.

Despite all that has happened to me, and most especially the events of that night, I still was not convinced that there was anyone, or at least not a single all-mighty being, to hear my prayers if I tried. But I had to at least have enough faith to try, I decided, and so I began to pray. I told whoever or whatever might be listening that I understood there had to be a balance between birth and death. That new life inevitably meant an old life was passing, that the balance of the universe required such an exchange. But not now, I prayed, not at this moment. The old butler had behaved with such courage and he had a wife who still needed him. It was only fair that he should be given more time. Take me, I told the universe, take me and send me wherever I must go, even if I have not yet redeemed myself. I have nothing else to offer, but I offer myself. Just please give the old man some more time.

Dry lightning split the sky and in that instant, the old man's body was silhouetted against the glare. A voice called out from the crowd, 'Man down by the trees.' A handful of officers sprinted toward the butler's body. A uniformed cop I did not recognize reached him first and rolled him on to his back. Kneeling by his side, he pressed both of his hands against the butler's chest and began to pump. A female officer reached them a second later and took her place near the old man's head. She tilted his chin up to clear his passageway, took a deep breath and began to resuscitate him. Others came up behind with portable paddles and gestured for them to make way. An EMT placed the paddles on the old man's chest, another adjusted the dials on a small black box connected to the paddles and nodded.

The butler's body arched up and fell back to earth. The EMTs waited, saw no response, and applied the paddles a second time. Once again, the old man's frail body arched as if presenting itself to the skies.

Still nothing happened.

Take me, I pleaded. Not him. Not him.

I felt something pass through me, something cold and in a hurry.

The EMTs applied the paddles to the old man's chest yet again.

This time, they were successful. The butler began to breathe on his own. The EMTs raised their arms to the skies in triumph and the crowd cheered once again, looking from Arcelia to the butler, unable to believe that two miracles had occurred in one night.

I was the only one who could see that, up in the night sky, below the pearly moon, a tornado of tiny swirling lights had formed in the trees above the old man's head. The constellation whirled and the darkness surrounding it deepened until the funnel rushed upward and exploded in a glory of fireworks that only I could witness.

I knew then that my fellow traveler was gone. That whatever needed to be given in exchange for the old butler's survival, he had been the one chosen to give it. Once again, I had been left behind.

I tried to tell myself to have faith, that my time would one day come. But I could not help feel I had been forgotten yet again.

That was when my fellow traveler gave me a gift.

I felt him within me and saw the world through his eyes once more. Only this time, instead of feeling the attacks of cruel men on my body, I was filled with a peace so profound it infiltrated every fiber of my being. I felt safe and exalted and uplifted as I found myself walking through a luminescent tunnel, drawn by a warmth ahead of me. A light glowed in the distance and I walked toward it without hesitation, drawn by the joy it promised.

Slowly, out of the fog, there emerged the faces and figures of those I knew my fellow traveler had loved – and been loved by in return. I saw ancient African warriors dressed in feathers and beads, paying homage to his courage. I saw a smiling old women with nothing but wisps of white hair left on her scalp beaming as she held her outstretched arms toward my friend. By her side, stood an old black man in a pair of worn overalls, his eyes filled with pride and enduring love for his son. And then, there by the mouth of the light, stood the woman I had seen in my earlier vision cooking over a fire in their cabin. She was younger and more beautiful than in my vision, her face free from worry or pain. Her eyes sparkled and her hands were wrapped around children on either side, who smiled up at my fellow traveler with such love and joy that I thought my heart might explode.

I was Icarus flying too close to the sun. And like Icarus, my fate was to tumble back to Earth.

This time, I knew, my friend was truly gone. But he had left me with the gift of knowing that, one day, my time would come.

THIRTY-FIVE

I t was not such a bad deal to be returned to the living, not this time around. What a glorious sight it was to see Arcelia and her baby being transferred to a stretcher in preparation for her trip to the hospital.

The EMTs had just finished wrapping a clean blanket around her and her baby, when I heard her name being called from across the lawn. 'Seely! Seely!' a voice shouted in the distance. The crowd parted like the Red Sea before Moses, making room for a man running full tilt across the grass. Danny Gallagher. His life was restored and with it, his strength. All he wanted was to be with his wife.

No one made a sound. No one tried to stop him. The entire crowd watched, transfixed, as Danny reached his wife, laughing and sobbing at the same time, unable to stop saying her name, needing to reassure himself that it was true – she was alive. He reached her side and froze, unable to take his eyes away from the baby in her arms. She whispered something to him and he cupped the baby's face in his hands, kissing its tiny brow and laughing as he ran his hands through her thick hair. True to form, he was crying. But this time, I just thought to myself, 'Aw, let the guy cry.'

When the time came to interrupt them, the EMTs were gentle with Danny Gallagher. They let him hold his wife's hand as they wheeled her toward the ambulance. He kept rubbing his thumbs over the red marks gouged into her wrist from where she had been shackled to the wall. Every few steps, he would raise her hand and gently kiss her wounds, as if he might heal them with his tears.

Arcelia balked when they tried to load her into the ambulance. 'Not yet,' she said to the people hovering around her. 'I must talk to the woman who helped me.'

'I'm here,' Alice said quickly. She had never been more than a few feet from her side. 'What is it?'

'There was someone else down there with me,' Alice explained to her, speaking in English so that the others could understand. 'When I was down there, I could feel him with me and I saw the bones coming out of the earth.'

'There was a body down there with you?' Alice asked. She, like the others, was wondering if Arcelia was thinking clearly. She had been through a lot.

'Yes,' Arcelia said. 'There is a body down there. I am sure of it. I felt the finger bone and I brushed the earth away from it. I know the rest of the body is there.'

Maggie had heard her and showed no hesitation. 'We'll send someone down and check,' she told her. She touched Arcelia's baby, her hand lingering on the clean white blanket that now bound the child from head to toe. 'I'll make sure they check carefully. You go now. Your husband can ride with you to the hospital. Go and show him your little girl.'

'What about him?' Arcelia asked Maggie, nodding toward the house. She could not bear to say Lamont Carter's name.

'There are officers taking care of that now,' Maggie promised. 'You don't have to worry about him any longer. No one does.'

THIRTY-SIX

I arrived back at the house in time to see Lamont Carter being dragged down the grand staircase in handcuffs. He had drawn in even further on himself and he radiated sullen hatred toward all. As he was hustled toward the foyer, I felt the house itself gather around him as if it were anxious to spit him out of its front door.

Carter was dragged into a night made bright by the glare of television lights. The media had arrived. It seemed as if every network covering Arcelia Gallagher's disappearance had been tipped off and were now crowded at the front gate, pressing against the bars or surging against the hapless line of uniformed men sent to guard the low fence on either side. Dozens of reporters and their crew members shoved for position, determined to bring their viewers the unexpected happy ending to the Arcelia Gallagher story. Lindsey Stanford stood at the front of the pack with her camera crew, resisting all attempts to share her premier spot in line. She would be first through the gate when it opened. Maggie's ex, Skip Bostwick, stood beside Stanford. He had become one of them. He threw elbows like an experienced reporter.

For days, the media had accused Danny Gallagher of killing his wife, and Aldo Flores of helping him. Then they had cast suspicion on non-specific illegal immigrants. They had, in fact, pretty much blamed everyone but the man now being dragged out to a waiting police car in front of them all. It made absolutely no difference. The reporters smelled blood. Better yet, they smelled a huge story: Hollywood and crime intertwined. It was a ratings dream.

As soon as Lamont Carter came into view, Lindsey Stanford went live with a pompous intro about the dark face of Hollywood fame. But an intrepid reporter had slipped past the guards and found the manual switch to the main gate. He flipped it before he could be stopped. Like a pack of hyenas falling on a dead beast, the journalists crashed though the front entrance, trampling Lindsey Stanford as they ran toward Lamont Carter.

Skip Bostwick stepped over Stanford as unconcerned as if she had been a boulder in his way and dashed toward Carter and his police escorts. The cops saw the crowd converging on them and practically threw Carter into the back seat, shutting the door just before a flood of reporters' overcame the car.

In the chaos, I was the only one, at first, to see the spooky figure framed in the front door of the mansion, looking out into the night, her eyes bleary and unfocused. At first, I thought it was an apparition. But it was Dakota Wylie, dressed in a nearly transparent negligee with her emaciated, decidedly non-pregnant body on full display. Her face was stripped of bandages and bare for all to see in its horribly altered state. She was barefoot and her hair was disheveled. She was also clearly confused about what was happening or where she was. The pills had hit her hard before the noise woke her from her drug-induced sleep.

'Lonnie?' Dakota called out into the night. 'Lonnie, where is the baby? You promised me a baby.'

When Carter did not respond, and I was not even sure he could see her through the crowd of reporters blocking his view, she began to scream his name again and again, attracting the reporters' attention. One by one, they fell silent and turned to stare at her standing in the doorway, looking for all the world like a young Blanche Dubois – wilted, frail and teetering on the verge of madness.

There was a moment of utter silence as they realized who they were seeing and then it sounded as if a thousand crickets and ten times as many locusts had descended on the scene. Whirring and clicking filled the air as every single camera leapt to action, their operators surging forward as they fought for a better shot of the star.

Dakota was too confused to move. She was too doped up to realize that her ravaged face had been exposed for all to see – the misshapen mouth, too wide and unnaturally thick; the bruised eyes, with the right one off-kilter; the strangely asymmetrical tilt of her right cheek; the ghastly pulled-to-one-side stretch of her skin.

It was awful. It was humiliating to think of someone once so beautiful, and still so fragile, trapped in the frames of all those cameras, exposed for the world to see.

'Is that Dakota Wylie?' Skip Bostwick shouted frantically. He was ignored by the others. They pressed forward, shouting questions at her. Dakota stared back, eyes wide, and reached a hand out to steady herself against the door frame. She was too stunned at what she had finally noticed to react.

Calvano came out of the blue.

Like a defensive lineman intent on sacking the quarterback, he shot out of the crowd and cut in front of the cameras, bent low. He scooped up Dakota Wylie and folded her over his shoulder, then raced back inside the house and slammed the door shut with his heel.

The crowd froze. No one moved. No one understood what had just happened. And I think more than a few thought that they had, perhaps, imagined it all.

But that one act of kindness would later become the defining moment in Adrian Calvano's career, long after the tabloid covers faded. It would lead to his new nickname – Sir Calahad – and, I suspected, be talked about for years, if not decades, to come. He'd had no white horse, but that had not stopped Sir Calahad from galloping to his lady's rescue.

I don't think Calvano cared what others were thinking when he did it, though. I think all he cared about at that moment, and all he would care about afterwards, was protecting someone he saw as too frail for this world, someone who was about to be thrown to the lions. If she had once been his dream girl, he would now be her knight.

Adrian Calvano, it turns out, really was a romantic.

I was not the only one who thought that.

That night, long after the media had left, long after Lamont Carter had been taken into custody and a psychiatrist called to attend to Dakota Wylie, when the crime scene crew was still deep below, processing the cave, and the moon above was giving way to dawn, Calvano stood alone on the edge of the great lawn, looking out over the grounds, perhaps wondering what was going to happen to his dream girl now.

Alice Hernandez had seen him walk out by himself to the edge of the lawn. She joined him there, in the shadows, with the smell of roses all around them.

'That was a very kind thing you did back there,' Alice told him. 'I confess I was impressed.'

'I didn't do it to impress anyone,' Calvano said gruffly. He jammed his hands into his pants pockets and would not look at her. Somewhere close by, a night bird trilled.

'I know you didn't, that's why I was impressed.'

'Don't mess with me, Hernandez,' Calvano said. 'I just don't have the energy tonight.'

Alice put her hands on his arms and turned him to her. Her voice was soft and she dropped all pretense of being the tough cop who liked to tease him. 'Adrian, there is nothing in this world that I would like better than to go out with you. OK? Just the two of us. And if you will agree to do that, to go out and be just you and me, then I promise you I won't make a single smart-ass remark all night. Not one. I mean it. I think we should try.'

'You mean it, Hernandez?' Calvano asked, a goofy smile spreading over his face.

'I mean it,' she promised. 'Do you want me to prove it to you now?'

'Sure,' he said, reaching for her.

Oh, to be alive.

THIRTY-SEVEN

Not everyone thought Dakota Wylie deserved rescuing. Especially not after the man and woman I had seen cruising the Delmonte House in a beat-up Chevy with Alabama plates stepped forward as exclusive guests on Lindsey Stanford's cable show. Turns out they were Dakota Wylie's parents – and Lamont Carter was not just her manager, he was also her brother. Their real names were Lonnie and Dixie Earle.

According to their parents, Lonnie and Dixie were ingrates who had turned their backs on a loving but poor family and traded Sundays at church for the money and bright lights of Hollywood, then left their parents to poverty once they found fame.

Not a lot of people bought it. Those two had hungry eyes and they couldn't quite keep the greed from their voices as they talked about their daughter's wealth. I know I didn't buy it. I thought back to the father snatching handfuls of cash from Lamont Carter and the mother whining about how ungrateful Carter was. Somehow I doubted they were the upstanding people Lindsey Stanford tried to present them as on her show. Besides, I had seen the way that

Lamont Carter slept, enfolding his sister to keep her safe, coiled as if ready to do battle against the entire world. He had grown up protecting her from *someone* and I was pretty sure it was those two. No one was born that hard or that angry. Life had made Carter that way.

I didn't know what would happen to Dakota Wylie without her brother around to protect her. I think he was the only person in the entire world who loved her, not for who she had been on the screen, but truly for herself.

Lamont Carter proved his love for his sister when he pled guilty to avoid her being forced to testify. It was with no small satisfaction that everyone involved in the case realized that his plea had also robbed Lindsey Stanford and her peers of the opportunity to wallow in the sordid details of the case.

Within months, Carter was to be in a prison outside Philadelphia, where he was initially kept in solitary confinement until his fame cooled down. His sister visited him often, arriving in a limousine and trailing a parade of cameras behind her as she marched in, dripping in diamonds and decked out in all the brand names that Lamont Carter could no longer have. She was a walking reminder of the life he had fought so hard to win and then had lost. But she was, of course, oblivious to what she was doing to her brother each time she visited, as well as oblivious to the difference in the way the world had treated her compared to him. And it had treated her very differently indeed.

Dakota Wylie was never charged in connection with Arcelia Gallagher's kidnapping. She insisted that she thought her brother had arranged a legitimate adoption and that she had simply been waiting for that baby to be born. Her helplessness and her insistence that she never paid attention to complicated legal affairs like adoption agreements convinced the grand jury not to indict her.

To be fair, she paid a price nonetheless. She cried for weeks after her brother was arrested, both for the loss of him and for the loss of the baby she had been promised, perhaps never once quite understanding what her brother was willing to do to get it for her. Or maybe she was just putting on the performance of her life? It was hard to say. She still seemed to have no awareness as to how she looked, and that required a *real* break from reality. She sat behind her brother in court, dabbing her ruined face with a Kleenex and reapplying lipstick to her misshapen lips for the cameras without a clue as to how she was now seen. Perhaps it was better that way. She had lost everything she had in the world: her looks, her career, her brother and even her husband, for Enrique Romero did not stand by her, not even for a day. In fact, he never returned to the Delmonte House again.

Dakota Wylie did not, however, lose her wealth. Someone – and my money was on Calvano – got her a very good divorce lawyer indeed. A lawyer who somehow knew to subpoena the photographs Gonzalez had stored away of her husband cheating on her in California. That was enough to invalidate the prenuptial agreement and make Dakota Wylie a very, very rich woman. She would never work again, not after what she had done to her face, but she would have enough money to live like a queen for the rest of her life. People would still photograph her, not because she was beautiful, but because she was a freak with an inconceivable amount of money. I'm not sure she could tell the difference, or if she would even care if she knew. She just needed the cameras trained on her. Without them, I suspected, she believed that she didn't exist.

Though others disagreed – most loudly, Lindsey Stanford, who called for her arrest nightly for awhile – I preferred to think of Dakota Wylie as an innocent. To do otherwise was impossible. It was simply too much for me to acknowledge that she might, instead, be a perfect storm of self-absorption meeting need and denial; a confluence created by poverty and covetousness, turned into a dangerous monster by the power her beauty gave her.

No, I told myself, Dakota Wylie had known nothing about Arcelia Gallagher's kidnapping. She had simply asked for what she wanted, as she had grown used to doing, and then waited for her brother to provide it, as he had long done.

Three months after entering prison, at his own behest, Lamont Carter was released into the general population. I figured he would thrive there. His hard outer shell and his capacity for violence would serve him well. But the very day he first joined the other inmates in the outside exercise area, he was stabbed sixteen times by a member of a Mexican prison gang who shouted the name of a well-known drug cartel leader as he plunged his home-made knife into Lamont Carter again and again. Carter died before the guards ever reached him.

No one could understand what had prompted the attack. Carter had not been in contact with the other prisoners long enough to make enemies. But I thought I knew. Deep beneath the earth, while fighting for her life, Arcelia Gallagher had told Carter, 'They will find you and they will kill you.'

I thought I understood who the 'they' had been. And with that realization, I also understood that there was more to Arcelia Gallagher's past in Mexico than her husband would ever know. She had paid a terrible price for Danny Gallagher's love. She had given up someone for Danny and the fallout had been those scars I once glimpsed on her body, long before she was even pregnant with their child. Those scars were from a spurned lover, a man used to violence and a man used to getting exactly what he wanted. It was not a miracle she had survived them, nor an accident the torture had been confined to hidden parts of her body. The man she had left for Danny had still loved her – or at least loved her beauty – enough to spare both her life and her face.

Perhaps he loved her still, for who else would have had the power to reach deep inside the prison walls and avenge her kidnapping?

I think Maggie understood what had happened as well. Shortly after Lamont Carter died, she took a brown folder from her desk drawer – the one that had arrived from her friend in the FBI – and shredded its contents in the squad room one night when no one else was around. If she knew the details of Arcelia's past, she was going to keep them to herself. She would let the beloved preschool teacher continue on with her new life.

And continue on she did. Arcelia Gallagher had a gift. She had learned to forget the past and to appreciate what she had.

In the months following her rescue, she fell into a routine that would seem mundane to most, but enchanted me. Each day, she would rise early and tenderly feed and clothe her little girl, without hurry, then make breakfast for her husband. After he left for the fields, she would often take a trip into town with her daughter – they had named her Angela – to visit the children who had been in her preschool class. They always loved a visit from their Seely and seemed to view Angela as the best toy ever invented. Arcelia would then pick up a few items from town and she was still as picky as ever when it came to what she was willing to buy. The Korean grocer who owned her favorite fruit stand seemed to consider her rescue a miracle of sorts and always pressed a special fruit on her as his gift. She would take it, knowing it made him happy. She would then return home, bundle her daughter against her in a sling and march out to the fields to find her husband so that they could share a lunch together beneath a wide open sky that was lifetimes away from the dark hole where she had been held. Her strength was breathtaking. Many afternoons, she would transform the sling into a papoose and stay in the fields to help her husband, bending and picking with the baby strapped to her back, just as her ancestors had done for thousands of years. Later, she and Angela would take a nap together on a blanket spread in the shade while Danny worked nearby, stopping often to check that they were safe.

I didn't know if they would always stay that close. I didn't know what dreams or fears the future held for her. But I did know that Arcelia was happy for now and that her baby would grow up much loved.

To me, the Delmonte House had been as much a part of this case as any person living in it. I roamed its halls soon after Lamont Carter was taken away. If the house felt rejected by yet another owner decamping from it, it didn't seem to care. It was bigger than any of its owners had ever been.

When Enrique Romero decided that the photo opportunity-rich life he had envisioned in the Delmonte House was never going to materialize, he ended up donating it to the Catholic Church as a publicity stunt that more than mitigated his connection to the seedy family his wife had brought to the table. His generosity, however motivated, allowed Father Sojak to successfully lobby that it be turned into a retirement home for priests and nuns. I'm guessing the old priest I saw snoring in the rectory's library was one of the first to move in.

The nuns, it was decided, would manage the property. Rodrigo stayed on as the gardener. Early one evening in late summer, he joined Father Sojak on the final walkabout of the house. Despite the nuns' protestations, Father Sojak was determined to clear the house and bring it peace. He carried a thurible of incense and a container of holy water. He stopped to say prayers every few steps and to sprinkle holy water around the mansion's perimeters. When he was done with the house, he and Rodrigo blessed the lawn above the underground room where Arcelia had been held. A man's skeleton had indeed been found beneath its floor and removed, then the cavern itself had been filled in forever. But Father Sojak blessed it and declared it consecrated ground just in case. He wasn't taking any chances.

I don't know if anything had lingered in the house after my fellow traveler left, but I do know that I could feel a peace settling over the house, as if all the greed and dissatisfaction that had filled it for over one hundred years was finally being put to rest. It is a beautiful thing to be satisfied with what you have, and truly the residents getting ready to move into the Delmonte House were more than grateful to be there.

The old butler and his wife were invited to stay on at the mansion as guests. The old man, who never quite recovered from that night on the great lawn, would never have to work again. He was free to look after his wife, who could wander the house at will as there were plenty of nuns to gently guide her to the right rooms.

As for Aldo Flores – held in jail on suspicion of Arcelia Gallagher's murder for nearly a week while in despair about his wife and child – Immigration came to question him at the jail, only to find an empty cell and Aldo long gone. Someone had checked him out late the night before. The handwriting on the visitor's log was indecipherable, the security cameras had mysteriously malfunctioned, the guard had been in the bathroom and the desk sergeant had no memory of who might have checked Flores out. Aldo Flores was gone for good. He disappeared into the underground world of illegal immigrants and was likely fast on his way to finding his wife and child by the time the morning sun rose.

Whether it had been Maggie or Calvano who made it possible for Aldo to join his family, or even someone else, was anyone's guess. But the fact that they never once discussed the disappearance of Flores between them made me believe that, perhaps, they'd both had a hand in his freedom.

Commander Gonzalez let the discrepancy go. He had been horribly wrong about Aldo Flores, and while he would never admit it, he was not willing to punish someone else for his mistake. Besides, he found a new object for his self-hatred. Enrique Romero's donation of the Delmonte House to the Catholic Church had provided an opportunity for publicity that the bishop could not ignore. Romero was honored at a lavish ceremony, along with four other prominent Latino leaders from the eastern states. Commander Gonzales was not among them, nor was he invited to the event.

He sat alone in his study watching the gala on television, a glass of scotch and a plate of brie beside him. A few rooms away, his wife and children laughed and teased each other over a table full of homemade tamales and a stew that smelled heavenly. How sad to think of what Gonzales was giving up each time he turned his back on who he was. Instead of being with his family, he stared at the screen, filled with resentment that his rival was being celebrated while he was being ignored. I almost felt sorry for him.

As for the people who worked for Gonzales – this case had moved their lives forward, albeit in very different ways. Calvano and Alice Hernandez were in love, though no one else knew it, a subterfuge that told me both were taking the relationship very seriously indeed. I found myself wishing my self-appointed rival well. Adrian Calvano had proved that he believed in love. It was nice he had now found it. Especially with someone who would kick his ass when he needed it, as Calvano always would.

While Calvano found love, Maggie buried hers. Or at least she buried a stand-in for it. Skip Bostwick, now firmly one of the pack, followed the other reporters to a new crime scene. From what I could tell, he did not contact her before he left. She had outlived her usefulness to him. And that was OK. Maggie was ready to forgive herself for marrying him and move on. She had a new cause in her life. When the bones that been found in the underground room with Arcelia Gallagher were analyzed, specialists reported back that they were likely over 150 years old and had belonged to a male of African descent. That was not enough for Maggie. She wanted a name. She began to spend her free evenings poring through the records of slave purchases, escape notices and even death announcements, in search of the man whose remains they had found.

If Maggie chose to spend her evenings with the dead instead of the living, who was I to judge? In truth, perhaps I should be flattered. Besides, I don't think Maggie was quite ready to embark on the future when it came to love. I think she still needed time to bury the past. The bones in the cave gave her that chance, even if they didn't belong to Skip Bostwick. Last time I caught up with her late at night in front of her computer screen, she had been at it for months, trying to find the identity of my fellow traveler, and she showed no signs of stopping. I had no doubt she would find out his name one day. Maggie never gave up.

As for me, I found a new home. No one ever discovered the room full of immigrants below St Raphael's and I checked in on them each evening on my rounds. I told myself it was an excuse to feel what it was like to be among the living. I told myself that what I really wanted was their hunger, their passion, their joy and their sorrows. But I knew I was only telling myself that to avoid the truth. For I had twice tasted the glory of what I hoped awaited me one day during the course of the Arcelia Gallagher case. Once while sitting in St Raphael's, when I had been filled with grace, and again when my fellow traveler allowed me to take his first steps into eternity with him.

Was that what it was going to be like when the day finally came that I was allowed to move on? If so, how could I get there sooner? What could I do to prove myself worthy?

I still did not know, but I did finally come to realize that it was time for me to make a choice. To find some meaning in my after-life. There was little I could do for most people in my current state, but there was a lot I could do for Father Sojak. Just as I suspected that I fed on the life force of others, I thought that, perhaps, I had the power to relieve Father Sojak of part of his burden. His gift had a dark side. I thought that all the pain and suffering he kept stored within him was too much for a human being to bear. I would help him. I would take away some of his darkness.

And so, I took to sitting behind Father Sojak each evening as he prayed, opening myself up and offering to take on as much as I could of the pain he had lifted from others. I don't know if he felt it. I don't know if it helped. But I do know that, at long last, in all of my years of both living and dying, and even wandering this earthly plane afterward, I finally felt as if I could be of use to someone. And that, I think, might be the point of it all.

EPILOGUE

A priest sits in a deserted church as the evening outside drains away and the stained-glass windows surrounding him fade to dark. He is, once again, weary beyond all weary. He walked among the rows of the needy tonight and their troubles still cling to him like wisps of cotton candy. There are so many people who need him. So many who come to him to lighten their loads. How can he turn them away?

Since he was a young boy, he has known that he has a gift. Perhaps, somewhere deep inside, he remains unsure as to its origin, but many years ago he decided it was a gift from God himself and that it was his duty to share it.

Since then, he has touched many lives. He has comforted the grieving, healed the sick and perhaps even banished true darkness at times. But all of it has taken its toll. He is forty-one years old and there are nights, like this one, when he feels as if he is one hundred or more. His body aches and there is a heaviness to his soul that he is not sure he can endure.

As always, he has sought refuge in the quiet of his church, where all the familiar symbols of his faith never fail to comfort him. This is where he feels solace. This is where he never feels forsaken.

The priest begins to pray. And as he prays, he can feel a presence there, almost as if God is with him. He is, the priest tells himself, of course he is here.

'Please, Lord, lighten my load,' the priest prays, feeling ashamed of himself for being so self-serving. 'I am here to serve you, but I do not know if I can go on. Please help me to serve you longer.'

As if in answer to his prayers, he feels a lightness flutter in his chest, grow hold and spread. His spirit dislodges from the muck that traps it and he can feel it rising once more. The misery, the despair, the hunger all seem to drain from the fortress that other people's sorrows have built in his heart. Hope floods through him. His heart beats stronger. He can breathe again. He knows that he, like life, will go on.